TURNING
POINT

OTHER BOOKS AND BOOKS ON CASSETTE
BY LAUREL MOURITEN:

The Passageway

For Love and Zion

TURNING POINT

a novel

Laurel Mouritsen

Covenant Communications, Inc.

Cover image © 2002 Photodisc, Inc.

Cover design copyrighted 2002 by Covenant Communications, Inc.

Published by Covenant Communications, Inc.
American Fork, Utah

Printed in the United States of America
First Printing: April 2002

08 07 06 05 04 03 02 01   10 9 8 7 6 5 4 3 2 1

ISBN 1-59156-015-2

Library of Congress Cataloging-in-Publication Data

Mouritsen, Laurel.
   The turning point : a novel/Laurel Mouritsen.
      p. cm.
   ISBN 1-59156-015-2
   1. Mormon women--Fiction. 2. Embezzlement--Fiction. 3. Illinois--Fiction. I. Title.
PS3563.O9215T87 2002
813'.54--dc21   2002023775
                                        CIP

Acknowledgements

The journal entries
in this book are taken
from the journal of
David Osborn.

CHAPTER 1

"Ready to ride, Anne?"

I hurriedly reread the last paragraph of Jaden's letter, folded it, and stuffed it into the zippered pouch of my backpack. "I'm just grabbing my camera," I hollered to Carly, who was standing outside the tent with the bikes. I rummaged in the pile of paraphernalia lumped in the corner of the tent until I found my Canon, threaded the loop of the camera case onto my belt, and adjusted it snugly against my hip. Slinging the backpack onto my shoulders, I stumbled out of the tent and zipped the flap shut.

My friend Carly was waiting on the roadside with our bicycles. She stood straddling hers, one hand on the handlebars, and the other hand steadying my silver Diamondback.

"Did you lock the car?" I asked Carly, settling myself on my bike.

She nodded. "We're set for a day of cruising. Isn't it an incredible morning?"

I squinted up into the morning sky. Not a trace of clouds obscured the May sun. The morning smelled of spring flowers and greening grass. "We couldn't have designed a better day to be on the road," I agreed. I was ready to start a day of biking over the swells and hollows of the Illinois countryside. Carly and I had spent the night at a campground outside Keokuk, Iowa, which marked the halfway point of our road trip.

We wheeled our bikes onto the road. The foliage was lush and green, though it was only the second week of May. I'd been astonished by the forests of trees and tall grass as we'd traveled east. Back home in Denver we had mountains, but not mile after mile of wooded hills like I saw here.

Carly spurted ahead of me, the rush of air coursing through her cropped, blonde hair. "I feel the need—the need for speed!" she whooped, facing into the wind.

I laughed. The phrase had become a private joke between us since starting our trip. Just before our graduation from the university in Colorado Springs, where we'd been roommates for the last two years, we'd made it a practice to relax from studying for finals by watching old movies. We must have seen a dozen videos during those final few weeks of school, one of which was *Top Gun*. The phrase from the movie had seemed suited to us as we had climbed into Carly's dilapidated Honda Civic, mountain bikes in tow, and set out on a three-week road trip to celebrate our graduation.

My bike had become my best friend in the last several months. For some reason when I was on my bike in the mountains, I felt free. With graduation from college behind me, the rest of my life loomed before me like a big black hole. I'd done well enough in school, and I wasn't afraid of hard work, but I had no idea what to do with my life or even where to start. I'd start thinking like this and then get anxious and fearful, which told me it was time for a ride in the mountains. As I usually did, I shoved my fears away, pedaling faster, as if I could escape my uncertain future.

Leaning into the breeze, I geared down and closed the space between Carly and me in seconds. Neither of us wore our helmets, though we carried them strapped to our bikes. We liked the feel of the air streaming across our faces and whipping through our hair.

I ran a hand through my tangled brown mane. It hadn't seen a curling iron and scarcely a comb for a week and a half. And it needed shampooing badly. Our living conditions on the trip may have been considered less than desirable by some people. Most nights Carly and I camped in a tent borrowed from one of Carly's friends at school. We'd stayed at a motel only twice since starting the trip. Yet in spite of the accumulated layers of grime and dust, we were happy with our living arrangements. Even though most of the time was spent traveling in the car, about every other day we left the car parked at camp and set off to do some exploring on our bikes.

Carly and I biked for the next hour, and I lost myself in the natural beauty around us. The country road was home to the scampering feet of chipmunks and other furry creatures, and the air pulsed with melodies from the meadowlark and wood thrush.

"I assume you know where you're going," I said to Carly, pulling up even with her.

She glanced over at me and nodded. "I asked the guy at the gas station last night which roads were best. He recommended taking this winding back road because it follows the river. We get a clear view of the Mississippi the whole way, and not much traffic. If we stay on it for twelve miles, it'll take us into the town of Nauvoo."

"Nauvoo?" I repeated. "What's in Nauvoo?" I fell back behind Carly's green Schwinn as a car whizzed past us.

"Not much. That's the beauty of it. Just a sleepy little town along the river. And it's half a day's ride to get there and back." Carly sped up again, weaving a zigzag pattern along the side of the road.

I hung back, admiring the view. The broad Mississippi sparkled in the morning sunlight. On the opposite side of the road, emerald hillsides harbored an occasional house, but buildings were scarce. I saw more squirrels than I did people.

"What did Jaden have to say in his letter?" Carly asked, her words flying against the streaming air.

In my mind's eye, I visualized Jaden's cramped, handwritten note. It had been mailed to me and had been waiting at the Keokuk post office when Carly and I stopped for a day's rest. I'd given my boyfriend of the last several months my itinerary, and we'd prearranged to exchange letters at certain points along the road as I traveled. This was the second letter Jaden had sent to me, and I'd relished every word of it.

"Well?" Carly asked pointedly. "Was it too private to share?" The tone of her voice implied an obvious curiosity.

I grinned. "Just the same old. He misses me. He can't wait to see me. Et cetera, et cetera, et cetera."

"It's the et cetera I want to hear about." She turned to look back at me, raised her brows, and smiled proddingly.

"No way," I laughed. "Besides, I'm sure you'd find it boring. Snoring boring."

"It's that bad, huh?" teased Carly.

I pedaled off the shoulder of the road just as a ramshackle, faded red pickup rumbled past. The letter in the pouch of my pack was burning a hole in my back. Jaden's suggestions that we marry were becoming more insistent. Although he had a charm I was certainly drawn to, I'd become aware of a nasty tendency toward jealousy and possessiveness on his part. That propensity had already caused disagreements between us.

"I wish I had your problems," Carly said. "Jaden is a major babe."

"As if you sit alone at home on Saturday nights," I quipped. "You have more than your fair share of hunks banging on the door."

Carly let go of the handlebars and tossed her hands in the air.

I chuckled under my breath. Carly was one of the most spirited and unpredictable people I'd ever met. In fact, the road trip had been her idea. Originally, six of us had planned to go, but as the scheduled date had drawn closer, our friends had backed out one by one until only Carly and I were still eager to take the trip. Carly had already made the excursion memorable with her crazy antics, particularly evident one night a week ago when we had stopped at a café for dinner. A young, shy waiter had served us—a babe, Carly had declared, her favorite term for any good-looking male—and she'd flirted with him unashamedly. After we had eaten, she had written him a flirtatious note on a dinner napkin and had left it on the table for him. It had been all I could do to swallow my laughter as we left the café.

"Oh, wow, look at that!" I exclaimed, my attention collared by a cottage resting in the shade of leafy trees, not far from the roadside. The small house was painted robin-egg blue, with white shutters on the windows and a stone chimney hugging the outside wall. A waist-high stone fence bordered the cottage, nearly hidden by the profusion of bright flowers growing beside it. I squeezed the hand brakes on my bike, pausing to savor the picture. A blue jay sailed across the yard, the sun glinting off its azure wings. I spotted a cat curled up on the front windowsill. "This is like a scene from a calendar," I said to Carly.

"When you're an important art dealer, you can commission someone to paint that scene for you and make a bundle off its sale," she quipped, braking to a stop beside me.

I reached for my camera. "Look at the way the shadows flicker across the stone hedge," I said admiringly, holding my bike upright between my knees while I snapped a picture. I'd seen some stunning scenery the past few days, and had already used up three rolls of film. Snapping a last shot, I reluctantly put away the camera.

"You're never going to be able to afford to get all that film developed," joked Carly as we started off again. It was true that I'd put my camera to good use. I could never resist photographing a scene where light and shadow played leapfrog, or when splashes of color spun a story rich in beauty and contrast. Though I longed to record such images on canvas, I possessed no talent for it and so I had to content myself with a camera. The artistic abilities of others I deeply appreciated; that's why I had majored in art history at the university. I'd relished in my classes, especially my study of the great painters of the Renaissance, who created masterful frescoes to adorn the walls of churches and palaces. What I planned to do with my degree in art history, I wasn't sure. Perhaps take a position with an art gallery or museum. My strongest desire, however, was to visit the great galleries of art in Europe, where I might see the masterpieces of firsthand. A romantic notion, I suppose, but I was a confirmed romantic at heart.

"When are your parents getting back from their cruise?" she asked, swinging her legs out from her bike, away from the pedals, as we coasted down a slope.

Her words yanked me out of my pleasant reverie and back into reality. "A couple of days after I get home from the road trip," I said with a trace of harshness.

"Have you heard from them at all?" she asked, apparently ignoring the warning in my voice.

"No, and I don't expect to," I said bitterly. "I'm sure they're having the time of their lives. They've been wanting to take a Caribbean cruise."

The face of my mother came to mind, with her faded blue eyes and tight smile. She and my father had both worked long hours at their jobs for as long as I could remember. They had planned the vacation for years, and it wasn't their fault that the cruise had coincided with my graduation from the university and they hadn't been able to attend. They'd promised a celebration when they returned home from the Caribbean, but the thought left me cold. It merely served as a reminder of dance recitals and soccer games when I seemed to be the only child there without a parent to support her. While the other parents led their children away afterward for ice-cream celebrations, I walked home alone with no one to share my success or my failure.

My relationship with my parents—particularly my mother—was one reason I was worrying about my life. I knew I could live with them as long as I needed to before I found a job, but I didn't relish the thought. My father and I had gotten along well enough as I was growing up, but my mother and I were at odds more often than not. We'd never really been close and, after sharing a close friendship with Carly, I knew how much more satisfying that was. But Carly was headed back home, and I needed to find a job and focus on my life.

Reflecting on my childhood, I didn't wonder that I had always felt adrift and alone while growing up. My brother, Brett, had ignored me for the most part, preferring his own activities and friends to the company of a little sister. Since he had moved out of the house to a place of his own, I hadn't heard a word from him. This stung, but it wasn't unexpected.

"Maybe your parents will bring back a Jamaican guy with dreadlocks and a scraggly beard as a souvenir for you." Carly's suggestion roused me from my thoughts, and I laughed. Carly's mind hinged on one topic.

"Let's stop for a second. I'm thirsty," I said, pulling over to the side of the road.

While we paused for a drink, I decided to slip on my bike helmet. The road was becoming more twisty, with loose gravel at the edges. Carly had already come close to losing control of her bike as we'd descended the slight knoll.

"Are you sure this is the road to Nauvoo?" I asked Carly, gazing up ahead.

"Yeah, I'm sure."

We climbed back on our bikes and set off. "Maybe I'll send Jaden a postcard from there," I mused. "Any interesting sights in the town?"

Carly shrugged. "Not that I'm aware of."

"Well, it'll at least have a post office." I steered to the shoulder of the road as a blue, midsize car crested the rise ahead of us and began heading down. "When we get back to camp this afternoon, maybe we can clean up our stuff and make a run to the laundromat."

"Good idea. These biking shorts could use a wash."

"Mine too. And all my T-shirts are grungy and beginning to smell like—" A big yellow Labrador suddenly came tearing across a fenced yard. It bolted through the open gate and, barking savagely, headed straight for me.

Carly was ahead of me by a foot or two. Impulsively, I swerved into the road to avoid the approaching dog. As I glanced from the dog to the street, I caught a blur of blue closing in on me. The driver sounded his horn and yanked the wheel, but I was too close. The blue car completely filled my field of vision. I cried out, frantically squeezing the hand brakes. The bike slid sideways into the road.

Then a tremendous blow turned everything black.

CHAPTER 2

The field was ablaze with color. I stood in a sea of blossoms, flowers of magnificent hue spreading in every direction. I'd never seen anything to match such brilliance. Blossoms of emerald green, olive, dusty brown, maroon, and ocher mingled with more familiar shades. The flowers were so fragrant they filled the air with perfume, with colors so vibrant they confounded the eye. As I gazed in wonder, it occurred to me that the flowers seemed almost alive and breathing. They appeared to sway and nod to a rhythm inaudible to human ears.

I bent down to examine an exquisite flower shaped like a seashell. The center was sky blue, and the blue darkened in concentric rings as the petals spread outward. The flower gave off the most unusual scent too, like a salty ocean breeze.

I spread my fingers over the close-growing flowers, ruffling their petals. The blossoms felt soft and silky, and when stroked gave off a tinkle of music. I was enthralled. The field of flowers seemed to extend to the horizon.

But wait a minute! Something was wrong with this picture. Where was the winding road I'd been following? And why wasn't Carly anywhere in sight? I whirled around, confused and anxious.

Then I saw a woman walking toward me through the field of flowers. The flowers rustled as she passed through their midst, emitting their peculiar, charming strain of music. I watched and listened in fascination as the woman approached me.

"Hello, Savannah Marie," she greeted me by my full name.

"Hello," I returned. The word was spoken calmly, belying the curiosity and surprise I was feeling.

When the woman drew closer, I noticed her unusual dress. She wore a full skirt the color of ripe apricots, which came to her ankles, and a crisp white blouse with lace at the cuffs and throat. A soft, green woolen shawl draped across her shoulders. In her hand she carried a bonnet with flowing, green ribbons.

"It's a pleasure to see you." The woman smiled.

I smiled back, intrigued by what was occurring. She came to my side and took my hand into hers. She had the softest hands I'd ever felt.

"Come join me," she said simply.

I couldn't take my eyes off her face. I followed willingly, happily, not even thinking to inquire who she was or where she'd come from. She was far more lovely than the myriads of flowers surrounding us. Her features were simple, yet the beauty radiating from within shone in her countenance. We walked wordlessly for a few moments, hand in hand, through the field of flowers. I couldn't tell exactly how long or how far we walked, but sensed that time seemed to stand still here.

"You have a great opportunity before you," the woman said softly, turning to face me as we strolled through the field. "Few receive such a blessing."

I smiled at her, and felt as calm and serene as a child in her mother's lap. "What blessing is that?" I asked, bewildered.

She pressed my hand. "You will see."

As I basked in the warmth of her smile, I suddenly found myself inside a building, lingering at the open door of a large room where many people were seated on simple wooden chairs. I looked curiously into the room. The people were attired in old-fashioned clothing, the ladies in long skirts and bonnets, the men in frock coats and vests, with top hats resting on their laps.

"Look," the woman whispered, nodding toward the front of the room.

I turned my gaze to the spot she indicated. There stood a man, gesturing as he spoke to the congregation. He was tall, with a fair complexion, and a somewhat prominent nose. His voice rose and fell with expression as he spoke, and though I was able to plainly hear him, I couldn't understand his words. I watched the congregation lean forward in their chairs, eager to catch every word the man said.

"What's he saying?" I asked the woman at my side. She only smiled, her eyes focused on the man at the head of the room.

I turned back to stare at him. He stood with regal bearing and spoke with power and authority. I felt awed by his presence, though I didn't understand why. There was no misunderstanding, however, the effect the speaker had on his audience. They sat listening intently, their faces shining. I could sense their excitement and anticipation, though if it was for the man himself or what he was explaining to them, I couldn't tell. The room pulsed with energy, joy, and light. Something was stirring these people to unspeakable joy, and I wished to know the reason for it.

The beautiful woman gently touched my arm, and I turned to her. "Remember what you hear, Savannah. Listen and remember," she whispered.

"But I can't understand what the man is saying," I replied in consternation.

It was as if she didn't hear me or chose to dismiss what I'd said. She leaned closer and spoke softly in my ear. "You have an opportunity to do a great work among these people." She gestured to the congregation in the room. "Be faithful to your trust."

I looked up into her face, my heart fluttering. "What trust?" I asked. She patted my hand. "You will know."

* * *

I opened my eyes with a start. A horrific pain thundered in my head, stealing my breath away. I gasped and sputtered.

"Anne? You're going to be all right. The doctor said you'll be all right."

I recognized the speaker's voice but couldn't put a face or name to it because of the throbbing in my head. I felt a cool hand cover mine.

"Anne, can you hear me? It's Carly. You're going to be fine."

Carly. That's who the voice belonged to. I tried to answer, but my tongue seemed to fill my mouth.

"What? What are you trying to say?" Carly sounded anxious.

I attempted to speak again. My throat was dry and sore, and my voice came out sounding like a growl.

"Don't talk now, Anne. Try to sleep. The doctor will be back to see you soon."

I let myself drift back to sleep.

I awoke again to the uncomfortable feel of poking and probing at my stomach. "Ouch. That hurts!" I blurted out.

The doctor stepped away from the bedside, his hands on his hips. "How are you feeling, Miss Lawrence?"

I tried to sit up, but a wave of dizziness overwhelmed me. I plopped back prone in the bed. "Oh, my head hurts. And my stomach. And everything else," I moaned.

The doctor stood staring at me. He was a tall reed of a man with horn-rimmed glasses and thin lips. "Can you tell me what month it is, Miss Lawrence?" he asked solemnly.

I frowned, trying to concentrate. My head felt stuffed with cotton candy. I tried to think through the cloud of pink fuzziness. "May," I fumbled. "Yes, it's May. And the flowers are all in bloom. Beautiful flowers."

Flowers? Where did that thought come from? I wondered. My subconscious dredged up an image of a field full of exquisite flowers. Then, just as quickly, the vision submerged again.

"That's right. It's May. How many fingers am I holding up?" He took a step backward and held up his hand.

What a silly question, I thought. *Does he think I can't count?* "Four. You're holding up four fingers. Is that significant of something?" I knew I sounded impatient, but I was tiring of this game.

A smile flitted across his mouth. "Just wanted to make sure you're feeling all right. And you seem to be. You're a lucky young woman, Miss Lawrence."

"Lucky? Why is that?" I groaned. I certainly didn't feel lucky. I felt worse than I'd ever felt in my life.

"You had an accident while biking with your friend." The doctor's professional demeanor returned, but was coupled with a gentle kindness. "Can you remember your friend's name?"

"Of course I can remember her name. It's . . ." I stopped. Though I knew her name as well as my own, I couldn't seem to make it surface. "It's . . . it's ah . . ." I felt a fluttering of panic inside. "It's Carly!" I said in a triumphant rush. "Carly Weller." Then another thought struck me. "Where is Carly? And where am I?"

I threw back the blanket and tried to get out of bed, but the doctor put a hand out to restrain me. "Not just yet, young lady.

You've had a nasty bump on the head, along with some bruising and internal bleeding."

"What?" I cried, stunned by the news. "What happened to me?"

"You were hit by a car. It could have been very serious, but you've escaped with few injuries."

I let out my breath with a whoosh. "Hit by a car? I don't remember anything about it. No, wait," I said, growing agitated. "I do remember something. A blue car. Yes, it was blue. I remember it was blue because blue was all I saw before I woke up and found myself here."

The doctor nodded, stroking his chin and gazing at me closely.

I glanced around the room. Everything looked sterile and glistening. It smelled of antiseptic. "Where is here?" I asked slowly.

"The hospital in Keokuk, Iowa. The ambulance brought you here after the accident." The doctor picked up a clipboard from the bedside table and quietly studied it. Then he started writing something down.

I stared at him for a moment before looking around the room. I saw a yellow, plastic pitcher and glass sitting on the bedside table, another bed across from mine partially hidden behind a curtain, and an array of buttons and gadgets set in the wall above my head. A stand with an IV bag full of clear liquid stood nearby. I was surprised to find the tube from the IV snaking toward my arm and disappearing beneath a layer of tape across my wrist.

When I turned to look in the opposite direction, the movement brought a wall of crushing pain. I gasped, bringing my hand to my head.

The doctor looked up from his chart. "Are you doing all right?"

"My head. It hurts horribly when I move it." My fingers came in contact with something soft and spongy on my head. "What's this?" I asked in alarm.

The doctor gently moved my hand aside. "It's only bandages, Miss Lawrence. You have a few cuts and some swelling we've been treating, but you're recovering nicely."

I wanted to explore the bandages with my fingers but didn't dare do it while the doctor was standing there watching me. "How long have I been here?" I croaked.

When he told me two days, I stared at him in shock. "You've been unconscious much of the time because of the sedatives we've been giving you and the effects of the blow," he explained.

His answer eased my mind somewhat. "Where's my bike?" I asked a moment later. I suspected it had taken quite a beating.

He blinked. "Your bike?"

"Yes. My gray Diamondback. I paid a lot for it." My imagination was creating a vivid picture of my ravaged bike, and I cringed at the thought of getting a new one.

"Just be calm, Miss Lawrence. I don't know where your bicycle is, but I'm sure your friend will. Though I don't imagine it's in any shape to ride." The doctor gave me what he thought was a reassuring smile, and patted my arm.

I sank deeper into my pillow and sighed. My shiny, silver touring bike. I could see it all twisted and broken, completely irreparable.

The doctor put away his pen and returned the clipboard to a wire rack attached to the foot of my bed. "If you need anything, the nurse's station is right outside the door. All you have to do is push this button." He handed me a buzzer-type contraption, its cord attached to the gadgets on the wall.

"Alright," I said, nodding slightly. I knew that even the slightest motion would cause the wall of pain to come crashing down again.

The doctor started to leave the room. "I'll check back with you later this evening," he said.

"Wait a minute," I cried out, feeling suddenly frightened about being left alone. "Where is Carly?"

The doctor paused in the doorway. "She's in the waiting room. I'll tell her she may come in to see you, but only for a few minutes. Then you need to rest."

"Okay." I relaxed, knowing I wouldn't be alone or surrounded by strangers.

"Oh, Miss Lawrence?" the doctor said, halting in the doorway.

"Yes?"

"When we asked Miss Weller for some information concerning you, she mentioned your parents are currently out of the country. If you'll tell the nurse where they can be reached, she'll contact them for you to let them know what's happened here."

I frowned in thought. "I don't think they can be reached, Doctor. They're on a cruise in the Caribbean. I have no idea how to get a hold of them."

A line creased the doctor's brow. "What about another family member? A brother or sister, perhaps."

"No. I only have one brother. And I don't know for sure where he's living. I haven't talked to him in months."

The doctor tapped a finger to his lips. "Alright. We'll see about all of that later. You get some rest."

After the doctor had closed the door behind him, I burrowed deeper into my pillow and closed my eyes. Two days. I'd been unconscious for two whole days. That thought concerned me more than the fact that I'd been involved in a serious accident. Now that the doctor was gone, I gingerly felt the bandages on my head. I seemed to have one big one across the right side of my brow and another toward the back of my head. I felt down along my arms and torso. I could feel numerous scratches and cuts beneath my fingertips. I moved my legs and feet and heaved a sigh of relief knowing I was able to do so comfortably. At least I wasn't paralyzed, and I hadn't even suffered any broken bones, it appeared. What had the doctor said? A nasty bump on the head, some cuts and bruises, and internal bleeding. I started thinking about how much worse it could have been. My body began shaking, and I broke out in a cold sweat. I pulled the blanket up around my chin as I trembled beneath it.

The door opened and Carly peeked in. "Hey, girlfriend," she called softly.

"Oh, I'm so glad you're here," I cried out. "Come in, come in."

She slipped through the door and came to my bedside. Her face looked pale and drawn, and deep circles shadowed her eyes. "How are you feeling?" she asked gently.

"Miserable. And my head hurts. But the doctor says I'm going to be fine." I grasped her hand. "How are you? You look tired."

She sank into the chair beside my bed. "I am. I haven't slept a wink the whole time you've been here."

"I'm sorry," I said. And I meant it. But I was glad she was here. I felt so much better now that she was sitting beside me, and the trembling in my body was subsiding.

"I've been a nervous wreck, Anne, being the only one here for you. They asked me to get in touch with your family, but I had no idea which cruise or even travel agency your parents had used . . ."

I gave her an empathetic look.

"I mean, what if you had died?" she whimpered, then her hands flew to her mouth. "I'm sorry. I didn't mean to say that."

Her words jolted me, but I tried not to let it show. "That's alright," I murmured, patting her hand. I didn't want to think how I would have felt if she were the one in the hospital and I was the helpless bystander. "I understand how difficult it's been for you. I'm sure this whole thing has been scary."

"That's an understatement." Carly leaned back in her chair, the anxiousness finally leaving her eyes. "I'm glad you're doing better. Does your head hurt awfully?"

I released her hand and leaned back into the pillow. "It feels like someone's taken a jackhammer to it."

Carly smiled. "At least you haven't lost your sense of humor. That's good to see."

I propped myself up in the bed as well as I could. "Carly, what exactly happened out there on the road? I remember a blue car heading toward us, but after that, nothing." It was driving me crazy, this absolute blank in my memory.

She sat forward in the chair, her eyes wide. "I didn't actually see everything because I was riding a few feet ahead of you. But all of a sudden this huge dog came tearing toward you, growling and snapping, and—"

"That's right," I broke in. "I remember that part now. The dog was coming straight for me, and I swerved to miss him. I swerved and . . ." I shrugged. "That's the last I remember."

"Yeah. That's when the blue Grand Am came barreling down the hill and you swerved right into his path."

Chills snaked down my spine at the sudden visual memory. "Oh my gosh. I can't believe I didn't get killed," I gasped.

"Me either. It was amazing you didn't break every bone in your body." Carly sat shaking her head thoughtfully.

"Then what happened?" I asked.

But that was the part she hadn't seen, she said. She'd heard the brakes screeching and had turned to see my bike catapulting through the air and me hurtling across the road.

I lay still for a second, trying to focus on something besides the recent event. Then a thought formed in my mind. "Did I land in a field of flowers?"

She stared at me. "What?"

"Flowers. Lots of them. After I was hit by the car, did I end up in a field full of flowers?"

"Nooo," she said slowly, drawing out the word and looking at me with a strange expression.

I furrowed my brow. Then why had I remembered flowers? "Were there flowers anywhere around?" I persisted. I was desperate to know about the flowers, although I had no inkling why it was so important.

"No, Anne. You landed in the middle of the road. There were no flowers anywhere in sight."

"Oh." The desperation subsided, leaving me feeling weak and confused.

"I found your bike helmet several feet away under some bushes. It was cracked, with a big piece crushed in."

I shivered. "Don't tell me anymore, Carly. I'm not up to hearing about it just yet, I guess." I closed my eyes, trying to block out the images her words had resurrected in my mind.

"I'm sorry. I didn't mean to upset you. It's just . . . I thought you wanted to know," she finished haltingly.

I waved my hand feebly to let her know it was all right.

"Maybe I should go now and let you get some sleep. The doctor told me not to stay long."

I closed my eyes and nodded. "Okay. See you later." I was drifting into sleep even as I spoke, exhausted by the effort of making conversation. I didn't hear Carly leave the room for I was already dreaming. Dreaming about flowers.

CHAPTER 3

"You're sure you feel up to this?" Carly asked, concern evident in her voice.

"Yes, of course. I need to get my strength back. Let's take one more turn down the hallway."

Carly took my elbow as I shuffled along the hospital corridor. It had been four days since my accident, and although I was still sore and weak, I was feeling better. The ferocious pain in my head had dulled to a constant sharp headache.

"Did you bring my jeans and T-shirt like I asked?" I said to Carly.

"Yeah. They're washed and packed in the bag I put in your room. But your biking shorts are trashed, along with the shirt you were wearing on the day of the accident."

I winced, thinking about that day. "What about my bike? Can it be repaired?"

Carly let go of my elbow to let me maneuver the hallway on my own power. "The guy at the bicycle shop said it would cost more to repair it than to buy a new one. I left the bike with him anyway, until you decide what you want to do with it."

"Thanks, Carly."

"You bet. What are friends for?"

"You've been terrific, sticking by my side like you have." I saw a frown flicker across Carly's brow. "What? What is it? Is something wrong?"

"I wanted to talk to you about that," she said slowly, averting her gaze. "I've been in Keokuk nearly a week now. I probably need to think about starting for home."

My heart sank. "Of course, you're right. I don't know why I didn't think of it. This accident has eaten up the whole rest of the time we planned to be gone on our trip. I'm sorry, Carly," I finished dejectedly.

"Hey, that's all right. We had fun while it lasted, didn't we?"

I tried to give her a cheerful smile. "Yes. We did."

"But I really do have to get moving. I've got a job at home waiting for me. I'm supposed to start at the first of next week."

Depression lowered like a black rain cloud. The doctor wouldn't release me from the hospital for another couple of days, and I dreaded staying there alone, without an acquaintance or friend in the world. "Don't give it another thought," I said in a deliberately light tone. "You get going. I'll be fine. And I'll be right behind you."

"Okay. You sure you're fine with that?"

"Yeah. Sure, I am." I smiled and airily waved a hand.

"I'll bring you the rest of your stuff from camp before I leave. And write down the address of the bike repair shop in Nauvoo for you. You'll be flying home in a few days?"

I nodded. "Winging my way across the sky," I said, wiggling my hand through the air. "Cause I feel the need—the need for speed."

Carly laughed heartily. "You're too funny, girlfriend," she said.

"Now get going. You have a lot to do. I hope that old Honda of yours makes it home in one piece."

"It's a deal. I'll walk with you back to your room."

As we started back along the corridor toward my hospital room, I caught sight of a young man rounding the corner of the hallway. His eyes were to the floor so he didn't see us yet.

"That's him," Carly whispered in my ear.

I glanced over at her. "Him who?"

"The guy who was a passenger in the car that hit you. He's come here several times to see you, but you've been either asleep or down in therapy."

I stared curiously at the tall broad-shouldered fellow as he strode with purposeful steps down the hallway.

"He's a babe, Anne. A real honest-to-goodness babe."

We watched the guy pause at the door to my room and look inside. Finding it empty, he glanced around.

"Hey," Carly called in greeting when he spotted us.

"Hey, yourself," the young man returned. His hands were stuffed in the pockets of his jeans, and he had on a steel-gray sweater. He waited for us to reach him, his eyes darting from Carly's face to mine. I felt myself redden under his stare. I knew I looked particularly unattractive dressed in my hospital gown and robe and my hair pulled back into a disheveled ponytail.

"Anne, this is Bridger Caldwell," Carly said, making the introductions. She turned to the fellow who towered several inches over us. "And this is Savannah Marie Lawrence, the girl you bumped into."

Bridger looked at me with a serious expression. "How are you feeling?" he asked me.

"Good. I'm feeling all right. Just a headache and a few bruises, but they'll heal soon enough."

The relief flooding his face was obvious. "That's great to hear. James and I have been worried about you."

"James?" I asked, raising a brow in question.

"James Baldwin. The driver of the car. I work with James and we were driving into Keokuk for a meeting. I'm relieved to see you're all right."

"I guess the fault was more mine than his. Please tell James I'm fine, and not to worry."

"She's definitely on the mend," Carly put in, favoring him with another smile.

Bridger was tanned and well built. His dark hair was cut in a short style, and his eyes were an interesting shade of gray blue. Carly was right. He was definitely cute.

"We've been here several times trying to see you, and to apologize for what happened. And to make sure you're doing okay," he said earnestly.

"Thank you for your interest. But I'm fine, I assure you." I wished we could talk about something else.

"Bridger is from Utah," Carly informed me. "And attends a university there. He's working in Nauvoo in connection with his schooling."

"Oh? You're from Utah?" I responded. I self-consciously put a hand to my head to smooth what I knew had to be matted and stringy hair. I could feel the bandages still covering the corner of my forehead.

"That's right. Have you ever been to Salt Lake?" He stared at me, waiting for my answer.

I shook my head. "No. But I bet it's a nice place. Lots of mountains. We've mountains in Colorado Springs too."

"Where you've been going to school, right?"

Carly had evidently filled in all the blanks for him. "Yeah. Carly and I just graduated." I figured he knew that already, too.

"How long are you staying in Illinois?" Carly asked him, placing her hands on her narrow waist.

"Through the summer. Until I'm through with my project."

"What kind of project are you working on?" I inquired, my interest aroused.

"I'm involved with the Nauvoo Restoration project to gain some field experience. Sort of a practicum required for a degree in architecture. Have you been to Nauvoo to see what's been done there?" he asked, glancing from me to Carly.

"No. What's been done?" I replied, curious to know.

"It's amazing stuff. A whole nineteenth-century town is being restored."

"Really," Carly said, obviously more interested in the speaker than in what he was telling us.

Bridger explained that some of the old homes had been repaired and restored, while others had been rebuilt on the original foundations. "It's all open to the public," he told us. "You ought to see it before you leave the area."

I was growing tired from standing in the hallway but I didn't want to end the conversation just yet. And I didn't feel comfortable about inviting this stranger, interesting as he was, into my room to visit. I shifted my weight and leaned against the door frame of my room.

"Hey, let me get you a chair," Bridger said quickly, noticing my slumping posture. He ducked into my hospital room and emerged with two chairs, then slipped across the hall to an empty room and reappeared with a chair for himself.

The three of us sat together in the hospital corridor.

"What is it you do exactly at the restoration site?" I asked him.

Bridger contemplated my question for a moment. "We're designing plans to reconstruct a stable on site."

"Sounds awesome," Carly volunteered.

"I think so," he replied. He thrust his hands in his pockets and leaned his chair backward until it balanced on two legs. "What about you? What are you going to do now that school's through?" he asked, eyeing each of us in turn.

Carly spoke up first. "I'm leaving for Wisconsin tomorrow. I've got a job lined up with an advertising agency," Carly answered.

"Doing what?"

"Fashion spreads. Merchandising advertisements. That sort of thing. I graduated in fashion design and merchandising, with a minor in marketing."

"And you?" he inquired, transferring his attention to me.

"Art history." I smiled. "There's not a whole lot I can do with that major."

"Don't let her kid you," Carly put in. "She'll end up being the curator at some famous art museum."

I chuckled. "Yeah, I wish."

"Seems like a noble ambition." A smile flashed across Bridger's face, revealing even, white teeth and a hint of a dimple in one cheek.

"Right. And about as likely as my becoming an astronaut."

He laughed at that remark, a deep, rich sound that brought out prickles along my arms.

"Actually, I don't have a job lined up yet," I said hastily, feeling a warmth flood my cheeks. "But I'll be going home to Denver in a few days." I wished he'd laugh again. I liked the sound of it.

"Denver? So the two of you weren't friends before college?" He wagged a forefinger between us as he spoke.

"Nope," Carly answered. "We met at the university in Colorado Springs."

"What made you decide to attend school there?" Bridger asked.

Carly answered for both of us. "Anne got a scholarship to the university. I wanted to go to a part of the country I'd never seen before."

Bridger turned to me. "So why'd you choose art history as a major?"

I brushed back a strand of hair falling across my cheek. If I'd known I was going to have a male caller this afternoon, I would have paid more attention to my appearance. I normally wore my hair straight and sleek, parted in the center with the bangs grown out to the length of the rest. At the moment, however, it was looking pretty scraggly. "Because it interests me," I replied to Bridger's question.

"What style of art most interests you?"

"I'd have to say Renaissance. Are you into art?"

Bridger smiled easily. "I appreciate it," he responded. "Which artist do you most admire?"

"You sure ask a lot of questions, don't you?" I said, unable to keep from smiling back at him.

"I figure it's the best way to get to know a person. Don't you?" A wry grin flitted across his face.

I laughed, amused by his directness. "Peter Paul Rubens. He'd have to be my personal favorite."

"What famous stuff did he paint?" Carly blurted, determined not to be excluded from the conversation.

"Portraits. Religious scenes. I can tell you the names of the pieces if you like," I answered, my lips twitching with a grin.

Carly's eyes traveled to Bridger. "And you chose architecture as your major because? . . ." Her sentence ended in a flirtatious smile. She swiveled in her chair toward him.

He gave a low chuckle. "My ambitions aren't nearly as noble as Savannah's. I figured I could make money from designing buildings."

I smiled at his truthful reply. He was direct and to the point, had a subtle sense of humor, and was definitely nice looking. My first impression of him wasn't tough to justify.

Bridger lowered the chair legs to the floor, and glanced at his watch. "I should get going. I'm supposed to meet James in a few minutes out at the site." He rose from his chair. "It was nice to finally meet you, Savannah. I'm glad you're doing well. I know James wants to ask you about insurance stuff because of the accident," he added.

"Sure. He can come by anytime and talk to me," I said.

Bridger reached for my chair as I stood. He carried all three chairs back into the hospital rooms, then joined Carly and me in the hallway. "Have a safe trip," he said to Carly. He gave us a half-wave, then thrust his hands into his pockets and strode away.

"Didn't I tell you he's gorgeous?" Carly grinned as soon as he'd rounded the corner and was out of sight.

"You did," I agreed.

"He could certainly give old Jaden Tanner a run for his money, right?" She didn't expect a reply, but her comment made me pause. Jaden had telephoned me at the hospital several times after Carly's phone call to him about my bike accident. He'd called again earlier that afternoon, insisting that he fly out to Iowa to be with me. I'd told him not to come, that it was unnecessary because I'd be leaving for home soon. Now I wished I hadn't been so quick to discourage him from visiting. I missed him. And with Carly leaving tomorrow, I'd be especially lonesome. The hours would drag cooped up in the hospital. I decided to talk to the doctor about letting me go home sooner than planned.

"Bridger is hot, but he's also a little weird," Carly said offhandedly.

I looked over at her in surprise. "What do you mean?"

"The way he said that prayer over you right after the accident," she replied. "That was kind of weird, wasn't it?"

"What prayer? What are you talking about, Carly?"

Her face colored. "Didn't I mention it to you? Oh my gosh, I'm sorry. I thought I did."

"Mention what?" I demanded, growing impatient with her.

"Right after you were hit, and sprawled out on the road bleeding and unconscious, Bridger and this James guy jump out of the car and run over to you. I really didn't know what to do. I thought you were dead."

"Okay," I said, holding my breath.

"Well, then Bridger knelt down beside you, put his hands on your head, and started saying sort of a prayer."

I was startled by what she was telling me. "What did he say in this prayer?"

"I don't know, Anne. I was too upset to listen. He only kept his hands on your head for a few seconds, then he was done."

I felt a flash of indignation. What right did this total stranger have to even touch me if he wasn't giving medical assistance? "Why didn't you tell me this before?"

"I forgot. It slipped my mind, Anne. Everything has been so hectic and crazy."

"It's okay," I said fuming. I wasn't angry at Carly for forgetting, but I was upset with Bridger Caldwell for what he'd done. And then not bothering to mention it to me.

"You're mad at me, aren't you? You're scowling like a screech owl."

I tried to wipe the frown from my face, but I wasn't completely successful. "No, I'm not mad at you. Only at that arrogant architect. If I ever see him again, I'll have a thing or two to tell him."

"Look, his saying a prayer over you probably didn't hurt anything. You're going to be as good as new. Maybe it even helped," Carly suggested brightly, trying to absolve herself from guilt. "The doctor said it was miraculous you escaped with so little injury."

I looked at Carly but I was barely listening to her. I kept thinking about Bridger Caldwell. I was particularly annoyed because up until now, I had liked him so well.

CHAPTER 4

The next afternoon, Bridger's partner, James, came to the hospital to see me. I was expecting someone Bridger's age, but James turned out to be a forty-something, balding fellow who worked for an architectural firm in the Midwest. He stayed only a few minutes to apologize for his part in the accident and to see firsthand that I was actually alive. We briefly discussed a few insurance issues before he left.

Afterward, Carly dropped by to bring me the last of my gear and to say good-bye. We promised to call one another often and visit whenever we could. When she gave me a final hug, tears surged to my eyes.

I sat on the bed after she left, going through my stuff. She'd taken the tent, sleeping bags, and camping gear with her in the car, and had left me with my clothing and personal items. I was sorting through my jeans and T-shirts when I heard a knock at the open door of my room. I looked up.

"Surprise, hon."

"Jaden!" I cried in astonishment. I started to get out of the bed, but Jaden closed the space between us in a few strides, and welcomed me into his arms with a tight hug.

"How's my girl?" he asked. He held me at arm's length to eye me up and down. Then he pulled me close and kissed me.

I clung to him, excited that he actually did come in spite of my earlier protests. "When did you get here?" I asked, breathless, giving him a squeeze.

"Just now. I drove straight from the airport in St. Louis. I couldn't stay away any longer. How ya feeling?"

"Perfect, now that you're here." I kissed him soundly on the mouth.

"You look good," he said.

I laughed, motioning to a chair beside the bed. He sat down and I eased back onto the pillows. "How do you like this get-up?" I asked him, gesturing to my hospital gown and robe. "Straight off the modeling runway, right?"

"Hey, you look good in anything." He reached for my hand.

I playfully pulled the bill of his baseball cap down over his eyes. "*You* look good." He did, too. He had on a pair of baggy Levi jeans, a dark T-shirt, and sandals. The ever-present hat fit snugly on his head, and under it was short, brown spiky hair, with the tips bleached yellow. A silver hoop in each earlobe glittered in the sunlight from the window.

"Oh, I'm so glad you're here," I exclaimed, squeezing his hand.

"Me, too. I should have come earlier. I don't know why I listened to you," he teased, tweaking my nose.

"Well, I'm glad you ignored my instructions to stay away. And you came at the perfect time. Carly left this afternoon to go home."

"Is she driving the limo?" he asked.

I laughed. Ever since I told him we were taking Carly's battered old Honda Civic, he'd referred to it as the limo. "Yes, she is. Actually, it's been a good little car. We didn't have any trouble with it on the road."

Jaden hunched over in his chair and put his hands together. "Seriously, how are you feeling? What did the doctor say?"

"Theriously?" I mugged.

"Come on, Annie. Be serious. What's up with the bang to your head?" With his other hand, he brushed aside my hair to gently touch the bandage on my forehead. I tingled at the pressure from his fingertips.

"The doctor said I suffered a bad concussion in the accident. He was worried about swelling and bleeding in my brain, but those problems never materialized. There was some concern because I was unconscious for a while, but now I'm fine, really. Sometimes I get a killer headache, though most of the time it's just a dull throbbing inside my head."

Jaden's green eyes took on a look of empathy. "What about the other stuff? Carly told me they were worried your spleen might be ruptured."

I leaned back in my chair and sighed. "I do have a bruised spleen and a sore leg where I landed on my side, but that's it. It's pretty much a miracle."

Miracle. The word seemed to jump out at me. I remember Carly saying the doctor thought it was miraculous that I'd escaped such a serious accident with so little injury, but this was the first time I'd given it more than a fleeting thought. A miracle. Goosebumps rose along my arms. If it was a miracle, I had no idea why I had been the lucky recipient.

"So, no lasting effects. Is that what you're telling me?"

My thoughts returned to the moment. I planted a light peck on Jaden's cheek. "That's what I'm telling you, babe." I laughed, borrowing Carly's term.

"That's good. When do you get out of here?" Jaden asked, letting go of my hand and leaning back in his chair.

"A couple more days. The doctor wants to keep me awhile longer to be sure nothing comes up."

Jaden took off his hat, raked his hand through his hair, then replaced the hat with the bill facing backward. It was an unconscious gesture, and it usually indicated nervousness. He was priming himself to express something difficult to put into words.

"Anything wrong?" I purred, sitting forward to stroke his cheek.

He took my hand and kissed it. "I wanted to fly home with you, but I can't stay past tomorrow."

"I think I can persuade the doctor to let me go home tomorrow," I replied, winking at him.

"Can you do that?" He looked doubtful.

"Are you therious?"

He laughed. "Then I'll make a reservation for you on the plane. The flight leaves at 4:30. I booked a round trip."

"Okay. Do it."

"Then, when we get home, I'm going to take care of you. At my apartment. Our apartment."

I knew what he was saying. I buried all objections I'd previously felt about marrying him. "Sounds good," I said, closing my eyes to receive his kiss.

* * *

I swiped at the tears burning in my eyes. "The doctor said absolutely not, Jaden. There's no way he's going to okay my release from the hospital until Monday." It was late in the afternoon of the following day, and the doctor had given me the bad news just minutes earlier.

Jaden tightened his arm around my shoulders, pulling me in close. "Two days from now." He swore under his breath. "Did you tell him you wouldn't be alone? That I'd be there to take care of you if you needed anything?"

"I tried every argument. He wouldn't listen. He just says I need rest and he wants to be sure the pain in my head isn't indicative of something more serious before he releases me."

Jaden began to pace the hospital room. "I can't wait, hon. My job is already on the line."

I sniffled, and looked up at him. "Why is that?"

He shoved his hands into the pockets of his jeans. "I've been late to work a few too many times. Late nights, ya know." He shrugged.

I bit my lip, wondering what he'd been doing during those late nights. Partying with his guy friends, I guessed. "I wouldn't ask you to stay, Jaden. You go home. I'll be all right here for a couple days more."

"I can't believe that dude," Jaden said, shaking his head. He seemed more upset with the doctor's insistence that I stay than with the fact that I wouldn't be accompanying him home. "I think you should get another doctor's opinion."

I shook my head, resigned to the verdict. "It's all right. I don't mind all that much."

He cursed once again. "I can't believe it," he spat out.

I got up from the bed and went over to him, and put my arms around his neck. "Hey, I'll see you in a few days anyway." I kissed his cheek.

He slipped his arms around my waist, resting his thumbs in the side belt loops. Today was the first day since the accident that I'd gotten dressed. It had felt so good to exchange the hospital gown for my own comfortable pair of jeans and a snug-fitting T-shirt. I looked up into Jaden's eyes. "I love you. Do you know that?"

He kissed me briefly. "I love you too, hon."

He released me sooner than I anticipated, his mind apparently on other matters. I stood next to him, my arm dangling around his neck. "When I get home, we can—"

"Excuse me. Ah . . . I can drop back later."

Jaden and I both turned at the sound of the male voice. I caught my breath in surprise to see Bridger Caldwell standing in the doorway of my room.

"Sorry. I can come back another time. I didn't know you had company," he said, glancing at Jaden.

"It's alright," I said hastily. I felt my heart skip a beat and didn't know if Jaden's kiss had affected me more than his past kisses had, or if it was the fact that Bridger had inadvertently witnessed it. "Come in," I invited him, trying to keep my voice from squeaking. "Come in and sit down."

I didn't really think he would after seeing that I was already engaged with a visitor—a very close visitor, obviously.

"Thanks." He strolled into the room and straddled a chair, the back of it turned toward us.

Surprised by his boldness, I eased back onto the bed. Jaden remained standing beside it. "This is Jaden Tanner, a friend of mine from Denver. Jaden, this is Bridger Caldwell. He was riding in the car with the fellow who accidentally hit me."

Jaden silently nodded an acknowledgment.

"Good to meet you," Bridger said to him.

I felt a sudden tension fill the room and was confused by the cause of it.

Bridger sat with his arms resting across the chair back. "How are you doing today?" he asked me.

I swallowed, feeling ill at ease. "Good. Much better. I'm getting released on Monday."

"That's great news." He nodded and smiled.

"Yeah, it is. How are you? How are things out at the project?" I asked.

"Coming along. We're just about finished with the preliminary surveys."

"So it's on to the business of architecturing," I said nervously, unsure if "architecturing" was even a bona fide word. Jaden moved closer and reached for my hand.

"So, Jaden, you're here from Colorado?" Bridger asked casually.

Jaden's grip on my hand tightened. "Yeah, that's right. Came down to see Annie."

I sensed some sort of power struggle developing between Jaden and Bridger and wanted to laugh at the juvenile way they were behaving. Bridger definitely had Jaden at a disadvantage on a physical level. He was taller, more muscular, and exuded confidence. Even though Jaden had a hold of my hand, Bridger was clearly in control of the situation.

"Bridger is working on a restoration project across the river in a town called Nauvoo," I said, looking up at Jaden. There was no mistaking the smoldering resentment in his eyes.

"Yeah? What kind?" he asked gruffly.

Bridger explained to him a little bit about the project, then he turned to me and said, "I was wondering if you wanted to see what we're doing out there. Take an afternoon or something before you leave for home. I think you'd like it."

I felt Jaden tense at my side. "She can't leave the hospital yet, dude. Doctor's orders. She was way hurt in that accident."

I glanced up at him in surprise. It was my call to reply, not Jaden's, yet it was amazing to see how quickly he switched sides regarding the doctor's mandate. "Thanks for the invitation, Bridger," I said. "I appreciate it. But I probably won't be able to take you up on it. As soon as I'm able to leave the hospital, I'll be going home."

"I don't blame you. You've probably had enough of this place," Bridger replied. "Hey, I brought you a little something to pass the hours until you get released from here." He stood up from the chair.

"You did? Thanks—you didn't need to do that." I smiled. Jaden leaned forward, his eyes narrowing.

"I left it out in the hallway," Bridger returned sheepishly. "Let me get it."

Jaden glared at Bridger's back hard enough to bore a hole into him.

"Jaden," I hissed. "Grow up."

Bridger returned with a large paper sack tucked under his arm. I sat up as he held it out to me. "Here you go," he said, nudging it into my hands. Jaden stepped forward to watch me open it.

I couldn't suppress a grin. No one had thought to bring me a gift while I recuperated in the hospital, and I was flattered by Bridger's kind gesture. I glanced at the printed words on the sack. "*Once Upon a Time Book Shoppe*," I read aloud. "Catchy name." I smiled at Bridger, and he grinned self-consciously.

I pulled a heavy object out of the sack, obviously a book of some kind. It was wrapped in pale blue paper and tied with ribbon. "What is this?" I murmured, unable to hide a pleased smile. Jaden leaned in closer to see.

When the paper fell away from under my fingers and I read the title of the volume, I gasped in surprise and delight. "Bridger, this is so nice of you. What a beautiful book. I don't know what to say." I looked up and found him grinning, the dimple in his cheek prominent.

"What is it?" Jaden asked, taking the book from my hands. He read the title, "*Masterpieces from the Metropolitan Museum of Art*. Is this some kind of art book?" he muttered, rifling through the pages.

"Bridger, you shouldn't have done this, but I can't argue with your taste in books. These are the kind I want but can't bring myself to pay for."

He laughed, the same laugh that warmed me earlier. It did the same thing now. "I figured you might already have the book, but even if you did, it would give you something interesting to browse through while you're waiting to go home."

Jaden handed the book back to me. "Nice gift, dude," he said, and I was half afraid Bridger could see Jaden fuming.

"I don't have this one. I'm thrilled with it. Thank you very much," I said to him, ignoring Jaden's bad manners.

"It's supposed to contain photos of some of the major pieces of art housed in the museum. But you'd know more about that than I would," Bridger commented.

"I'll enjoy it. Thank you."

Bridger wished me a safe trip home and turned to Jaden. "Nice to meet you," he said. Jaden nodded imperceptibly.

We silently watched Bridger leave the room, but as soon as he was gone, I wheeled on Jaden. "What was that all about?" I demanded.

Jaden feigned innocence. "What? What are you talking about?"

"You came on like a tiger with Bridger," I accused him. "He just stopped by to be polite."

"Yeah. And drop off a little gift." Jaden jerked the bill of his cap down over his eyes. "I don't like him. He's too smug."

"Smug?" I repeated in disbelief. "You were downright rude." I stopped myself before saying something I'd really regret and instead turned the book over and looked again at the title. The volume was an expensive edition, full of color photographs. I was thrilled to have it, even though it *was* a little much for a casual gift from a veritable stranger. Of course, I'd never voice that to Jaden.

"You know," Jaden began, his mouth forming into an ugly scowl, "maybe you hit your head harder than you thought if you believe that dude wasn't after something from you."

My jaw dropped open. I was astounded to hear him say such a cruel thing to me.

"I'm out of here. Maybe I'll see you later." He strode out of the room, not even casting a backward glance.

CHAPTER 5

That night, alone in my hospital room, I cried bitter tears into my pillow. I was hurt and angered by Jaden's harsh words, especially so after all I'd suffered in connection with the accident. Though I loved Jaden, I was well aware of his negative traits. His volatile temper was one of those traits. When he got mad, he didn't care what he said or who he hurt with his words. I knew he'd feel sorry about what had happened and eventually he'd apologize to me, but what he'd said seemed beyond token apologies.

There was also the book Bridger had given me. The more I thought about it, the more inappropriate I believed it to be. I knew I shouldn't have accepted it, but his generosity had been so unexpected—I'd had no time to think it through. And I was secretly pleased with his thoughtfulness. Yet I knew the book would become an issue between Jaden and me if I took it home, and so I finally decided to return it to Bridger.

The next morning, Jaden came to visit me at the hospital, bringing half a dozen red roses as a peace offering. He stayed until after lunch, then left to catch his plane home. I'd promised him we'd see each other soon. The following day crawled by, though I felt stronger and better. My head still hurt, but the disabling headaches were less frequent. In the next day or two, my parents would be arriving home from their cruise. They'd be surprised to hear I'd spent half my vacation in the hospital.

Monday morning the doctor permitted my release. My flight home was Tuesday evening out of St. Louis, and I planned to travel by bus the 160 or so miles to the airport.

As I closed the hospital doors behind me, I soaked in the warm May sunshine, then stood on the sidewalk with my eyes closed, luxuriating in the feel and smell of the outdoors. I had the whole day to myself and decided to take a taxi into Nauvoo to see about my bicycle and also to drop off the book at Bridger's work. I didn't want to face him, and planned to leave it at his desk with a note expressing my regrets.

I had just the one bag Carly had packed and left for me. I clasped it firmly and stepped to the roadside to wait for the cab coming to pick me up. The short trip from Keokuk to Nauvoo took only a few minutes' time. The taxicab drove the same route Carly and I had taken with our bikes, and when we passed the spot where I was hit, I averted my gaze, staring out at the river instead.

I gave the cab driver the address of the bike shop, and he let me out in front of the building. As the cab drove away, I tried the handle at the door. It was locked solid. I cupped my hands around my eyes and peered inside the window. The shop within was dim and deserted. I consulted the sign posted in one corner of the window—*Closed for Lunch*. The hands on the little clock printed on the sign pointed to one o'clock. I looked at my wristwatch; I had an hour to wait. "Drat," I muttered under my breath.

I picked up my suitcase and began walking down the sidewalk of Mulholland Street, which appeared to be the main street of the town. I passed a candy store where sticky yellow taffy was being stretched and pulled on mechanical rotating arms in the window, then wandered inside a gift shop, browsing through display shelves of blown-glass figurines, ornaments, and pottery. I purchased a postcard for Carly, and one for my parents.

Back out on the street I paused, considering which direction to go next. The most prominent landmark in town seemed to be a tall, white water tower with the word *Nauvoo* painted on it. I noticed many of the shops along the street were closed: not yet open for the day or out of business. Soon my stomach rumbled, and my injured leg started to hurt from walking. I figured I'd better start making arrangements for a place to spend the night. Hopefully, the motel would have a café or restaurant.

A few blocks farther on I spotted a small, white-framed motel with a vacancy sign posted in the window. When I went inside to inquire, the clerk told me the place was being renovated and was not yet open to the public.

"You should take your vacancy sign out of the window, then," I said, not bothering to hide my annoyance, "so people won't be misled."

The clerk shrugged.

"Can you tell me where I might find a motel that is open?" I asked, trying to sound more cordial.

"You might try the red brick one down the road a few blocks. I know they're open."

"Would you mind calling there for me to see if they have a room? I'm without transportation and recovering from an accident, so I'm having a little difficulty walking very far," I explained.

"I'm sorry, miss," the clerk replied. "We have no phone service yet, either. But I'll bet Agnes at the quilt shop two doors down would be happy to make the call for you."

"Thanks," I replied. I picked up my suitcase and made my way to the quilt shop, which hardly justified the title since there were only three quilts on display for sale. But the elderly woman behind the counter was kind enough to place the call to the motel for me. I watched her with a sinking heart as she tapped a forefinger on the counter, waiting for someone to answer.

"They seem to have stepped out momentarily," she said, replacing the receiver. "I can try again later for you."

"I really hate to take up your time, but could you call another motel for me?" I asked apologetically.

"There's only one more place in town that I know of, dear," Agnes said. "And they close for the winter. They won't be open for another week or two."

"There're only three motels in this whole place?" I exclaimed in exasperation.

"No, there're one or two more. But they aren't open yet for the tourist season."

I left the quilt shop without further conversation, feeling anxious to locate a place to stay. I looked up one side of the street and down the other. A few people were hurrying along the sidewalk, cars traveled by on the narrow road, but the town was far from bustling. My stomach was growling constantly now, and my head had begun to pound. If I didn't find a place soon to eat and rest, I'd have to return to the hospital at Keokuk and plead for my old room back for the night. *That* was a gloomy thought.

I started down the sidewalk toward the west, where I could see

Mulholland Street curving and dropping in elevation. I was curious about where the street led. As I was squinting down the road, not paying attention to the passersby on the sidewalk, I bumped into someone. "Oh, I'm sorry," I said automatically. "I wasn't looking where I was going."

"Savannah?" the person exclaimed. "You're out of the hospital!"

My eyes widened as I stared Bridger Caldwell full in the face. "I didn't see you on the sidewalk. How are you?" I said, flustered by his sudden appearance.

"Great. But how are you?" he answered.

"Much better. But a bit exasperated at the moment."

"What's wrong?" His expression immediately registered concern.

"I'm taking the bus to St. Louis tomorrow, but I can't find a room in this whole town to spend the night. What's up with this place? Haven't they ever heard the word *tourist*?"

Bridger chuckled at my response. "This town caters to tourists. But you're a couple of weeks too early. They haven't opened up shop yet."

"You can say that. Literally. I saw all kinds of businesses along this street with their shades pulled down."

"The tourist season doesn't start full swing until about the first of June, I'm told. Then this town quadruples in population."

I glanced down the street. "Why is that?"

"Because the summer months are when most people come to see what makes Nauvoo famous."

"The restoration project, right?"

Bridger nodded and placed a hand on my shoulder. "Are you serious about needing a room for the night?"

"I was thinking about taking up residence on the nearest street corner," I answered.

"Then you've bumped into the right person. I can arrange to get you lodging and food. How about that?" He raised his brow expectantly. "There are quarters for the people who live and work at the restoration site. And most of the BYU students have already left, so there's plenty of room."

I cocked my head. "BYU?"

"Brigham Young University. The main campus is in Provo, a town about fifty miles south of Salt Lake City. Ever heard of it?"

"I have actually."

"I'm sure it will be fine for you to stay the night." He gestured up the street. "My car is parked over there. I'll give you a lift and introduce you to the director of the Semester in Nauvoo program."

"Alright. Thanks."

"I have to stop at the post office first to pick up our mail because James is expecting a check from his firm. I told him I'd run up to get it. Lucky for me I came when I did," he added, smiling easily.

"You mean lucky for me," I corrected him.

"Both of us. Now you'll have to visit the project with me. Let me show you around the place. In return for rescuing you from a life on the streets." He took my suitcase and led me toward his car. He stopped at a candy-apple red Toyota Paseo.

"Here we are," he said, opening the car door for me. I slid inside. The car smelled faintly of men's cologne. I breathed out a long sigh, grateful to have my worries for the night's stay resolved. Bridger climbed in the car, turned on the ignition, and began backing out of the parking space along the road.

"Eternity?" I queried, raising my brows.

He glanced over at me with a puzzled expression.

I sniffed, my nose tilted meaningfully. "Eternity or Obsession. I'm not sure which. I noticed it when I got in the car," I said.

"You were right the first time. Eternity. I use far too much of the stuff. That's why I'm always broke."

"We all have our little vices," I quipped.

"Maybe it says something about our meeting today," he replied keeping his eyes on the road.

I turned to look at him. "Now you've stumped me. What does that mean?"

He wheeled the car into the flow of traffic. "Nothing, most likely," he answered.

He drove the short distance to the post office and pulled into the parking lot. "If you want to wait in the car, I'll be right back," he told me. He pocketed the keys and strode inside. I watched him go, appreciating the sight of his broad shoulders and narrow waist. He had on a solid blue, button-down shirt tucked in the waist of his khaki slacks, and a blue tie. He obviously hadn't been sifting through the dirt on site today dressed like that.

I was seized by a mischievous little demon who urged me to snoop through his glove compartment while he was away from the car, but my conscience prevailed and I sat quietly in the seat. I thought about his remark concerning the cologne, of it saying something about our meeting on the street, and tried to figure out what he'd meant. But it made absolutely no sense. I recalled Carly saying that she thought he was a little bit peculiar. I tended to agree with her. Though he was personable and nice looking, there was something different about him that I couldn't put my finger on. I hadn't forgotten, either, about the prayer Carly said he'd offered right after my accident. I was curious, and resolved to speak to him about it, and to return the book he'd given me. After I got situated into my quarters, if he wasn't mistaken about how easily it could be managed, then I'd address those two issues with him.

My musings were cut short by his appearance exiting the post office. He walked to the car carrying a single white envelope and let himself in. "Alright, we're all set," he remarked. "Ready to go see your new home away from home?" he asked me.

"If you're sure they'll take in a stranger."

"You'll just have to trust me on that." He drove west along Mulholland for a couple of blocks, then followed the road where it rounded a curve and descended toward the river. In seconds, a vast grassy area dotted with trees and buildings came into view. I watched curiously as we came to a sign proclaiming *Nauvoo Restoration Incorporated* and *The Church of Jesus Christ of Latter-day Saints.*

"Is this property affiliated with some sort of church organization?" I asked, looking back at the sign.

Bridger nodded. "Have you ever heard of the Mormons?"

"Mormons? Yeah, sure. I knew some Mormons at the university."

He wheeled the car down a quiet, tree-lined road. "Mormon is kind of a slang term for a member of The Church of Jesus Christ of Latter-day Saints," he explained. "The Church has developed and restored most of what you see here." Bridger gestured to the landscape.

"Wow. This is quite a project," I responded, twisting in my seat to look out the car windows. "This is where you're working?"

"Yup. We're taking measurements on a spot you can see right

through the trees there."

I looked to where he was pointing but couldn't identify anything specific. I watched with interest as we continued along the shady road for a few more blocks before we pulled into the parking lot of a large, two-story brick building.

"This is it. I'll take you inside and introduce you," Bridger said. He opened the car door and stepped out. I did the same. The beauty and serenity of the place was instantly appealing. Wide stretches of green, manicured lawn were interrupted by more than a dozen scattered red brick and log structures, and orderly crisscrossing roads. I heard a bird chirping from a nearby tree, and the scent of spring flowers wafted through the air. I accompanied Bridger into the red brick building, and followed him up the stairs to the second floor.

"This is the Nauvoo Visitors' Center. On the ground floor are historical exhibits and a film presentation explaining about old Nauvoo." Bridger indicated the various features as we walked.

When we reached the top floor, Bridger ushered me into a room with a long front desk and rows of bookshelves and cabinets in the rear.

"Afternoon, Sister Parker," he greeted a middle-age woman behind the desk. "I'd like you to meet a friend of mine." He turned to me. "Savannah, this is Sister Parker. She and her husband are here from Pocatello, Idaho, serving a mission for the Church. They're helping out the administrators who oversee the project."

I stared in surprise at the woman. She was wearing an ankle-length, blue cotton dress with a white apron covering the front of it. Dangling down her back on ribbon streamers was an old-fashioned straw bonnet. I put out my hand and greeted her.

Bridger continued his introductions. "This is Savannah Lawrence. She's been visiting in the area and is on her way home to Denver, but she needs a place to stay for the night. I told her you might be able to scare up some room here."

The woman gave me a friendly smile. "Well, of course we can. Savannah, it's so nice to meet you." She shook my hand warmly. "Is this your first trip to Nauvoo?"

I nodded.

"Well, I hope you enjoy your stay. You'll find this is a remarkable place." She turned to Bridger. "Most of the students have already left for home, but there are a few still here. Why don't you take Savannah over to the William Weeks home. Three or four of the girls will be there through the weekend."

"I'll do it," Bridger replied.

"You have Bridger show you around," the woman instructed me. "You won't want to miss seeing a single thing."

As Bridger and I left the building, I felt a stirring of anticipation. The woman's kindness and generosity warmed my heart, and the idea of exploring such unusual surroundings fueled my curiosity. As we walked back to the car, I whispered to Bridger, "Does she always dress that strangely?"

He burst out laughing. I stared at him, wondering what was so funny.

"Well?" I said, growing annoyed with him.

"It's a costume, Savannah—to lend historical authenticity to what they do here."

"What is it, exactly, that they do here?" I asked, my hand on the car door.

"This is a living museum of sorts, like Williamsburg, only with a spiritual dimension to it."

"A spiritual dimension?" I replied, cocking a brow.

"Let's get in the car and drive around the place, and I'll explain it better to you."

CHAPTER 6

Bridger and I sat in the shade of a tree near one of the restored homes. "So, what do you think?" he asked me.

I leaned back on my elbows. What *did* I think? That was difficult to answer in a single sentence or two. Bridger had bought me lunch, and then we'd spent the afternoon visiting some of the buildings in old Nauvoo. Each house tour came with an explanation about the home's original occupants and a brief overview of some facet of Mormon doctrine, presented by a person dressed in period costume. My head was whirling with all the new information, which was entirely different from what I had expected.

Bridger glanced over. "So?"

I smiled up at him. "Perplexing. That's what I think."

He laughed. "What's perplexing about it?"

I thought for a moment. One question stood out above all the others. "Well, for one thing, why did all these people leave their homes and families to follow Joseph Smith here?"

Bridger didn't flinch. "They believed Joseph Smith to be a prophet of God."

I sat silently, trying to digest what he told me.

"The early Saints believed Joseph's account of seeing God the Father and His son Jesus Christ. They believed the gospel had been restored and the Church organized according to God's plan. They believed Joseph Smith was God's prophet." Bridger smiled at me.

I plucked a blade of grass and stuck it between my teeth. "I've never been religious myself, so I have a hard time identifying with such notions."

"Do you believe in God?" Bridger asked.

I glanced at him and realized his question was asked in earnest. "I didn't say that. I said I'm not religious. There's a difference between the two."

"Well, we believe God is our Father, and He loves us and wants what is best for us. We believe He wants us to live with Him after this life."

"I guess that makes sense," I murmured, sucking on the sliver of grass. "I haven't given it much thought."

"Does it make sense for God to give us a blueprint to follow in order to return to Him?"

I snatched the blade of grass from my mouth. "Blueprint? What are you? Some sort of architect?" I asked with a grin.

Bridger laughed. I'd grown accustomed to the deep, rich sound and found myself liking it. "Would you be interested in seeing the displays at the Visitors' Center and watching a film there about the restoration of the gospel?"

"Why do I have the sneaking hunch that you're a Mormon, and are trying to turn me into one, too?" I asked, trying to look stern.

Bridger smiled at me. "Yes, I am a Latter-day Saint. But I'm not trying to convert you. I would like to give you an understanding of what we believe. So long as you're here in Nauvoo . . ." he added, with a wink.

I got to my feet and Bridger followed suit. "Well, I have no intention of joining your church on this trip," I said. "I've already been clobbered by a car, spent half of my vacation in the hospital, and wandered the streets wondering where my next meal would come from. That's enough excitement for one vacation."

Bridger chuckled at my rendering of the events.

"And my head is aching," I added dismally, noting the fierce throb beginning to take hold inside my head. I was tired from the afternoon's excursion and wanted to get my belongings situated, then rest for a while.

"You're worn out. Let me get you over to the Weeks's home," Bridger said in concern.

"Wait a minute, Bridger." I put a hand on his arm. "I need to talk with you about something. I really appreciate that book you bought me while I was in the hospital, but it probably would be better if . . ."

I paused as a sudden strong smell of flowers drifted in on a breeze. The fragrance triggered an immediate image in my head. I closed my eyes, trying to concentrate, to shut out everything else around me. I visualized a woman wearing a long, apricot-colored skirt and a white blouse, with a shawl the color of ripe, green apples hugging her shoulders, and a wide-brimmed bonnet tied at the chin with green ribbons. I recognized her warm smile, and sensed that she knew and loved me. And then, as suddenly as the image had come, it was gone, and I was left feeling alone.

I opened my eyes, bewildered by the picture presented in my mind. And what was that sweet scent, like a field of blossoms, lingering on the breeze? I turned to find Bridger staring at me, waiting for me to finish my sentence.

"You started to say something about the book," he prompted, nudging my arm.

"What?" I mumbled, consumed by the puzzling feelings awakened in my heart.

"The book. *Masterpieces from the Met.* Or is it *Met Masterpieces?* I've forgotten which," he said, scratching his head. The title Bridger was trying to remember was unimportant to me at the moment, for I still couldn't shake the strange impression I'd had.

We started walking toward the car. I concluded that the unusual sensation I'd experienced must have been due to the lingering effects of my bike accident. My head was hurting and my body ached.

Bridger apparently noticed the weariness in my face. "Let's get you settled in for the night."

I nodded, forcing myself to focus on what he was saying. "You've done too much for me already. I've taken your whole afternoon."

"I was nearly through with the stuff I needed to do, anyway," he replied. "It's been a nice break."

We walked the remaining distance to the car in silence, then Bridger opened the door for me, and I slid into the seat. I was quiet as he backed onto the road, lost in my thoughts, and Bridger didn't press me to speak.

* * *

The Weeks's home was a beautiful old house with an arched front doorway and three pairs of chimneys gracing the roof. It housed four girls on a study program from Brigham Young University. The one I liked most was a pretty girl with short, bouncy brown hair and lively brown eyes named McKell Hunt, from Portland, Oregon. She'd invited me to share her room for the night.

"We're going for a moonlight picnic," McKell said, bobbing into the room where I was unpacking a few things from my suitcase for the night. "Come with us."

"A what?" I said, looking up.

"A picnic in the dark," she grinned. "With starlight for candles. Some crazy idea, huh?"

It didn't sound crazy at all, but I considered declining her offer. I was tired and my head still ached, though a warm supper at the house with the girls earlier in the evening and a catnap on a comfortable couch had somewhat rejuvenated me. "Okay. But I haven't anything to contribute in the way of food."

McKell waved her hand. "You don't need to bring anything. All we're taking is doughnuts and pickles."

"Doughnuts and pickles?" I laughed. "What kind of a picnic is that?"

"It's all we have left in the cupboards," McKell giggled.

"Then it sounds perfect."

"Good. We're gonna be leaving in just a few minutes."

I looked at my watch. It was nearly ten, and dark outside. "Where will we be having this picnic?" I asked.

"We thought we'd walk over to the temple site and have it there," she replied.

I detected a reverent tone in her voice. "Okay," I said slowly. I had no idea where this temple was located or what it was used for; but I'd heard the term mentioned occasionally throughout the afternoon while with Bridger, always with the same mixture of reverence and excited anticipation.

Ten minutes later the four girls and I started off. The night was clear and warm, with a canopy of starlight glowing overhead. I was soon caught up in the girls' carefree banter and easily slipped into a comfortable camaraderie with them. The temple site turned out to be only a couple of blocks away. We approached it from the west and spread out our "picnic" on the grass across the street in the shadow of a large, unlit building. The temple site itself was surrounded by a wrought-iron fence. In the sprinkling of starlight, I could easily see the stones marking the foundation of what once must have been a grand edifice. The girls' conversation grew subdued as we sat on the grass munching our pickles and doughnuts.

"It's awesome here, isn't it?" one of the girls remarked. The others nodded their heads in agreement.

"What's this building behind us?" I asked, craning my neck to look at the sprawling building cloaked in darkness.

"It used to be a Catholic boarding school for girls, but the Church bought the property last year. They're turning it into a study center for Semester in Nauvoo students. It opens next fall," answered McKell.

"So it will be like a campus for students?" I asked, selecting a fat, dimpled pickle from the pickle jar.

"Yes. And I think a residence hall, too. You know what? This will be the last time students have the opportunity to live in the restored homes during their study program in Nauvoo."

"You're right," one of the other girls, a tall blonde named Sierra, remarked. "We were lucky to get to stay in the Weeks's home."

"It's been so nice to live in that old house," another girl named Kaitlyn said. "You really get to feel the spirit of the place when you're walking on the very ground the early Saints did." Her voice was soft and quiet.

"Yeah. They left a great legacy," Sierra remarked.

"It's incredible to see what is happening here," Hailee, a blue-eyed, strawberry blonde pointed out. "Everyone is so excited about President Hinckley's announcement."

I bit into my stump of dill pickle, wondering what all the fuss was about.

"I can't imagine how the Saints who once lived here must be feeling," McKell suggested softly. "After all their hard work and sacrifice, they must be proud of the legacy they've left behind."

"And thrilled to know that the temple is to be rebuilt," Kaitlyn added.

Finally I spoke up. "A temple's going to be built here?" I asked, noisily swallowing my mouthful of pickle. "On this spot?"

McKell wiped away a crumb of chocolate doughnut clinging to her lips. "Yes, right here. And it's going to look nearly the same as when it was first built 150 years ago."

"What's it going to be used for?" I asked. "A place to hold church meetings?"

McKell set down her partially eaten doughnut. "No, not exactly. Latter-day Saint temples are special places where sacred promises are made between a person and God. We believe that those promises are binding in this life and in the next."

"Really" I replied, genuinely interested in what she was saying. "What kind of promises?" I glanced at the stones set in the ground on the temple site.

"Well, eternal marriage is one," Kaitlyn replied. "Marriages performed in the temple don't end in this life. They go on forever."

Her explanation startled me. "Wow. That's something. What do you have to do to get married in the temple?"

"Well, you have to be a member of the Church who lives according to its beliefs and standards," McKell answered, blinking. My heart missed a beat. Even though I wasn't a regular church-goer, I knew about the Ten Commandments. And some of my activities with Jaden didn't strictly meet their criteria. I felt my face grow red and was glad the darkness concealed me from the girls' sight.

"I've been taught a lot of things about the temple and these historic old homes since we've been here," McKell said thoughtfully, her fingers caressing a gold, braided chain at her throat. Whatever was attached to the chain lay concealed under her blue T-shirt. "But my testimony has been strengthened most from what I've learned about Joseph Smith."

Sierra nodded, her blonde hair shimmering in the light of the countless stars. "I know. His spirit seems to permeate this place, doesn't it? Nauvoo, the beautiful. The City of Joseph."

"This has been one of the best experiences of my life. I'm going to hate to leave this place," said Kaitlyn.

The girls lapsed into contemplative silence. I found myself wishing I knew more about Nauvoo's history and the people who had once lived here.

"I'm so grateful to be a member of the Church," Hailee said

quietly. "I've made some mistakes in my life, but the principles of the gospel have always been there, constant as the North Star, to guide me." Her eyes traveled across the starry heavens.

I listened silently to the conversation taking place. The girls talked about their experiences over the last few months, and how they had enriched their lives. I couldn't relate to most of what was said, though they tried to include me and explain concepts I didn't understand. They spoke about their love for their families, their plans for the future, and their hopes for marriage and children. McKell said when she was married, she wanted it to take place in the soon-to-be-constructed Nauvoo Temple.

I couldn't help but admire their lofty goals and desires, and the manner in which they conducted their lives. I gathered that none of the girls drank alcohol, smoked, or used drugs, and I found that very courageous. I almost wished I had conducted my life in a like manner.

By the time we'd polished off the last doughnut and cleaned the last pickle from the jar, I had learned a number of things about their church just from listening to the girls. As we walked back to the house together, McKell slipped her arm around my shoulder for a moment. "I'm so glad we got the opportunity to meet you," she said with genuine feeling.

"Thanks. I'm glad, too."

"I wish you could stay for a couple of days with us. Until we have to leave," Sierra said wistfully. "We could have some good times together."

"Hey, why don't you stay for a few more days?" Kaitlyn echoed. "Do you have to catch your plane tomorrow? Couldn't you wait until the weekend?"

The other girls clamored in a chorus of agreement.

"I don't think that would be possible," I stammered. Their kindness and acceptance of me was touching.

"Oh, come on," Hailee said, slinging her arm around my neck. "What's so important that it can't wait for a few days more?"

I thought about Jaden and the arrangements awaiting me. Suddenly, I wasn't so sure that those plans were really what I wanted. Should I stay a day or two longer? Jaden would be furious if I did. But I liked what I felt here in Nauvoo, associating with these people who set such high standards for themselves, firmly believing they were following God's laws. There was something about them that drew me to them. I wanted to know more about the way they lived.

"How many more days are you planning to be here?" I asked the girls.

"Four days. We leave Saturday morning to catch our plane in St. Louis," McKell answered.

I looked from McKell to Sierra, and then at the other two girls, all standing elbow to elbow in a clump. "Do you have any more doughnuts in the cupboard?" I deadpanned.

McKell broke out laughing. "No, but I promise we'll buy some more first thing tomorrow for you."

"Then I might consider staying." I grinned.

CHAPTER 7

The next morning Bridger Caldwell was standing on the front step of the house at nine o'clock. He'd volunteered the day before to drive me to St. Louis rather than let me take the bus.

"'Morning," he greeted me brightly when I opened the door to his knock.

"Good morning yourself," I returned. "You're going to be upset with me."

A look of surprise crossed his face. "Why is that?"

"Because I'm not leaving for St. Louis today. I've decided to stay in Nauvoo for a few days longer. Are you angry?" I asked. "After arranging time off from work to take me?"

The dimple in his cheek sprang into view. "Angry? Are you kidding? That's great news." His grin penetrated the farthest corners of his face.

I smiled, too. "The girls here at the house are so awesome. They invited me to stay awhile longer with them, and I think I will. I'm sorry to inconvenience you this morning."

Bridger leaned against the door frame. "You know what this means, don't you?" His face was solemn, but his eyes danced.

"No. What?"

"You're obligated to spend the morning with me. To make up for the inconvenience."

"Oh, really?" I grinned. "You think I owe that to you?"

"Most definitely."

I opened the door wider. "Then I guess I have to invite you inside."

He stepped through the doorway, his hands in his pockets.

"Hey, Bridger. 'Morning," McKell said to him as she drained a glass of milk at the kitchen table.

Bridger crossed through the small living room into the kitchen. "How's it going, Kellie?" he asked, lowering his tall frame onto a chair.

"Fine. Has Savannah told you the good news?"

I followed Bridger into the kitchen and took a chair across from him. He glanced at me and smiled. "About her staying for a few days? Yeah, that's great."

I rested my chin in my hand. "Are you living in one of the restored homes here, too?" I asked him.

"No, the company I'm with arranged for me to stay at a motel in town."

When I asked him how long he'd been in Nauvoo, he said three months.

"And I'm staying until the end of August," he added. "I'll tell you what. I have to stop at the office first to speak to James, then how would you like to have your very own, genuine Nauvoo red brick to take home as a souvenir?"

"A brick? You mean like a building brick?" I asked, puzzled.

McKell chuckled. "I think he wants to take you to see the brick-making exhibit here on the grounds."

"Oh. Okay. Just what I've always wanted, my own personal red brick," I joked.

Bridger and McKell laughed at my comment. "You ready to go, then?" Bridger asked.

"Yeah. Just give me a minute to drag a comb through my hair." I stood up and went to the bedroom I shared with McKell, quickly changed clothes, and put my hair into a clip to keep it off my neck. Then I smudged on some blush and lip gloss and took one last look in the mirror. Satisfied with my appearance, I grabbed my camera and hurried back to the kitchen. "All set," I announced.

Bridger got up from his chair. "Okay. Let's go."

"See you in a while, Kell," I said over my shoulder as Bridger and I headed for the door.

"Have a good time," she called.

"I feel guilty about taking your morning," I said to Bridger as he opened the door of the Toyota for me. "You already spent all yesterday afternoon away from your work because of me."

"Yeah. James will probably discharge me," he said, sober faced.

I punched his shoulder. "I mean it. I'll go see the brick making whatever-it-is with you, then you go back to work. I can see the rest of the stuff on my own."

"We'll discuss that afterward," he hedged, hiding a grin. "I'll drop the car off at the office, and we'll walk from there."

The office turned out to be a portable trailer parked on the edge of the Nauvoo Restoration property, close to the river. Bridger pulled up next to James's Pontiac Grand Am and parked. A shudder passed through me as I gazed at the blue Pontiac. It was the same car James had been driving when I veered my bicycle into his path. I took a deep breath and followed Bridger into the trailer office, where we found James hunched over a desk littered with papers.

"'Morning, James," Bridger said to him. "You know Savannah Lawrence," he added by way of introduction.

James reached across the cluttered desk to shake my hand. "Of course. How are you feeling, Miss Lawrence?"

"Fine. I'm much better than when we met at the hospital."

The older man's face reddened. "I'm glad to hear that. I can't tell you how sorry I am about what happened."

"It wasn't your fault, Mr. Baldwin. I rode right into your path."

"Savannah was planning to take a plane out of St. Louis, and I offered to drive her there, like I mentioned to you," Bridger said. "But she's decided to stay a few days. So I thought I'd take the morning anyway, to show her around some, if you don't need me."

James rocked back in his chair and put his hands behind his balding head. His shirt stretched tautly over a bulging belly, gaping open between button holes. "Sure. You two go and have a good time. We can get started on that layout when you get back this afternoon."

"Alright. I'll be back before one."

"That'll be fine," replied James. "Nice to see you again, Miss Lawrence."

Bridger and I exited the trailer office and started off on foot. "Was he really okay with you taking the morning off?" I asked.

"I think so. Sometimes I get the feeling he'd rather not be saddled with me at all." Bridger glanced at me. "He's supposed to be providing me with some hands-on experience, but he prefers to do things himself."

"So you mostly stand around and watch, huh?" I teased.

"Something like that." We walked down the road and started across a grassy square.

"Does James live at the motel, too?" I asked.

Bridger shook his head. "There's a small bedroom area inside the trailer, behind the office. James sleeps there. He's been in Nauvoo working at the site for about eight months."

"Doesn't he ever go home for a visit?"

Bridger reached in his pocket for a stick of gum. He offered it to me, but I shook my head. "He's divorced and has a couple of grown children. I don't think he has much contact with his ex-wife or his kids." He popped the gum into his mouth.

We walked across the grass toward a display area where rows of seating faced a small red brick kiln. A few tourists were seated on the benches listening to a man dressed in coarse trousers, shirt, and a leather apron address them.

"I thought the exhibit might not be open yet for the season, but it looks like we're in luck," Bridger whispered as we slipped onto the end of a bench.

The man in period costume was explaining how the brick used for building in old Nauvoo was made of clay taken from local pits. "There were half a dozen brickyards in Nauvoo during the Mormon period," the husky fellow related, "most of them located east of the temple. As brick buildings replaced log structures, brick making became an important industry." He explained how the clay was shaped and formed, then fired in the kiln.

I sat next to Bridger, my shoulder touching his, as we listened and watched the brick-making demonstration. I could feel the rise and fall of his shoulder with each breath. The sensation was a little distracting.

"After the bricks were formed, they were heated in the kiln to a temperature of 2,100 degrees," the man continued, holding a formed lump of clay in his hand. "It took about twenty-one days for a brick to dry after firing. The bricks needed to be turned every other day to allow them to dry uniformly."

I sat forward, concentrating on what the man was saying. "Bricks were used to construct larger and more permanent homes and public buildings. This same red brick was employed to pave the temple's baptismal rooms."

I blinked. There it was again, mention of the temple. My thoughts turned to the previous night when the girls and I had picnicked on the grass overlooking the temple site. Because of the girls' comments, I'd been able to sense something of the sacredness of the place. I planned to go back there in the daylight, by myself, to walk the perimeter of the temple's foundation and view the exhibits on display at the east end of the site. The talk of the temple, and the special feeling I had sensed there, had awakened something in my heart. I wanted to identify what that something was and why I was feeling it. And I thought a return trip to the temple site might give me some insight.

"Here comes your brick," Bridger whispered, nudging my shoulder with his.

My attention returned to the speaker. He was holding a finished brick, smooth and hard, the color of red sand at sunset. "We want each of you to have a brick to commemorate your visit with us," the brick mason was saying.

I watched him distribute the bricks. When he handed me the lump of hard red clay, I studied it, noting its weight and texture. The brick, smaller than normal, was etched with the words, *Old Nauvoo*. I closed my fingers around it, thinking it a quaint novelty.

The brick mason made a few concluding remarks, and then Bridger got to his feet. "What did I tell you?" he said. "It's not everyone who acquires a genuine Nauvoo brick."

I handed the brick to Bridger to examine as we strolled together across the lawn. When he was through looking at it, he returned it to me, and I stuffed it in the pocket of my jeans.

"I want to take you next to the Jonathan Browning house. That's my favorite place of all. Do you know who Jonathan Browning was?" Bridger slowed his stride to match mine.

"The gunsmith? He invented the Browning rifle, didn't he?"

"Good girl. You know your history. Browning patented one of the first repeating rifles," Bridger told me.

"The guy was a Mormon?" I asked in surprise.

"A convert to the Mormon Church. He lived in Nauvoo with the Saints until they were driven out. Would you like to see his shop?"

"Of course."

We spent over an hour touring Browning's reconstructed home and gunshop, built on the original site, and viewing the many guns on display. Then Bridger took me to see the restored post office, and after that the printing office. I snapped a whole roll of film during the morning, and when we paused to take a break, I stole a shot of Bridger perched on the top rail of a split-log fence.

"Hey! At least let me pose if you're gonna take my picture," Bridger protested. He turned in profile and flexed the muscles in his arm. His bicep muscle bulged under his shirtsleeve. I snapped in quick succession as he moved from one muscle-man pose to another.

"Okay. That's enough," he said, laughing. "Stop with the camera."

I took one last picture and then put the camera away. "When you're a famous architect, I can sell these photographs and never have to work again," I joked.

Bridger hopped down from the rail fence. "What about your job as the curator of the Met? Wouldn't you miss that?"

"That's right. The Metropolitan Museum of Art. Carly believes I'm going to own that place one day," I laughed. My thoughts lingered on Carly. I hadn't heard from her since she returned home. I wanted to call her. And I needed to telephone Jaden and tell him of my plans to stay in Nauvoo for the time being. That was going to be a disagreeable task.

"You're frowning. What's wrong? Aren't things going well at the Met?" Bridger teased.

I looked up into his face. His eyes were the color of blue smoke. His hair, cut short and stylish, was like thick rich earth. He was wearing a pair of denim jeans and a sky blue T-shirt. I smiled at him. "I was just thinking about what I have to do when I get home. I'm going to have to get a job. A real job. Not a pretend one at the Met."

Bridger returned my smile. "Why don't you think about getting a job here?"

"What?"

"Stay here for the summer. This town balloons during the summer months. You could find work easily."

"No way," I said hastily. "I've got plans at home."

Bridger dug the toe of his shoe into the grass. "Those plans include your boyfriend, right?"

My head whipped up. "Jaden? Yeah, partly."

"You planning to marry him when you get home?"

I averted my gaze, pretending to study some scene in the distance. "I don't know. Maybe." I paused and put my hands on my hips. "You know what? You haven't told me which one of these sites you and James are working on."

Bridger looked reluctant to change the topic of conversation. "The stable. There was a red brick stable near Joseph Smith's Mansion House. It was unusual because it was a two-story."

"A two-story stable? Really." I sensed the tension spring between us. His remark about Jaden had flung up an invisible barrier.

"Yeah. They probably kept the feed and tack on the upper level. It was a good-sized stable for the time."

We walked to the spot without making much conversation. Bridger kept his hands in his pockets and his eyes on the ground. His jaws moved rhythmically as he chewed his gum. He stopped at a grassy spot near the river, across the street from Joseph Smith's Mansion House. "You can see we've done some preliminary excavation here," he said, rippling the grass with his shoe. "We know where the cornerstones were, and thus the dimensions of the building."

"Are there plans to reconstruct the stable?"

"Yes, eventually. After the archaeological and engineering work is done. And when financing is available."

I paced the grassy area where the stable once stood. "Who provides the funding for the rebuilding?"

Bridger explained that this project was different from the others because the stable, along with the Mansion House, the Nauvoo House, and the log Homestead, originally belonged to the Joseph Smith family. The sites were currently owned by a break-off organization called the Reorganized Church of Jesus Christ of Latter Day Saints. "They get their funds from church headquarters and donations of the members. James's firm has been hired by the Reorganized Church to do some preliminary work on this particular site."

I listened with interest to Bridger's explanation.

"The bulk of the sites are owned and maintained by the Mormon Church," he went on. "The umbrella organization is called Nauvoo

Restoration Incorporated, a nonprofit corporation owned by the Church. It was organized to restore and operate the facilities here. Monies are used from Church funds and the donations of individuals."

"Well," Bridger said after a moment's silence. "I'd better be heading back to work." He glanced at his wristwatch. "It's nearly one."

"I should get going, too. I promised to hang out with McKell and the girls this afternoon."

We sauntered across the grass, heading for the trailer office which was situated nearby. I enjoyed the feel of the sun splashing across my back.

"How's your headache been today?" Bridger asked me as we walked side by side.

"No trace of one yet. This place must be good medicine for me," I added, partly in jest.

"Yeah. There's something special about this place," he said quietly.

We reached the trailer office, parked on the grass beside the road, and Bridger reached for the door. "Come in while I speak to James for a minute. Then I'll give you a lift home."

When we stepped inside, we found the office empty. James was apparently away on some errand. On his desk lay scattered papers and an open ledger book.

Bridger moved to the desk and briefly sifted through the papers, then he glanced at the ledger. I saw a puzzled look cross his face.

"Something the matter?" I asked.

He bent closer to the open page of the ledger book, and ran his finger down a column of figures. "This isn't right," he muttered. "I saw the amount of the check myself when I set it on the desk for James."

I kept silent while he studied the figures running down the page.

"Have you got a second while I check something out?" he asked me.

"Sure. Take your time." I found a chair and sat down.

Bridger seated himself in front of the computer and punched a couple of keys. While he waited for the computer to boot up, he turned through a few pages of the handwritten ledger notes.

I glanced around the office while he worked at the computer. The one desk and a couple of chairs filled the small room. The walls were unadorned except for a plat map tacked to a spot above the desk. The door was ajar to an adjoining room, which looked to be even more cramped than the one in which we sat.

Suddenly, I heard Bridger draw a sharp breath. As my eyes darted to his, I saw his face looked taut and pale. I leaned forward in my chair. "What is it?"

He turned wide, startled eyes to me. "These numbers have been tampered with."

CHAPTER 8

"What do you mean?" I asked, startled by his words.

"The numbers have been altered. The amounts changed." He stared at the computer screen, then punched the keys some more. Rows of numbers flowed across the screen. "I don't understand this," he muttered. "This can't be right."

I stood up and peered over his shoulder. The screen changed each time Bridger jabbed at the keys. I could make no sense out of what I was seeing. Finally he paused and looked up at me with a stunned expression. "Someone has entered false information."

"A mistake?" I asked.

"I don't know. Either that or someone has doctored the numbers."

"Who? Why?" I stuttered.

He shook his head. "James is the only one who enters these amounts. But the whole financial program can be accessed at the company headquarters in Omaha." Bridger turned his attention back to the screen.

As I leaned to take a closer look at the computer screen, I heard the office door open, and turned to find James crossing the threshold. A look of surprise skittered across his face. Bridger looked over his shoulder too, and his face went gray as slate.

"You're back," James said, forcing a smile. "Good. We've got work to do." He nodded to me as he stepped around the desk and glanced quickly at the computer screen. I noticed that the screen had suddenly gone blank.

"I was just about to drive Savannah to her house. I'll be back in ten minutes," Bridger said as he hastily got up from the chair.

"Alright," James replied, darting a glance at me. The look carried a hint of suspicion.

Bridger ushered me outside. He didn't speak until we were both seated in the car. "Don't say anything about this to anyone. Not until I've had a chance to do a little digging."

"You're not going to mention the mix-up in numbers to James?"

"Not yet. Not until I'm sure he's not involved in any way."

I gasped with surprise. "You think James is the one falsifying the numbers?"

Bridger put the Toyota in gear and pulled out onto the road. "I didn't say that. There's a chance I could be mistaken about this whole thing. I need to look over the account balances carefully."

Bridger's expression was grim as he drove me the short few blocks to the Weeks's home. He pulled to a stop and I got out of the car. "Thanks for the morning's tour. I enjoyed it," I said, trying to lighten his mood.

"Me, too. I'll talk to you tomorrow, okay?"

"Sure." I could plainly see he was distracted by his thoughts. "See you later." He drove away as I walked to the front door of the house.

"Hi," Sierra greeted me as I entered the living room. She was seated on the couch, a paperback book in her hand, and her blonde hair pulled into a ponytail. "How was your morning?"

I sat down next to her. "Really nice," I responded, blocking out the tension of the last few minutes. I showed her my genuine Nauvoo brick. "Bridger took me to see the brick making exhibit, the Jonathan Browning house, the post office and printing office. It was very interesting."

"You've seen a lot of stuff in two days' time, haven't you?" she smiled.

"Yeah, I have."

"Are you glad you decided to stay longer?"

I nodded.

Sierra closed her book and set it on the couch. "Bridger's nice, isn't he?" she commented.

I remembered Bridger mentioning that he'd met all four of the girls living at the Weeks's home. "He seems to be. How long have you known Bridger?" I asked.

"Just through the semester, since we've been here. We met him the first week or so."

I grinned slyly. "Did you date him?"

Sierra laughed. "I would have liked to. But he and Kell hit it off right away."

"McKell?" I said in surprise. "Kell and Bridger dated?"

"They were a hot item for awhile," Sierra answered. "Didn't you know that?"

I shook my head. "No, I didn't. Kell has never mentioned it." I pictured Bridger and McKell together, walking hand in hand or stealing a quick kiss under the trees. I was surprised to find myself experiencing a twinge of envy.

"Yeah. They were tight for about three months."

"What happened?" I asked, trying to sound nonchalant.

"Nothing in particular. They just decided mutually to call it quits. I guess the spark went out."

I silently mulled over Sierra's explanation.

"You still want to see the Visitors' Center this afternoon?" she asked brightly.

"Uh-huh." My thoughts remained centered on Bridger and McKell, trying to visualize them as a couple.

"Okay. Hailee and Kaitlyn are at the grocery store, but they'll be back right away. We'll go as soon as they get home. I think Kell is in her room."

I nodded and stood up. "Do you think I could use the phone to call home? I'll give you guys the money for the long distance charges."

"Sure. No problem," Sierra replied, picking up her book again. "You can use either the kitchen phone or the portable."

It took me a few minutes to track down the portable phone. I finally found it in Hailee and Kaitlyn's room, under a pile of laundry heaped on the floor. I took the phone outside with me onto the back porch and sat down on the step. First I dialed Jaden's apartment, but there was no answer. Then I phoned my parents at home. I talked with Mom for about ten minutes, telling her what had happened to me and where I was staying for the time being. She was shocked to hear about my accident and was concerned for my health. But by the time we finished talking, she'd calmed down. As I hung up, I couldn't help but wonder why my mom and I had never been close. Had we ever really talked? I didn't think so.

I tried Jaden's place again, and this time he picked up the phone. My heart was in my throat as I tried to explain my decision about remaining in Nauvoo for a few days longer. He was angry with me; but to his credit, he tried to bridle his temper. He told me that he missed me and loved me, and was anxious to see me. I said the same to him. The words leaving my mouth, though, sounded hollow. We hung up a few moments later.

I sat staring at the phone, trying to analyze how I felt after my conversation with Jaden. I expected to be pining away for him after hearing his voice and wondered why I wasn't. The lack of intense emotion took me by surprise. Had my feelings for Jaden changed? If so, when did it happen? And why?

The sound of Hailee's and Kaitlyn's voices inside the house put an end to my introspection. I joined the two girls in the kitchen where they were tucking groceries into the cupboards.

"Look what we bought for you," Hailee said, thrusting her hand inside one of the plastic grocery bags. She withdrew a plain white paper sack and opened it under my nose.

"No way." I laughed. "Doughnuts. Just what I wanted."

* * *

Our excursion through the Nauvoo Visitors' Center awakened a million questions in my mind. My four companions tried to answer them for me as we moved through the exhibit. We watched a short film about Joseph Smith, his role in the organization of The Church of Jesus Christ of Latter-day Saints, and the emergence of an unusual book called the Book of Mormon. I viewed with interest the artifacts, documents, and paintings on display, and was intrigued by a large scale model of old Nauvoo situated in the center of the room. An imposing statue of Christ particularly impressed me.

But none of it moved me as deeply as the lush garden park where we now wandered, set behind the Visitors' Center, and called the Monument to Women. As I tread the brick plaza, I was awestruck by the dazzling display of flowers and life-sized statuaries gracing the garden. Placed at intervals along the brick path stood a series of polished bronze sculptures characterizing woman in her various roles. One grouping, titled *Joyful Moment*, depicted a mother and her children in a ring of joined hands. Another showed a woman on her knees in prayer. An exquisitely executed pair of statues, gleaming golden in the sun, represented Joseph Smith and his wife, Emma.

I moved from one piece of statuary to the next, reflecting on the message each portrayed. Crafted with skill and touching realism, I savored every detail. I marveled at each individual piece, and how the whole blended into one supernal masterpiece.

"This is amazing," I said to McKell, who stood at my elbow.

"Beautiful, isn't it?"

"I've never seen anything so lovely," I returned. I bent to inhale the sweet scent of a delicate blossom. The variety of flowers growing in the garden park in all their diversity of color and form was astonishing to me. Present were large, cone-shaped blossoms, and tiny multipetalled ones. Colors ran the spectrum. Many of the flowers gave off an exquisite odor which perfumed the air. I moved to a bench in the center of the garden park and sat down to enjoy the scene surrounding me, feeling a profound peace I had seldom experienced.

Few people in addition to my friends and me strolled the grounds. As I sat on the bench contemplating the beauty around me, and wishing I'd remembered to bring my camera, I felt the stirrings of a gentle breeze. The breeze sighed softly in my ears, like the tinkling of music. I closed my eyes, savoring the sweet smell of the blossoms and the soft sound of the breeze. Behind my closed lids, an image began to assemble. I seemed to see the kindly face of a woman. Her light brown hair was drawn back into a bun at the nape of her neck, and the long skirt and spotless white blouse she wore revealed a slim figure. She had eyes the color of a summer sky; clear, warm, and brilliantly bright.

Her visage in my mind's eye produced a feeling of serenity and comfort. I smiled to myself, feeling at peace with my surroundings. "How have you found your stay in Nauvoo thus far, Savannah Marie?" the woman behind my closed eyes seemed to say.

"I'm enjoying it here," I responded.

Her lovely eyes gazed into the distance and a shadow curtained them. "Remember your promise, and be faithful to your trust," I thought I heard her say in a voice as faint and inaudible as the rustling leaves in the wind. I opened my eyes with a start. My head felt fuzzy, as upon awakening from deep slumber. Had I drifted off to sleep for an instant, sitting here on the bench in the midst of the garden? If so, what a peculiar dream I'd had.

Strange, I thought. I stood up to join McKell who was admiring the delicate petals of a rose. I'd taken only a step toward her when I sensed the tinkling of a melody which seemed to rustle through the flowers. As I strained to listen, the sound evaporated. It was as if the woman had gathered the strains of music and taken it away with her. Perhaps my mind was playing tricks on me. I wasn't completely well from the bike accident, and at times my head still felt woozy. Or perhaps being here in this lovely garden with its myriad of fragrant flowers had only triggered my overactive imagination.

When it came time to leave the Monument to Women garden, I was reluctant to go. I glanced behind me as the five of us exited the plaza. I accompanied the girls out onto the sidewalk while they chatted together, though I didn't feel much like joining in the conversation. The things I'd seen and heard while at the Visitors' Center had left an impression on me, and I wanted a moment to ponder them. I decided to retire to a place where I could be alone to think about what I'd experienced.

As we started away from the building I said to McKell, "Hey, Kell, I think I'm going to hang around here a while longer."

She slowed her step. "Okay. I'll stay with you."

"No, you don't have to do that. I just want to wander around a bit more. See some stuff on my own, you know."

"Sure thing. We'll see you later at the house, then."

"Okay. Later," I returned with a smile.

She and the other girls waved as they started off again without me. I watched them for a moment before angling off in a different direction. I planned to visit the temple site, this time with more serious intent. I wanted to find out exactly what the temple had been used for and the meaning that it held in the lives of the Nauvoo Latter-day Saints.

I walked briskly across the grass, out to the road leading to the temple site. It was nearly supper time and my stomach was rumbling. It took me a few minutes to reach the site, and when I did, I found myself alone there. I walked along the perimeter of the temple's excavated foundation, then moved to a large model of the original Nauvoo Temple set out on display. I studied the replica, noting its shape and features. I wandered next to a pair of display cases standing nearby, one of which held a carved stone from the early temple.

I contemplated the scene before me, thinking about what I'd learned in the Visitors' Center that afternoon, the things the girls and Bridger had told me about their religion. The principles of their church seemed to make sense. Their standards and morals were strict, and I admired the character it took to keep them. Most of all, I was intrigued by their temple and the promises made there between God and man. To be married for this life and on into the next was a concept that had never occurred to me.

As I stood pondering these ideas, I noticed two fellows dressed in suits pull up on bicycles. They had packs strapped on their backs and wore white shirts and ties. I watched them park their bikes and remove their bicycle helmets. One of the young guys spotted me and waved. I nodded in return. An instant later they were both walking toward me.

"'Afternoon," one of them greeted me. He held out a hand and said with a broad smile, "My name is Elder Gardner and this is my companion, Elder Witt. We're missionaries for The Church of Jesus Christ of Latter-day Saints."

I shook each of their proffered hands, amused by their eager smiles and bright eyes. "Hello. I'm Savannah Lawrence."

"It's nice to meet you, Savannah," Elder Gardner said, pumping my hand.

"Are you here visiting Nauvoo?" the other fellow, Elder Witt, asked.

"Yes. I've been here a couple of days."

"Have you had a chance to see the restored homes down on the flats?" he asked.

I nodded at the friendly young man. He sported a thatch of unruly blonde hair and a generous sprinkling of freckles. His wide smile revealed slightly crooked front teeth. I thought he looked like a young farm boy dressed up in his daddy's Sunday suit. Both wore a black plastic tag on the front of their suit coats with their names printed on it and the name of their church.

"Is this your first time to the temple site?" Elder Gardner asked. He was shorter than his companion, and slighter in build, but he possessed the same friendly smile.

"It's actually my second visit. The first time I was here on a picnic." I thought that comment would startle them, but neither blinked an eye.

"A picnic, huh? Well, you're probably not the first to have a picnic here. Did you know this area was used as a place to hold outdoor meetings back in the 1840s? And I'll bet people brought their picnic lunches on more than one occasion."

I smiled indulgently at them. "Is that right?"

"You bet. The spot over there," he nodded toward the building which once served as a Catholic boarding school, "was called the West Grove, and the people would meet there to listen to their prophet speak. His name was Joseph Smith. Have you ever heard of him?"

I chuckled. "About a dozen times just since this morning."

Elder Witt pounced on that. "Then you've learned about how Heavenly Father and Jesus Christ appeared to young Joseph in the woods near his home in Palmyra, New York, after Joseph went there to pray. He was concerned about which of all the religions was right and which one he should join."

Elder Gardner took up the narrative without missing a beat. "God told young Joseph not to join any of the churches, that they were all wrong, and the true church wasn't on the earth. But the gospel would be restored, and Joseph would be an instrument in the Lord's hands in bringing it forth."

"Whoa. Hold on a minute, guys," I said, putting out a hand. "I've been to the Visitors' Center and some of the restored homes already. I know this stuff you're telling me." I went on in a singsong voice. "Joseph Smith prayed in the grove. The Father and Son appeared to him. He dug up some gold history books. He organized your church. He and his followers got driven out of Missouri, or wherever it was, and came here to Illinois where they built Nauvoo."

"That's right," Elder Witt exclaimed. He was rocking on his toes with excitement.

I lowered my voice, surprising even myself with the earnestness of my next comment. "But what I really want to hear about is the temple. What was it used for? Why did your people build it? How come all the excitement surrounding its rebuilding?"

Elder Gardner and Elder Witt exchanged a breathless glance. "Why don't we sit down together here on the grass? Elder Witt and I will explain it to you and try to answer all your questions."

I folded my legs beneath me and watched the two missionaries reach for their packs.

CHAPTER 9

At James's response to my knock, I stepped through the door of the trailer office.

"Come in," he repeated as I moved inside.

"'Morning, Mr. Baldwin. Is Bridger around? I wanted to talk to him for just a second."

James pasted on a false smile. I shivered involuntarily as he studied me from behind his desk. I knew my reaction was colored by the discovery Bridger had made yesterday on the computer, and I felt guilty for letting that influence me. After all, Bridger had said that he needed to check the balances more carefully before pointing any fingers. But something about James's demeanor chilled me. Maybe it was only that his presence brought back unpleasant memories of my bicycle accident. "No, he's not here, Miss Lawrence. He's out taking a few measurements for me."

"At the stable site?" I asked, feeling uneasy under his stare.

"That's right."

"Okay. Thanks," I said nervously. "I'll go talk to him there." I started back out of the room.

"Wait a minute, Miss Lawrence."

I froze in my tracks, my hand turning icy on the doorknob. "Yes?" I stammered.

"You and Bridger have become good friends, haven't you?" His smile was false. "That's nice."

"I guess so," I answered slowly. I wondered what he was leading up to.

"Bridger's been doing a fine job here. I plan to give him a good recommendation when he's through."

I nodded, not knowing what he expected me to say in reply.

"If he continues to work hard and tends to his end of the business, he can leave here with high marks. That will go a long way toward his future success. Academically speaking."

I felt a frown cut across my brow. I sensed his words were shrouded with another meaning that I couldn't interpret. "I'm sure he must appreciate the experience you're giving him," I replied cautiously.

James smiled again, a brief, tight movement of his lips. "Nice to see you again, Miss Lawrence."

I turned and let myself out, glad to be away from him. I swiped at my forehead as I hurried down the portable wooden steps and was surprised to find my fingers come away wet with perspiration. As I hurried to the site where Bridger was working, I saw him from a distance crouched on all fours. He was wearing knee-length shorts and a baggy, blue T-shirt smudged with dirt.

He looked up when he heard me approaching. "Hey, look who's out and about," he greeted me, rising to his feet.

"Working hard, I see."

"You bet." He dusted off the loose soil clinging to his shorts. "Doing some prepping before we take measurements. Want to help?"

"No, thank you. I'll leave rummaging in the dirt to you."

He smiled at me as he shaded his eyes with his hand against the glare of the morning sunshine. "What are your plans for the day?"

"That depends."

His smile deepened, revealing the dimple in his cheek. "On what?"

"On whether you might be willing to give me a ride into town when you're finished here for the day. I want to visit the bike shop to see how badly my Diamondback is mangled. Carly arranged to have it taken there after the accident to see if it could be repaired."

"Well, I don't know. That depends," he said, parroting my words.

I pulled a face at him. "On what?" I shot back, mocking his earlier remark.

"On if you let me accompany you, then take you out for dinner after."

I snorted. "You mean there's actually a restaurant open for business in this place?"

"I know the perfect spot. A little country café tucked away on a corner of Mulholland Street."

I rolled my eyes. "I've got to see that."

"Does that mean you'll go with me?"

"Do they have pecan pie?"

He grinned. "If they don't, I'll personally bake one for you."

"Do you promise?" I asked.

"You have my word of honor."

"I'll remember you said that."

Bridger chuckled, a slow rumbling sound. "I'll be through here around four o'clock. I'll pick you up at the Weeks's house then."

"Okay. And, really, I appreciate the lift. The girls at the house don't have access to a car or I'd ask one of them to take me."

"No problem," Bridger said. "If the bike is repaired, we can bring it back in the car."

"That'll be good. Thanks."

"What are you going to do in the meanwhile? Have you seen everything on the property?"

My gaze drifted across the meticulously groomed grass. "No. I still haven't visited the Joseph Smith log cabin or the Mansion House. I'll probably do that."

He reminded me that the properties were owned by the Reorganized Church, which was begun by some early members who apostatized from the Mormon Church and set up their own organization.

"I'll still be able to tour the properties, right?" I asked.

"Sure. It's just that members of their church who are the tour guides will have their own interpretation of Joseph Smith and some of the events surrounding his life."

A frown flickered across my eyes. "Are you telling me that what they have to say isn't the truth?"

Bridger sucked on his lower lip as he pondered his response. "Not exactly. I'm saying that we, as members of the LDS Church, believe they have been misled or misinformed about some doctrines and historical events. And that they have wandered away from correct principles."

"You sound pretty sure of yourself and your beliefs. What if your church is the one that has strayed from the truth?" I pointed out.

"That's something each individual has to find out for himself,"

Bridger said without flinching.

"And how would a person go about finding the truth of it?" I knew I was challenging him partly for the sport of it, and partly out of annoyance with his attitude. But deep inside, I really did want to know.

"That's not something I can answer in a few words. Why don't we talk about it tonight during dinner?"

"Okay. You're on."

A solemn look settled in his eyes.

"I'm going to let you get back to work, now. Before James comes along and finds you loitering," I said, kidding him. I turned to leave, then paused after taking a step. "Speaking of James, he said a peculiar thing to me when I stopped at the office to see if you were in."

Bridger's brows knit together. "What was it?"

"Actually, it wasn't so much what he said, though his words did strike me as a little odd. It was more the way he said it. Like there was a double meaning intended."

Bridger looked genuinely concerned now. "What did he say?"

"He told me if you tended to your end of the business, you can leave here with a good recommendation from him. But it came across sounding almost like a threat. And why would he say something like that to me?"

"I don't know. That does sound weird."

I nodded.

"Thanks for letting me know," Bridger said. "I'll see you later this afternoon."

It was only a short distance from the stable site to the Reorganized Church's visitor center, where the tour of the Joseph Smith properties would begin. I soon put all thoughts of James and Bridger out of my mind as I entered the building that housed a collection of Smith family memorabilia and waited for the tour to begin.

* * *

When I returned to the house I found McKell eating ice cream at the kitchen table. "Hi, ya," I said, plopping down on a chair across the table from her.

"Hey, how you doing? How was your morning?" she asked,

setting down her spoon.

"Pretty good. I did a little more looking around. Visited the Joseph Smith homes."

"Yeah? How did you like them?"

"The Mansion House was awesome. But I wouldn't want to live in a log house like the Smiths did in the beginning. Too cramped."

"That's for sure. Did you see the graves of Joseph and Emma?"

"Uh-huh. Big stone tablets marking the graves."

She nodded, then picked up her spoon again and dipped it in the bowl. "Want some ice cream? There's plenty."

I helped myself to a bowl of ice cream, which I took back to the table. "All I've done since I've been here is eat doughnuts and ice cream. I'm going to go home looking like a balloon," I joked. "And Bridger promised me a piece of pecan pie." I blew out my cheeks to make them look fat and round.

As she laughed at my remark, chocolate ice cream dripped onto her chin.

"You're drooling," I squealed, pointing at her.

She grabbed a napkin and held it to her lips, her shoulders shaking with laughter.

"That's the last time I'm eating ice cream with you," I said, suppressing a giggle.

She gulped another mouthful and grinned at me. "You're hilarious. Do you know that?"

"You think so, huh?"

"I can see why Bridger likes your company. You're fun to be around."

I smiled at her, wondering if she realized that I knew she and Bridger had once been a couple.

"So he's taking you out for pie?" she questioned, grinning. "Umm. Lucky you."

"Because of the pie, or because of Bridger?"

She laughed. "I meant the pie. But being with Bridger is a nice treat, too."

I leaned my elbows on the table and prepared to ask her a serious question. "I heard you dated Bridger for a while. Do you still like him?"

She brushed a strand of dark hair from her cheek, and her

brown eyes were clear and frank. "I like him a lot, but not in the way you mean. We did date and for a while I thought I was in love with him."

My eyes grew wide. "Really?"

"Yeah. We even talked about getting married."

"Wow. I didn't know it was that serious. What happened? Do you mind talking about it?"

McKell leaned back comfortably in her chair. "No, not at all. It wasn't any one big thing that caused us to break up. We just realized that we weren't right for each other."

I silently pondered her reply for a moment. "How did you know he wasn't the right one for you?" I asked, thinking of my own relationship with Jaden.

She shrugged her shoulders. "It just didn't feel right. And when I prayed and fasted about it, I felt like the answer I got confirmed what I'd already been thinking."

Her explanation left me confused. "You prayed and fasted about whether or not you should marry?"

McKell nodded. "I try to include Heavenly Father in all the big decisions I make in my life."

I wanted to question her more concerning that line of thinking, but for the moment I deferred my inquiries to pursue another course. "What was it that didn't feel right about you and Bridger getting married?"

McKell puffed out her lip in thought. "Well, it wasn't that he was lacking in any specific quality that I wanted in a husband. In fact, at the time, I thought he was everything I ever wanted. He's intelligent, great looking, and has a good sense of humor. And he's a returned missionary with a strong testimony of the Church, which is important to me. He comes from an active family and has high standards and goals."

I interrupted her. "You want an athletic husband?"

I was surprised by McKell's chuckle. "I'm sorry. Sometimes I forget that you're not a Mormon and aren't used to our Mormon terminology. I just meant that Bridger's family are faithful, church-going Latter-day Saints."

"Oh." I felt a little foolish for misinterpreting her meaning. "So he sounds perfect. What was it about him that you didn't like?"

"Nothing, actually. He treated me great and was sweet and

thoughtful. But I just knew he wasn't the right one."

That explanation wasn't very specific, but I let the subject drop. There were a lot of things I didn't understand about these people who called themselves Latter-day Saints.

"What about you? Do you like Bridger?"

I was taken back by her question. "Me?"

She gave me a slow, sly grin. "Uh-huh. You."

"I hardly know him," I fumbled. "He's a nice enough guy, but probably not someone I'd ever feel serious about. Besides," I added, "I already have a boyfriend."

"You do?" McKell exclaimed, sitting forward in her chair. "What's his name? How long have you been dating him?"

"His name is Jaden Tanner. I met him at the university in Colorado Springs."

"And?" McKell's brown eyes sparkled.

"Oh, I don't know." I shifted, suddenly uncomfortable with her expectation that I would explain my relationship with Jaden when even I didn't know what to make of it.

McKell leaned her chin in her hands, gazing steadily at me. "What does he look like?"

I was tempted to describe him as a babe, as Carly had once done, but somehow the term seemed shallow and immature. "He's cute. Bleached hair, blue eyes. A good build. He likes to work out at the gym."

"He sounds awesome," McKell returned, grinning.

"Yeah. I guess so." I smiled, but inwardly I didn't feel as assured as I let on. I thought about McKell's description of Bridger and couldn't help but compare his traits to Jaden's. Was Jaden everything I had always wanted?

"I'll bet Bridger will be disappointed when he finds out you have a boyfriend," McKell remarked.

I looked up at her, startled by her words. "Why do you say that?"

"Because he sure likes you. Can't you tell?"

I shook my head.

"Well, he does. I know him well enough to read it in his eyes when he looks at you."

I was dumbfounded by this revelation. I knew Bridger sought out my company, but it never occurred to me that he had an interest beyond a casual acquaintance. I felt my face turning red. "He already knows about Jaden," I said quickly, trying to hide my embarrassment. "In fact, he's met him."

"Met him?" McKell repeated in surprise.

"Yes. At the hospital. After my bike accident."

McKell looked confused.

"Bridger came to the hospital to see how I was doing because he was riding with his boss when the car hit me," I explained. "That's how I met him."

"And Jaden was there?"

I nodded. "Jaden had flown out to visit me in the hospital. He'd hoped we could fly back together to Colorado."

"Oh, I see," said McKell. "Does Jaden know you've decided to stay in Nauvoo for a few days longer?"

"I phoned him yesterday. He wasn't very happy about the news."

"No, I guess he wouldn't be."

I wanted to bring the conversation back to the subject of Bridger feeling an attraction for me and to hear McKell's reasons for believing so. It wasn't a topic I could easily resurrect though, without arousing her suspicions that I might like Bridger after all, and without confronting my own feelings about him.

CHAPTER 10

"How's your burger?"

"It's perfect," I replied with my mouth full.

Bridger took another big bite out of his own double cheeseburger.

"How's yours?" I asked, reaching for my napkin.

He stopped chewing, lifted the bun an inch or two, and peered at the meat and dressings inside. "Yup. It looks as good as it tastes."

I chuckled. "How did you come across this place? I never would have noticed it because it's so small."

"James brought me here once for lunch."

"Well, it's certainly quaint," I replied. Bridger and I, and another couple sitting a few tables away, were the only ones in the cramped little café.

Bridger popped a cluster of french fries into his mouth.

"Have you looked into the numbers thing anymore since yesterday?" I asked, thinking about his comment concerning James.

He shook his head. "James is always in the office. I want to go through the records when he's not around."

"I hope it's just a mix-up," I said, not wanting to consider the alternatives. "Oh, and before I forget to tell you, thanks for driving me to the bike shop."

Bridger set the burger on his plate and wiped his mouth with his napkin. "You're welcome. I'm sorry the bike was a total loss."

"Me too. I paid over $300 for it." I tried to make light of the subject, but wasn't very successful. The clerk had led me to the twisted and broken bicycle leaning against the wall at the back of the shop. It had made my blood run cold to see the condition of the bike, to realize

I'd been riding it when the damage occurred. Even now, thinking of it, a chill pierced through me. I shivered and hugged my arms to my body.

"That was a shock to see the bike, wasn't it?"

I was grateful for Bridger's sensitivity. "I have to admit it did shake me up a bit. It probably brought back bad memories for you, as well."

"At the time of the accident, it scared me more than it did you," he said with a tight smile. "I hope I never experience that again."

"You and me, both." We looked at one another across the table, pasting on smiles we didn't feel. "There's something I've wanted to ask you about that day at the accident scene." I hugged my arms tighter against my chest, feeling awkward about the matter I needed to discuss with Bridger. I hesitated, licking my dry lips.

"Go on." Bridger rested both arms on the table. "What did you want to ask?"

"Well, Carly mentioned that you said some sort of prayer while I was unconscious. Before the ambulance got there." I paused, swallowing hard. "I was kind of surprised and angry when I first heard about it."

Bridger didn't blink. "She's right. I did offer a prayer. But it wasn't just an ordinary prayer. I gave you a priesthood blessing."

I held my breath, sensing something important in his words. "Tell me what that means," I said.

Bridger leaned closer and lowered his voice. "When a Latter-day Saint young man is twelve years of age, he receives the priesthood from one having the authority to confer it on him. The priesthood is the power and authority that God delegates to man to act in His name."

I nodded, paying close attention to what he was saying.

"A man who receives the priesthood uses its influence and power for good. If he is striving to live righteously and has faith, he can employ his priesthood to bless individuals who are sick or may need special help. He also uses his priesthood in carrying out assignments in the Church."

"So you saw I needed help and blessed me. Is that what you're saying?"

"Sort of. But it's not exactly what you may be thinking. It's not a prescribed blessing like a priest or a pastor pronounces."

"How is it different from that?" I found myself holding my breath, waiting for his reply.

"It's different because a priesthood holder is entitled to receive inspiration from God in carrying out his priesthood responsibilities. He can receive inspiration to bless his own life or to bless the lives of others." He paused and drew a breath. "I asked our Father in Heaven to keep you alive until medical help could arrive, and spare your life."

"Why did you do that?" I whispered in awe. "You didn't even know me."

"That didn't matter. I felt inspired to do what I could to help. Do you believe the blessing helped you?" he asked.

I glanced away. "The doctor said it was a miracle I survived the accident . . . and with so few injuries."

Bridger was silent for a moment, his eyes searching mine. "But do *you* believe God spared your life?"

My mouth was dry and my heart hammered in my chest. "I don't know," I answered honestly.

Bridger cleared his throat before saying more. "This morning you asked me about the truthfulness of the Church."

I nodded.

"You wanted to know how one goes about finding the truth for himself. I've been thinking about that question most of the day."

"And have you found an answer?" I asked.

"Oh, I know the answer. I've experienced it myself, and taught it for two years on my mission."

"Then tell me."

Bridger glanced down at his plate. The half-eaten cheeseburger was growing cold beside a pile of ketchup-stained fries. "I grew up in a family that was very involved in Church activity. My father was the bishop when I was a teenager." Bridger paused to define the word for me. "A bishop is the spiritual leader of his congregation."

"Uh-huh," I replied, listening closely.

"My mother, too, served in many Church capacities, especially the Relief Society which is an organization for women in the Church."

I knew a little something about the Relief Society from my experience at the Visitors' Center and its Monument to Women gardens. "Go on," I responded.

"I have three sisters and one brother. I'm kind of sandwiched in the middle." A quick smile lit his otherwise sober expression. "I idolized my older brother, Lincoln, while we were growing up. He was just an awesome guy. Even though he was five years older than I, he treated me like his equal. He included me many times in his activities with his friends, even though his buddies must have been annoyed at my tagging along. If they were, they never mentioned it in my hearing because Linc wouldn't have allowed it."

I was interested in what he was telling me, but I wondered what it had to do with our discussion about the Church. I rested my hands in my lap, giving Bridger my full attention.

"Linc was an outstanding athlete in high school. He excelled in just about every sport." Again, the smile came into play. "He had a pile of trophies sitting in his room for team sport championships and individual competition. He was especially good at baseball and won a scholarship to BYU, where he played on their baseball team."

"Wow. He sounds terrific."

"Yeah. And not only was he great at sports, he was just a natural leader. Personable. Outgoing. Energetic."

"Sounds like the perfect big brother."

Bridger nodded. "When Linc was nineteen, he left BYU to serve a mission for the Church in New Zealand. I was fourteen at the time. The night before he was to leave, he came into my room where I was lying in bed sobbing into my pillow because I was so unhappy that he was going away. I wouldn't see him for two years, and at the time it seemed like two years was an eternity to be separated from my big brother."

Tears nearly started in my own eyes as I listened to Bridger's account.

"Because I'd been crying, I didn't see that he'd carried something with him into my room. He set it down on the floor beside my bed. When he realized how upset I was, he put his arms around me and hugged me for a long time. Then he talked to me about the reasons he was going on his mission, and how important it was for him to serve Heavenly Father. He must have talked to me for thirty minutes, until I had calmed down and was able to come to terms with his leaving."

I was riveted to Bridger's account now. I leaned forward, resting my elbows on the table.

"Then Linc bent down and grabbed the object he'd brought into my room. 'I want you to hang on to this for me while I'm away, Bridge,' he said. He put into my hands his biggest, tallest trophy, the one he'd won at BYU for outstanding player on the baseball team. It was shiny gold, cast in the figure of a player with his arm wound up ready to pitch the ball. It was beautiful." Bridger's smile widened with the memory.

"I kept that trophy in a place of honor on my bedside table for a year and a half while Linc was gone. Every time I looked at it, I thought of Linc and the things he'd said to me that night in my room. I was so proud of my brother."

I nodded, smiling broadly right along with Bridger.

"Six months before Linc was due to come home, he was transferred to Wellington, the capital city. He and his companion were driving with a member of the Church to a conference on the other side of the city when a car drifted over the median and sideswiped them."

"Oh," I gasped, sitting up straight in my chair.

"The car Linc was riding in flipped and slid to a stop at the side of the road. Fortunately, the other missionary and the member, who was driving, were unhurt. But Lincoln took the full force of the blow. He was killed instantly."

"Oh no!" I exclaimed, shocked by this horrifying outcome. "I'm so sorry." I instinctively placed my hand over Bridger's, trying in some small way to assuage his grief.

"Needless to say, I was devastated by his death. I was sixteen by that time, and his death threw me for a loop. I couldn't understand why God had let such a terrible thing happen to someone who was so good and talented. Why he had let such a terrible thing happen to me—losing my only brother like that.

"The only way I could deal with Linc's death was to put it out of my mind. I threw myself into academics and sports, keeping a grueling schedule from the time I woke up until I dropped into bed at night bone tired. And I put Linc's trophy away on the top shelf of my closet, hidden in a box, where I couldn't look at it. I didn't want to see that trophy ever again."

I didn't know what to say. I had no words of comfort for him. His experience was something I couldn't even relate to. I removed my hand from his and sat up straighter in my chair.

"When I graduated from high school, my parents urged me to enroll at BYU. But I couldn't do it. That was where Linc had attended school and it would resurrect too many painful memories for me. So I headed off to Utah State University, located in a town called Logan, about eighty miles from Salt Lake City. While I was there, all my feelings about Linc's death that I'd kept submerged began to surface, and I started to question the truthfulness of the Church."

I sucked in my breath, surprised by this intimate revelation Bridger was sharing with me.

"When it came time for me to think about going on a mission, I was confused and undecided about my feelings for the gospel. I probably would have chosen not to serve a mission if it hadn't have been for a wonderful, wise bishop in Logan. He met privately with me every Sunday for about three months, helping me work through my grief over Linc's passing, encouraging me to bolster my own testimony of the truthfulness of the gospel."

My heart hurt for him. "How did you get through all that?"

Bridger's tight expression eased, and his shoulders relaxed. "I did what my bishop asked, even though I didn't want to at first. I prayed often, and fasted many times. I pored over the scriptures. I started attending church meetings again. I tried to listen for the whisperings of the Holy Spirit."

"And all of that helped you?"

Bridger nodded his head. "Yes. Eventually. I began to remember the teachings of my parents and the lessons I'd heard at church. But it was my brother's fervent testimony that night beside my bed before he left on his mission that finally brought me around. I knew I couldn't turn my back on something that had been so important in his life. He didn't get a chance to finish his mission. I determined to take advantage of mine, and in some crazy way in the back of my mind, I figured serving my mission was an extension of his."

I was speechless with emotion. Bridger's account so stirred me that I was unable to utter a word. I sat and stared at him, amazed by his strength.

"I was called to serve in Argentina, and it was one of the greatest experiences of my life. The struggle I had gone through to regain and strengthen my testimony before the mission helped me empathize with those investigating the Church, to understand their questions and problems. On the anniversary of my year-and-a-half mark, I wrote a long letter to my parents telling them how much I appreciated all they'd done for me and what a tremendous example and influence

Lincoln had been, and still was, in my life. And then I asked them to go in my closet at home, get down the box from the top shelf, and set Linc's trophy on my bedside table so that when I got home in six more months, it would be one of the first things I'd see."

I bowed my head, nearly overcome with the power of Bridger's story. I felt him take my hand from across the table, and when I looked up he was smiling into my face. "So the answer to your question, how do you go about finding the truth, is a simple one. The hard part is putting it into action."

I stared wordlessly at him. His face seemed full of light, as if a ray of sunshine flooded his countenance. "You want me to pray about it," I said simply.

Bridger squeezed my hand. "Yes. And read the Bible, as well as another book I'd like to give you called the Book of Mormon. You've already become acquainted with many gospel principles from your experiences here in Nauvoo. Now you need to find out if what we've been telling you is the truth."

"I already have a Book of Mormon," I told him. "These two young guys I met at the temple site day before yesterday, Elder Gardner and Elder Witt, gave me a copy."

"The missionaries!" Bridger exclaimed. "You met the missionaries serving here?"

I nodded my head. "They answered some questions for me about the temple and the doctrines of your church."

"Good for them." Bridger grinned. "What do you think about it all?"

"Like I said before, I don't know yet. Sometimes, when I'm talking to McKell and the girls about the Church, I get this sort of prickly feeling inside that nearly brings tears to my eyes. Not a bad feeling," I hurried to amend. "A good feeling. A peaceful feeling. I felt the same kind of thing while talking to the missionaries. But then the feeling goes away, and I'm not sure if I'm interested in learning more about your church or not."

"That warm, peaceful feeling you've been experiencing is the Holy Spirit, or Holy Ghost, testifying to you that what you are hearing is true and correct. That's the job of the Holy Ghost, to testify. To witness of the truth. And that's what you're feeling."

I withdrew my hand from his and leaned back in my chair. "I don't know, Bridger. Your church has a lot of strict doctrines and rules that have to be followed. I don't know if I even want to live my life by those kind of regulations."

"Every commandment our Father in Heaven has given us is to help us live happier lives. The gospel is a pattern for living. It's a plan for returning to dwell with our Heavenly Father and Jesus Christ after we leave mortality."

I shook my head and looked away. I felt a wall building up around my heart, shutting out the message Bridger was so earnestly imparting.

"Savannah, look at me." Bridger took my chin in his fingers and gently tilted it upward until my gaze met his. "I know my brother is happy and at peace. I know he accomplished everything he needed to do in this life in order to live with God again. And that is the reason why I can accept his death," Bridger said quietly.

As I looked in his eyes, the wall started to crumble. But although I admired Bridger's devotion to his church, I couldn't accept the same plan for myself. It was just too foreign to anything I had experienced or personally believed. I knew I could never follow its precepts no matter how hard I tried. But it was nearly impossible to put that into words for Bridger to hear. So I sat silently, saying nothing at all.

"Will you at least read the book the missionaries gave you?" Bridged asked.

"I don't know. I can't promise you that I will."

"That's good. At least you're not promising that you won't."

"Do you remember the other day on the grass, after seeing the restored homes? You said you wouldn't try to convert me to your church. I hope you'll keep that pledge. Please don't pressure me, Bridger."

"I understand how you feel. I honestly do. There'll be no pressure from me."

"Thanks." I glanced at his plate. "Are you going to eat the rest of that burger?"

"Naw. I think I'm through. What about you? You ready to go?"

I nodded. We got up from our seats and walked to the counter where Bridger paid the cashier. Then we went out to the car.

"Do you have to get back to the house right away?" Bridger asked as he held the car door open for me.

"Not particularly. Why?"

"Have you seen the river at sunset yet?"

"No," I answered, sliding into the passenger seat.

"It's awesome. Want to take a walk along the riverside with me?"

"Okay. Sure."

He closed the door and walked around to the driver's side of the car. While I waited for him to climb in, I noticed the faint scent of cologne that clung to the inside of his Toyota. I smiled slightly. Eternity. That was the brand of cologne he wore, and the smell of it on him sent a tingle racing along my spine.

CHAPTER 11

"I've never seen the Mississippi at night in the moonlight," I said as Bridger climbed into the car. "I'm looking forward to it."

"Then you'll be disappointed because there's only a crescent of moon visible tonight. But the sunset on the water is incredible." He backed the car onto the road and headed toward the flats.

He turned off of Mulholland and made the curve onto Durphey Street, and from there onto Parley Street. We drove past the red brick Riser boot and shoemaker shop, the blacksmith building and the elegant two-story Seventies Hall, all of which I had toured. Bridger continued down Parley Street toward the river, then pulled over beside a small, open-fronted structure near the water's edge.

We got out of the car. "This is called the Exodus to Greatness Monument," he informed me. "It was erected here to memorialize the spot where the early Nauvoo Saints crossed the river after being driven out of their homes in the dead of winter."

We entered the three-sided structure and read the information on the back wall about the exodus that began in February of 1846. I learned how the people and their wagons were ferried across the river on flat-bottomed boats in nearly zero degree temperatures, and how others crossed on the ice when the Mississippi froze solid.

I shivered, thinking about how cold and miserable it must have felt out on the river, and how terrible it must have been to be forced from home and farm, from the beautiful city you had helped to build.

We moved to the center of the room and let our eyes roam over the many names etched into the walls of those persons who had lost their lives on the trail to the Salt Lake Valley. It was a sobering experience.

After some moments of quiet reflection, Bridger and I exited the memorial and walked to the river's edge.

The sun was slipping in the sky, though it was still some time before dusk would envelop the gray, slow-moving river. Bridger threw a pebble into the water and watched the ripples move outward in an ever widening circle. I knew he was thinking about his people and their past, and I remained silent, not wanting to disturb his quiet contemplation.

My thoughts wandered from the people who once crossed this river in cold and desperate circumstances, to the Mississippi herself. My gaze stretched across her great girth to the shore on the opposite side. I could see up and downstream for only a short distance before her waters gracefully curved around the bend, but I thought about the hundreds of miles this mighty river flowed from her headwaters to the sea.

Bridger scooped up more pebbles, then took my open hand and poured them into it. "Let's see how far you can throw," he said.

I took one of the pebbles, wound up my arm like a pitcher readying the ball, and let the stone fly. It landed with a soft plunk on the water a few yards away.

"That's not bad," Bridger acknowledged, raising a brow.

I tossed a second pebble, but it fell shorter than the first. "How far can you throw?" I quizzed him.

He selected a smooth, round stone, eyed the river as he carefully calculated the distance, then heaved it. The pebble skipped and skimmed across the water.

"Nice," I commented.

He skipped another stone across the murky water. "Was it Huck Finn or Tom Sawyer who claimed a man could grow corn in his stomach from drinking Mississippi river water?"

"I have no idea."

"Imagine all the towns this river flows past, from its headwaters all the way to the gulf. Nauvoo is just one of them. Each place with its own slice of life, shaped and influenced by the river."

"Wouldn't it be awesome to board a boat at the head of the river and float all the way downstream. I wonder how long it would take?" I mused.

Bridger emptied the rest of his pebbles into the water. "How would you like to take a paddleboat ride on the river?"

"Really? Is there one operating in Nauvoo?"

"No, but across the river at Fort Madison, about ten miles upstream, runs an old-fashioned steamboat that caters to tourists. I've never been on it, but I've wanted to go."

"Sounds like fun," I responded.

"Let's do it. Tomorrow afternoon, maybe around 3:00?"

"Fine." The prospect sounded inviting, and I was excited to take a trip on the river.

Bridger thrust his hands into his pockets. "Want to walk along the shore?"

"Sure." I dumped my pebbles into the water, and together we started along the riverfront. The sun was settling in the west, staining the waters crimson. We kept our eyes trained on the river as we strolled, watching the ripples spread across its surface. Soon the red faded to amber, and dusk cloaked the water. I wished I'd brought my camera with me. The interplay of light and shadow on the river intrigued me and would have made an enchanting photo.

Bridger walked beside me, studying the water. He was correct about the moon. A thin, golden slice appeared on the horizon, offering a slender finger of light to lift the mist from the river. I thought it an altogether romantic setting, the sliver of moonlight above the water and the last rays of color, fading now, in the darkening sky.

I remembered what McKell had said concerning Bridger's feelings for me. If he did care for me, now would be an ideal time to let me know by reaching for my hand or whispering a tender word in my ear. And I think I would have enjoyed it. If he harbored any affection for me, however, he wasn't letting it show. He strode unperturbed by my side, his attention fixed on the river. I suppose I was disappointed by his lack of passion. I'd spent much of the past week with him and hadn't caught a glimmer of encouragement beyond friendship—except for that one moment when he came to the hospital while Jaden was there. I'd felt a definite rivalry in the air between them.

"So. What do you think?" Bridger asked, pausing to look at me. "Didn't I tell you the river was spectacular at sunset?"

"You were right about that," I replied, keeping my eyes on the water. "Do you come here often at dusk with your friends?"

"My friends?"

"Uh-huh." I was thinking about McKell's and Bridger's relationship, wondering if he'd brought her to the river to watch the sun set.

"Which friends?" he asked.

I could feel his eyes on me, but I didn't lift mine from the river. "Oh, I don't know. McKell, maybe?" I immediately regretted the words. I hadn't intended to say anything remotely related to the two of them. I frowned and bit my lip, wishing I could recall the query.

"Oh. McKell." He paused, pursing his lips. "So you've heard about Kellie and me."

The words were a statement, not a question, and I wasn't sure how to respond. I decided to act blasé about the subject. "Yeah. Kell mentioned it the other day. I thought it was cool. You and Kell."

"You did, did you?" he said. I heard the amusement in his voice.

I turned to glance at him. His face wore a sober expression, but his eyes were teasing. I poked an elbow into his side. "I think it's a fair exchange. You asked me about Jaden."

"And you wouldn't divulge a single detail."

"I told you that we'd considered marriage."

"Uh-huh. Well, I'm not planning on marriage with McKell."

"She's pretty. And smart. And a member of your church," I baited him.

"True. But I'm not in love with her, in spite of her many fine qualities."

He was still making light of the conversation. "Well, what kind of girl do you want to marry?" I pressed.

"Why do you want to know?" He started walking again, following the edge of the water.

I hurried to catch up with him. "I'm curious."

He glanced at me as I came to his side and matched my stride to his. "Well, let me think about it," he said. "I guess I want a girl who's fun to be with, has a sense of humor, and doesn't take things too seriously. Except for serious things."

"Like the Church?"

"Right. And I want a marriage in the temple. To last into eternity."

Eternity. The word hung in the air. *Or more like cologne?* I thought with a start. What was it Bridger had said the other day when I commented on his cologne? I scrunched my brows trying to remember. Something about eternity and it being symbolic of our meeting. My mouth abruptly dropped open. I stopped midstride, shivers coursing down my spine like the ripples on the river. Had Bridger's remark been intended as a reference to eternal marriage? *An eternal marriage with me?* The thought brought a wave of dizziness.

"Are we through walking along the river?" Bridger asked, pausing a step ahead of me.

"Yes. I should get back to the house now," I answered, flustered. I couldn't bring myself to look at him for fear he'd see the astonishment in my eyes. I didn't know how to deal with the possibility that had presented itself to my mind. If I was right, why wasn't he demonstrating any sign of affection for me? Perhaps it was because he knew about my relationship with Jaden and he didn't want to interfere with that relationship; although I had a hunch he didn't think much of Jaden after meeting him at the hospital.

We retraced our tracks along the riverbank. Only the pinpricks of light coming from the homes on the flats guided us. I walked rapidly, wanting to distance myself from Bridger as quickly as possible. My head was reeling, and my stomach felt as if I'd taken a hard punch. I grimaced, remembering my thoughts of only moments earlier; those romantic notions where I imagined Bridger holding my hand or kissing me under the moonlight. Now it all seemed possible, and I wasn't prepared for the consequences.

"I don't see a stampede," Bridger quipped. "Why are we suddenly in such a hurry?"

"I told you. It's later than I thought and I need to get back."

From the corner of my eye I saw Bridger shrug his shoulders. We arrived at the car without further conversation and traveled the few blocks back to the Weeks's home in silence.

* * *

The next morning I helped McKell and the girls with breakfast, then collected the art book Bridger had given me and headed for the river. I had discarded the idea of returning the book to Bridger and had decided to browse through it and then pack it away when I got home so Jaden wouldn't see it.

It was a beautiful spring morning, warm but not humid. I followed Young Street under a bright sun and puffy white clouds. I waved to one of the groundskeepers who was out mowing the grass. Tourists were already roaming the lawns, their cameras snapping. I'd brought along my own Canon this morning to capture the river. The camera hung around my neck on its strap, bouncing against my chest as I walked. I smiled ruefully, thinking how similar I looked to the other tourists.

It was seven or eight blocks to the river, but I enjoyed the walk in the warm sunshine. I felt good this morning, with no trace of the headache that had plagued me since the accident. My injured leg, too, was feeling stronger. I picked up my pace, breathing in the smell of freshly mown grass, and the faint perfume of flowers. I paused once to take a photo of close-growing trees in a wooded lot. The sunlight filtered through the leaves, weaving a pattern of shifting shades of light.

Soon the river came into view. The waters were silver, and the surface glimmered and sparkled with the reflection of the sun. I stood on the bank watching the Mississippi roll past. It struck me how unending the river was, flowing constantly to the sea. It had followed this course for eons of time, and would continue to flow long after my brief existence. The continuity instilled a feeling of serenity and order inside me.

I sat down beside the river on a patch of velvety moss, my elbows on my knees and my hands under my chin, watching the water glide past, letting my thoughts meander with it. In the glare of the morning sun, my head had cleared of all the romantic notions I'd harbored the night before concerning Bridger Caldwell and me. I'd reacted foolishly to the phantom idea that Bridger cared for me. The glamor of the moment, with the sun setting the river on fire and Bridger's talk of eternal love and marriage, had temporarily blinded me. In the morning sunlight, reality and logic stripped away such fanciful thoughts. I allowed myself a deprecating smile. I'd known Bridger little more than a week, and had already been swept away by thoughts of romance. Such fantasizing was a failing I needed to root out of my character.

After a time I opened my book, turning to the table of contents. The photographs of paintings, sculptures, and other art works were arranged chronologically. I began to slowly turn the pages, savoring the exquisite illustrations.

As the river purred beside me, I paged through the masterpieces housed in the Metropolitan Museum of Art, from prehistoric art forms to modern day representations. My favorite pieces stemmed from the period of the Great Masters who painted in Italy, Spain, and the Low Countries. Enraptured, I studied the photographs of paintings and sculptures executed by such geniuses as da Vinci, Michelangelo, Raphael, Titian, El Greco, Hals, Rembrandt, and Holbein.

The "prince of painters" in my opinion, however, was Peter Paul Rubens. His works breathed with vitality, color, and movement, executed within a framework of technical brilliance. He painted saints and angels, scenes from mythology and history, portraits and landscapes. His brush knew no limits.

I stared at a self-portrait of Rubens seated with his wife, both splendidly dressed, holding hands in a bower of honeysuckle; the features so lifelike I expected Rubens and his sweetheart to rise from their bench and step off the page to greet me, the colors so vibrant I yearned to stroke their velvet garments with my fingertips. The conformation of the piece, and the attention to detail—from the lady's bracelets of multihued gems to the gold, rosette buckles adorning Rubens's shoes—enchanted me.

As I gazed at the painting I imagined myself seated in the bower clothed in the rich violet skirt, the ebony jacket with lace cuffs, and the stylish hat tilted to one side. The lady's small smile of contentment could have been my own.

Without conscious bidding, Bridger Caldwell's face replaced Rubens's handsome features. How resplendent he looked dressed in his doublet of sunflower yellow, black velvet breeches, and rakish hat, with one hand resting comfortably on the hilt of his sword, and the other nesting under my fingers. I giggled at the mental picture as I closed my eyes and imagined threading my arm through Bridger's as we rose to stroll the broad lawns and formal gardens of our estate, and stopped to steal a kiss under the arbor.

Reining in my rampant imagination, I turned the page and continued looking through the photographs. I sat beside the river with my book for over an hour. When I closed the cover my legs were numb from the pressure of sitting on them. I stood up wobbly, shaking out my legs and coaxing the circulation back into them. With the book tucked under my arm, I started up the road.

I hadn't gone far when I felt a strange impression come into my mind. I paused, then turned to glance back at the river. The gray waters of the Mississippi lapped softly at the shore. I stood staring out over the water, trying to remember something that I knew was important and shouldn't forget. But what that something was eluded me. I closed my eyes, listening, breathing in the smell of the water. And yet, there was something else as well. In my mind I could see a woman standing with her back to me, looking out across the water. Her hair, pulled back in a knot, glistened like amber. She was dressed in a pale orange skirt, a white, long-sleeved blouse, and a green shawl. A bonnet hung down her back.

The woman turned to look at me, and I saw the melancholy expression in her eyes. As our eyes met, a communication passed between us, so indelible and surreal that I couldn't identify exactly what it was. We stood exchanging a glance for a long moment. So real was her image that I started toward her, intending to introduce myself and at the same time learn who she was.

As I took another step forward, I stumbled. I had forgotten that my eyes were closed. Instinctively I looked around, bewildered. The scene was the same as before with one notable exception. The woman was gone.

I clutched my book to my chest. What was happening to me? Had I only imagined the woman's appearance? I'd always been somewhat fanciful and could lose myself in a beautiful scene or a painting before I'd even realized I'd stepped into another dimension. But now it seemed as if the other dimension was reaching out to me. I squeezed my eyes shut, searching for the lost memory that had haunted me ever since my arrival in Nauvoo.

CHAPTER 12

I leaned back in the deck chair and adjusted my sunglasses. The Mississippi swirled around the keel of the paddleboat. Steam puffed out of the twin stacks and every so often the captain sounded the horn, a blast that made our ears ring. Bridger and I sat on the top deck, overlooking the broad river. At Fort Madison, where we boarded the Catfish Bend Casino riverboat, the river was nearly a mile wide.

Bridger slapped at an insect crawling along his arm.

"Did you get him?" I asked lazily.

"No, he got away," Bridger replied, trying again by flicking at the insect in flight.

I lifted my camera from my neck and snapped a picture of Bridger as he leaned forward in his chair, slapping at the air in pursuit of the insect. "The mighty hunter," I teased him.

He eased back and grinned at me. "Hand me that camera, and I'll take a shot of your red, sunburned nose."

"Uh-uh. No way." I put the strap of the camera safely back around my neck. "I'm the photographer here, not the photographee."

"Photographee?" Bridger laughed. "Is there such a word?"

"If not, there should be."

Bridger shifted his sunglasses to the top of his head. "Look at that island in midstream." He gestured upriver.

I turned in my seat to view it. "That's the biggest one we've seen yet, isn't it?" I commented.

"It looks like it."

The land mass, covered with brush and shrub and jutting from the river, seemed to glide toward us.

"The Mississippi must have been a tough river to navigate at times for the old steamboats," Bridger remarked.

We watched the island slide by as our boat chugged upriver. "Yeah, and I'll bet the passengers didn't enjoy ice cold lemonades and hamburgers during the ride," I quipped, taking a sip from my own frosty glass of lemonade.

"They didn't lack for a game of chance, though, while aboard the riverboats."

"Those notorious riverboat gamblers," I said lightly, "making a fortune off unsuspecting travelers." I set my glass on the floor of the deck beside my feet. "Want to try a hand of cards downstairs?"

Bridger replaced the sunglasses over his eyes. "You're a gambler, huh?" he teased me.

"Sure. I'll bet I can beat you at cards five hands in a row."

"You sound pretty confident," he joked.

"Uh-huh. I used to win nearly every game when we'd play poker in our apartment at the university. I made quite a reputation for myself."

"That's it, then. You stay the summer and get a job on the Catfish Bend Casino riverboat as a professional gambler. You can make a fortune."

"Umm. Don't tempt me. I could learn to enjoy life on the river."

Bridger chuckled.

"So what about that hand of cards? Are you chicken? Cluck, cluck, cluck," I said in a falsetto, flapping my elbows.

Bridger laughed at me. "Not chicken, just cautious. I know when I'm outclassed."

"Oh, come on. It's getting hot up on deck anyway."

"I thought you wanted to get some pictures of the river?" Bridger returned.

"I have. With you chasing insects as the focal point."

Bridger made a face at me.

"So let's go downstairs," I insisted. I was anxious to showcase my gambling skills.

"You're serious about this? You really want to?"

"Of course."

He started to rise from his chair. "Alright. You play and I'll watch."

"Wait a minute," I protested, putting out an arm to prevent him from standing. "What do you mean, you'll watch? Aren't you going to play?"

"Naw," he returned, shaking his head.

"Why not?"

He shrugged his shoulders. "I'll have more fun watching you."

I frowned, trying to figure out the real reason why he was hesitant to play a game of cards. "This doesn't have anything to do with your religion and the restrictions it places on its members, does it?" I asked, feeling vaguely irritated.

"I guess you could say the Church discourages gambling," he replied, smiling.

"Do you mean to tell me you've never played a single hand of poker?" I asked, incredulous.

"That's not exactly what I said."

His eyes held mine, and I shook my head.

"And what about you? Have you read anything in that book the missionaries gave you?" he asked.

"No. I haven't looked at it yet."

"But you intend to," Bridger said, smiling so that his dimple showed.

I grinned back at him. "Do you think we could go one afternoon without discussing your church and its beliefs?"

"Hey, you brought it up with your rabid desire for gambling," he joked with me.

"Okay. Okay. I'm not going downstairs to gamble. I doubt I'll ever gamble again, in fact, if you're anywhere near. It's just too exhausting to deal with."

"The gambling or me?" he quipped.

I looked him steadily in the eye. "Both."

He threw back his head and laughed heartily. I couldn't refrain from chuckling a bit too. "So, what shall we talk about that doesn't hark back to the Church?" I asked.

"Let's return to the topic of a summer job and the possibility of your staying in Nauvoo for the summer." His eyes, the same shade of gray-blue as the river, sparkled.

"There is no possibility. I need to get home. I told you that once before," I said quickly.

"What's a couple of months going to hurt?"

I gave him a wry look.

"What does that wicked glance signify?" he laughed.

"It means the subject isn't open to negotiation."

"Why not?" he persisted. "Oh, yeah," he replied, nodding his head as if suddenly remembering. "Your boyfriend."

"That, among other things. My parents are expecting me home. I haven't seen them since Christmas."

"That's a legitimate consideration," he acknowledged. "But you could phone them throughout the summer. Send them postcards and letters."

I stared at him through squinted eyes. "Why do you want me to stay so badly?"

"There're a lot of reasons. For one, I won't have any excuse for taking afternoons off from work if you leave."

"Be serious," I chided him.

He extended his legs and crossed them at the ankles. "Okay. The truth is I like spending time with you. I'd enjoy getting to know you better."

I hadn't expected that. I swallowed and looked away. The river was green behind my sunglasses, and ripples glided across its wrinkled face. I bit my lip, staring at the water, not sure how to respond.

"Does that scare you?" he asked. When I didn't immediately reply, he flapped his elbows and smiled. "Cluck, cluck, cluck."

I grudgingly returned his smile.

"If you stayed the summer, then we could see how we felt," he said, his face solemn.

"About what?" I asked flippantly, though I knew exactly what he was getting at. For some perverse reason, I wanted to force him to spell out. Or perhaps I only wanted to hear him speak his feelings openly. I stared at him without blinking.

He squirmed uncomfortably in his chair. Both of our eyes shifted momentarily to a passenger walking past our deck chairs. When he was out of range, our gaze fixed on one another again. "The thing is . . ." Bridger began hesitantly. He cleared his throat before continuing. "The first time I met you, I thought, 'Wow, she's really awesome.' I still feel that way."

"When you first met me at the hospital?" I asked in surprise.

"Yeah. As a matter of fact."

I could see he was becoming annoyed. I guess the conversation wasn't going in the direction he'd anticipated.

"Look, maybe I'm way out of line here," he said, a frown building between his brows.

"I'm not sure what it is you want me to say, Bridger," I started to respond.

He cut me off with his hasty reply. "Just forget it. It was a bad idea anyway, your staying for the summer." He turned away from me to stare at the cold, murky river.

* * *

"Did you have a good time on the boat this afternoon?" McKell asked me as the two of us sat curled in front of the television set in our pajamas. We were watching a late night mystery movie, and our attention repeatedly wandered from its inane dialogue and thin plot.

"Yeah, I did. But my face is totally sunburned."

McKell cast me a glance. "Looks like you forgot your sunscreen," she smiled.

"That's for sure."

"How long were you out on the river?"

"It was a ninety-minute ride, but it went by like that." I snapped my fingers. "Bridger said someone should start up a riverboat ride here in Nauvoo. It would be a gold mine during the tourist season."

"I'm sure some enterprising entrepreneur has been thinking of that exact thing. I bet it won't be long until the old steamboat landing at the foot of Main Street is resurrected."

"Was there more than one steamboat landing in the old town?" I asked, thinking about the Saints' departure point on Parley Street where Bridger and I had visited.

McKell nodded her head. "I know of at least three. One at the end of Main Street, another on Hyrum Street, and a third at Parley Street."

I gazed at her in amazement. "How do you know all that stuff?"

Her eyes drifted back to the TV. "It was part of the course work we were required to learn during our semester in Nauvoo."

"I'll bet you studied all kinds of interesting facts about old Nauvoo."

"We did." Her gaze came back to me. "Did you know that the original owner of this house, William Weeks, was the architect for the Nauvoo Temple?"

I raised my brows in surprise. "Really? He drew up the plans for the temple?"

"Joseph Smith was the one responsible for the temple design, but Weeks provided him with sketches and drawings and was in charge of the construction."

I glanced around the room, subconsciously searching for any visible clue that the Weeks family once resided here.

Kell went on to say that William Weeks had also designed the Nauvoo House, the brick-and-stone building near the river. Although originally designed to be a hotel, it was never finished during the Prophet Joseph Smith's lifetime.

"Have you been inside it?" McKell asked.

"No, I haven't seen the inside of it yet. Was it completed after the Prophet's death?" The word *prophet* fell cumbersomely from my lips since I wasn't accustomed to using the term.

There was a twist to the story, McKell added. After Joseph's death, the property went to his widow, Emma, who later remarried. Her husband built the two-story house from portions of the uncompleted structure. He and Emma called it the Riverside Mansion

The Riverside Mansion. The name elicited a romantic picture in my head.

"Is there anything else you want to know about the city?" McKell asked, grinning.

I frowned in thought. "Actually, there is one thing. Are you familiar with most of the staff working here?"

McKell's brown eyes registered surprise at my question. "Most of them, I guess. Why?"

"Well, I wonder if you know a woman who dresses in a peach-colored skirt, a white blouse, and a green shawl. She has blue eyes and brown hair that she wears in a bun."

McKell laughed. "Well, that describes about half the women who work here." She paused, looking at my face. "This is really important to you, isn't it?"

I could feel the heat rise in my cheeks. "It's so weird. It's like she's there in my mind, only I'm not sure if she's real or imaginary. I wondered if I might be confusing her with someone I've met here."

McKell's brow furrowed. "Are you certain you weren't dreaming when you thought you saw her?"

"That's just it. I don't know." I glanced at McKell, wondering if she thought I was a little bit crazy. She had been watching me carefully and giving me her full attention. "I don't know what to make of it," she said sympathetically. "But perhaps it will make sense to you sooner or later."

"Yeah, I guess so." I tried to shrug off my feelings. "I won't have much time to solve the mystery anyway, 'cause we're leaving the day after tomorrow."

"That's right. Gosh, I really hate to leave. I've gotten so attached to this place."

"You know what? I think I have, too," I said, feeling an odd sense of peace even though I hadn't really come up with any answers to my questions. McKell was proving herself to be a wonderful friend, easy to be with, sympathetic, and kind. She was a lot of fun too, and I knew she would go for the idea that had suddenly popped into my head. "We ought to have a going away party to celebrate our last night here."

"What a great idea!" McKell exclaimed. "A party. That's just what we need. Let's throw a big bash tomorrow night. Invite everyone we know."

CHAPTER 13

This was the tamest party I'd attended in a long time. About twenty people milled around the Weeks home, chatting and laughing, and not one of them carried a container of alcohol or smoked a single cigarette. I sat on the couch between two of McKell's friends from the Semester in Nauvoo program, listening to them talk about their plans for the summer.

"Are you going home for the summer months?" I asked the one on the right, a short, freckle-faced girl of about nineteen.

She shook her head. "I'm spending the summer at my brother's place in Sacramento. He's starting a mail order business and wants me to help him get it off the ground. I'm not sure he plans to pay me for my services," she added, laughing.

"Is your brother married?" I inquired.

"No. But he's living away from home and I think he's homesick. And though I'd never tell him so, I miss him an awful lot. It will be awesome to hang out with him for the summer."

I leaned back in my seat, pondering her remark. She and her brother apparently enjoyed a close relationship. I thought about my own brother, Brett, and how it would never occur to him to invite me out to visit at his new place. Nor would I be comfortable in doing so. Though Brett was only three years older than I, we'd never been comrades. I nibbled at my thumbnail, thinking about my relationship with him. Brett and I had lived under the same roof for eighteen plus years, until he moved out and I went away to college, yet we were strangers to one another. I didn't know anything about Brett's future plans for himself, or even about his goals and desires. I wondered how

I could live with someone that long and still feel like he was a mere acquaintance. The feelings for my parents were similar, and yet I'd be going home soon and might live with them for several months while I looked for work. The thought didn't enthuse me.

My attention shifted away from the conversation going on between the two girls beside me on the couch as I caught sight of Sierra engaged in conversation with a blonde-headed fellow. His blue eyes were alert with her every word. I smiled to myself. Sierra accumulated admirers as effortlessly as gathering wildflowers for a bouquet. She was undoubtedly the prettiest of my four new friends with her sun-streaked, long hair and striking hazel eyes. Tall and pencil thin, she carried herself with a grace that invited a second glance. She had a boyfriend back home, she'd told me, but she was not averse to making new acquaintances. I liked Sierra a lot because she was friendly and gregarious, but I preferred McKell's company. While McKell was fun to be around, she also had a quiet, reflective nature that I appreciated.

I excused myself from the company of the girls on the couch, stood up, and began sifting through the people in the room. Though McKell said she'd invited Bridger to our party, I hadn't seen him. I slithered through the living room into the kitchen, weaving around knots of people in conversation, keeping an eye out for Bridger in case he'd arrived without my noticing.

I found Hailee in the kitchen eating a slice of pizza. "Having a good time and introducing yourself to everybody?" she asked.

I nodded. "Yeah, I am. Have you seen Bridger come in?" I asked.

"Bridger Caldwell? No, I don't think so. He'll probably show up, though."

"Probably so," I agreed. I was about to say something more to her when an attractive, brown-eyed girl grabbed her elbow and launched into a story. I stood by listening. Even though I knew none of the guests, I'd been enjoying myself. Being timid around strangers was not one of my traits.

After a time, I drifted away from Hailee and her acquaintance and went to the table to get myself a thick, gooey slice of pizza and a glass of soda. McKell, the other girls, and I had spent most of the day housecleaning, not only in preparation for the party, but because we were leaving the next morning for our homes. All of us had been a little disheartened about going. No one really wanted to leave Nauvoo.

I licked a stringy piece of cheese off my fingers and took another bite of pizza. A tall, string bean of a fellow said hello to me as he passed through the kitchen. I brushed a straying strand of hair off my forehead. Tonight I wore part of it pulled back and caught in a bright red plastic clip. The rest flowed down my back, straight and sleek. I'd chosen from my few belongings in the suitcase a cherry-red tanktop to wear, the hem resting at the waist of tight-fitting jeans. I rather liked the look of myself in red. I thought it complemented my chocolate brown hair and dark eyes.

I was standing in the entrance of the kitchen chewing a big mouthful of pizza when I saw Bridger walk through the front door. He was accompanied by two guys who looked to be about his age. One was blonde and good looking, and the other short and a bit pudgy, with an unruly mop of brown hair, and glasses that drooped onto the end of his nose. I watched the three of them blend into the crowded living room.

I gulped down the rest of my pizza and swigged the last of my soda, then headed for the living room. I spotted Bridger talking with McKell and made my way toward them. "Hi," I greeted Bridger. "I was wondering if you were going to make it."

"We just got here," Bridger replied. He gave me a quick half-smile instead of his usual warm grin. Then he turned back to McKell.

"So, do you want to go with us later to the river?" he asked her. His two friends stood silently next to him.

"Sure. But not till after the party's over," she responded. She faced me and said, "Bridger and his friends found a great fishing hole and want us to come with them night fishing on the Mississippi."

I glanced at Bridger, expecting him to coax me into accompanying them. But he didn't. He just regarded me with a disinterested stare. I was taken back by his indifferent manner. "I don't know," I hedged, waiting again for him to extend a personal invitation to me.

One of the guys standing at his elbow, the one with the glasses and dense thicket of hair, spoke up. "Have you ever been night fishing?" he asked me.

I shook my head. "Nope." I waited for Bridger to introduce me to his friends, but he seemed oblivious to the fact that I'd never met them. It was McKell who came to my rescue.

"Savannah, do you know Travis and Bronson?" she asked me, nodding at the fellows standing beside Bridger.

"No, I don't think so."

"Well, this is Travis Perry and Bronson Cunningham. Guys, this is Savannah Lawrence."

"Sorry, I thought you'd met," Bridger said.

"No, we haven't," I returned stiffly. There was no mistaking Bridger's attitude. His coolness toward me was intentional. I guessed he was annoyed by my rebuff yesterday on the paddleboat, when he'd suggested I stay the summer in Nauvoo so we could get better acquainted.

"Do you want to go fishing with us?" the guy with the glasses, named Bronson, asked. His spectacles kept sliding down his nose and he had to repeatedly push them up with his finger.

"I don't know. Maybe."

"Come on, Savannah," McKell urged me. "It'll be awesome."

I smiled at her. "We'll see, okay?" I started to move away from them. "It was nice to meet you guys."

Travis and Bronson made a parting remark, but Bridger only glanced at me and nodded. I'd been looking forward to spending my last evening in Nauvoo in Bridger's company, and now it wasn't going to happen. I was disappointed and angry as I walked away from him. I joined a group of girls talking together and made an effort to join in the conversation, but I couldn't keep my eyes from drifting back to Bridger. He'd moved closer to McKell and was engaged in conversation with her. I watched as he leaned over and whispered something in her ear. She threw back her head and laughed heartily at his comment. He grinned, and nudged his shoulder against hers.

My stomach clenched. Bridger was flirting with McKell! And she wasn't doing much to discourage it. Had they both lied to me about their feelings for one another? I wondered. Did they still have a spark for each other? I forced my eyes away, feeling upset and betrayed.

"Want a soda?" Kaitlyn asked, coming up to me with a tray of soda pop. "I have Sprite, root beer, or Orange Slice."

I shook my head. "No thanks. I just had one a few minutes ago," I said, trying not to sound as miserable as I felt.

I walked to the couch and dropped onto it. I felt sick to my stomach. Maybe it was too much pizza, I told myself. I deliberately kept my gaze away from Bridger and McKell, looking anywhere but the spot in the room where they stood close together talking. What did it matter to me if they wanted to be together? After tonight, we'd all be going our separate ways and never see one another again.

I sat on the couch for a half hour or so, putting on a smile for anyone who stopped to speak. I didn't see McKell approach until she bounced down beside me on the couch.

"You're never going to guess what!" she exclaimed, her brown eyes wide and shining. "I've decided to stay in Nauvoo for the summer. What do you think of that?"

"What?" I looked at her in surprise.

"I love it here, and I'm not ready to go home yet. I said to myself, exactly why do I have to leave just yet? And I couldn't come up with a single pressing reason." She giggled and snuggled into my shoulder. "So why not stay?"

"Yes, why not?" I returned, still dazed by her announcement.

"It will be so much fun to be here through the summer," she said. "Oh, I just thought of something else. I'll be here for the *City of Joseph* production. I can try out for a part in it!"

I grinned at her enthusiasm.

"Savannah, oh my gosh! I've got the best idea," she turned sparkling eyes to me. "Why don't *you* stay the summer, too? We could all have such an amazing time together."

I stared at her, startled by her suggestion.

"What do you say?" she jabbed me in the shoulder.

One thought burned in my brain. "Did Bridger suggest this to you?"

"Bridger?" Her expression went blank for an instant. "No. I haven't even told him yet. The idea just came up while I was talking with Sierra a minute ago. She mentioned that she wished she could stay in Nauvoo longer. I told her I felt the same way. So she said why don't we just do it? What a terrific idea, huh? Sierra is going to stay, and so is Hailee. And Kaitlyn is thinking about it."

"You're all staying?" I asked incredulously.

"Uh-huh. We're going to get jobs in town and throw in together to buy a car. Maybe they'll let us rent this house for the summer. If not, we can find a place in town to live. What do you say? You game for a summer adventure?" Her grin stretched from ear to ear.

I said nothing for several seconds, my mind racing. If I *did* stay for the summer, what would I tell Jaden? And my parents? And could I really find a job in this tiny town that would support me for three or four months in an apartment? "Are you really serious about this, Kell?" I asked.

"Totally." Her voice was firm. "We're gonna do it."

I bit my lip, vacillating back and forth before I decided to throw caution to the wind. "I'm in," I said.

She shrieked and threw her arms around me in a tight hug. "The five of us are going to have such a great time!"

"Such a great time doing what?"

McKell and I looked up to see Bridger standing before us. He had a slice of pizza in one hand and a root beer in the other.

McKell popped up from the couch and grabbed his arm, nearly knocking the pizza out of his grip. "The five of us are staying in Nauvoo for the summer," she squealed.

His eyes grew wide. "You are? All of you?"

"Yes. Can you believe it?"

His gaze shifted from her face to mine. "That is surprising," he said. His eyes held mine for a second longer, and I thought I saw a hurt look flicker across them.

"We just decided it," I said quickly to let him know it had happened on the spur of the moment.

"Is that so?" It was as if a curtain drew across his gaze, shutting me out. "You girls are going to have a good time."

"We're going to have a *terrific* time," McKell corrected him. "*All* of us. We can hang together all summer long."

"I'm glad you've decided to stay," he said genuinely.

"Thanks," I replied, not certain if his sentiments included me.

"The guys and I are heading out now. If you want to meet us at the end of Main Street, we'll have fishing poles for you."

"We'll be there," McKell assured him.

"Are you coming too?" he asked me.

"Is that an invitation?"

"Sure. You're invited. If you want to come."

Why wouldn't I want to come? I asked silently. What did Bridger mean by that remark? I wondered if he'd prefer that I *didn't* come along. I avoided his gaze and instead focused on a couple swaying to the music blaring from Sierra's CD player.

Bridger and McKell exchanged a few words more about the impending fishing expedition, and then Bridger walked off to join his guy friends. I supposed they left the house soon afterward, though I didn't see them go.

The party lasted until well after midnight. By the time the last guest left the house, I was hiding a yawn behind my hand. I still wasn't up to my normal level of stamina since the accident, and was accustomed to retiring early. My head, too, had started to pound.

After McKell ushered out the last party guest, she turned to the four of us. "Let's go fishing!"

The girls nodded enthusiastically.

"Bridger said to meet him at the river near Main Street."

The girls moved as a group toward the door. I remained where I was standing.

"Aren't you coming?" Sierra asked, glancing over her shoulder at me.

"I don't think so. I'm pretty worn out."

"You don't feel up to joining us?" McKell asked.

"I guess not."

"I'll come back early with you if you want to go for just a while," she offered.

"Thanks anyway. You guys have a good time." I smiled at them.

"You sure?" Kaitlyn echoed.

"Yeah. I'll be here when you get back."

"Okay," they said as one. McKell waved as she went out the door.

After they left, I stood in the center of the living room glancing around at the messy remains of the party we'd thrown. Plates of partially eaten pizza littered the living room and kitchen. Empty soda pop cans lay strewn on the floor and chairs. I cleaned up the trash and wiped off the kitchen table and counters, emptied the garbage outside in the can and turned off the music blaring from the CD player. The house became still, with only the sound of my own padding feet on the carpet to break the silence.

I switched off the lights and headed for the bedroom I shared with McKell. As I sank down onto the bed, I felt a twinge of regret about my decision to remain behind. Though I was tired, I wasn't yet sleepy. I stretched out on the bed in my clothes, with my hands underneath my head, staring at the ceiling. I couldn't help but recall how Bridger had behaved toward me. His frostiness hurt my feelings and was the real reason why I decided not to join the group at the fishing hole. I imagined McKell and Bridger side by side at the river's edge. He would help her bait her hook and show her how to reel in a catch. The moon would be shining on the river, filtering the water with liquid light; and perhaps, under the spell of moonlight, Bridger and McKell's affection for one another would kindle anew.

I blinked and turned over onto my side. What did I care if McKell and Bridger got back together? If they spent all summer long in each other's company? I tried to tell myself that it didn't matter one iota to me if they did. But I was lying to myself. I did care. I hadn't realized before how much I cared.

CHAPTER 14

Early the next morning McKell and I hugged our roommates good-bye. Sierra, Hailee, and Kaitlyn, who last night had been swept up in the excitement of spending the summer in Nauvoo, had a change of heart with the morning's light. They left the Weeks's house with their baggage in hand to travel to St. Louis where they'd board planes for their separate destinations.

After they left, McKell and I looked at each other, grinned, and enveloped each other in a big bear hug.

"Can you believe this?" McKell squealed. "We're really staying for the whole summer!"

I nodded. "It would have been cool if the others could have stayed, but you and I will have enough fun to make up for it."

"Right! And the first thing we need to do is cancel our plane reservations, then go see Sister Parker to ask if we can stay here in the house for the summer."

We changed out of our pajamas into shorts and T-shirts and left the house, heading for the second floor of the Visitors' Center. We spent a half hour with Brother and Sister Parker making arrangements for our stay. They consented to let us remain in the Weeks's home, charging us a nominal fee for the summer months.

Afterward we walked to the store, located in town on the bluffs, and purchased some groceries. We carried the sacks of groceries home in our arms.

"Getting a car needs to be the next order of business," McKell puffed, setting her sacks on the kitchen table, then swinging her arms to get the kinks out.

I plopped my sacks next to hers. "Absolutely. We need wheels for shopping and getting back and forth from work."

We began putting the groceries away, all the while laying plans for our life in Nauvoo. McKell suggested we ask Bridger if we could borrow his car to drive around town in search of jobs.

"That's a good idea. He'd probably let us use it," I responded. I put a package of cookies in the cupboard and the gallon of milk in the fridge. "Did you have fun last night fishing?" I asked, striving for a casual tone.

"Yeah, we sure did. I wish you could have come with us. Only Bronson caught a fish because we spent most of the time just laughing and fooling around."

"I wish I could have gone too. But I was dead tired. I fell asleep before you got home."

"You did. Asleep on top of the bed with your clothes still on from the party. Do you remember me nudging you awake so you could change and climb into bed?"

"Barely. I was pretty much a zombie."

"Must have had too much to drink last night," she said, grinning.

"Right. One too many cans of Sprite," I teased. I folded up the brown paper grocery sacks and stuffed them away in the cupboard. "Have you ever even tasted a drop of alcohol, Kell?" I inquired with a grin.

"You're asking me to divulge my guilty secret."

"Actually, I'd be relieved to hear that even Saints occasionally tumble from their lofty pinnacles."

McKell laughed. "I don't claim to be a saint, but trying to conduct myself like a Latter-day Saint is important to me. I make plenty of mistakes, though."

"Hence, your guilty secret," I whispered dramatically.

"Yes. Do you want to hear about it?"

"Are you kidding? I'm dying to."

We sat down across from one another at the kitchen table. "When I was in ninth grade we moved from Arizona to Portland, Oregon. It was hard for a kid my age to break into a new social situation and make friends. I had a hard time for a while."

I nodded. "Yeah, I hated moving when I was growing up."

"I made friends with a girl I thought was cute and popular with the boys. She always had guys hanging around her. I felt lucky to be adopted into her circle of friends." McKell tucked a lock of hair behind her ear. "But I soon found out that this particular group of kids were partiers. Most of them habitually went to weekend keg parties."

I whistled. "I bet that threw you for a loop."

"At the time, I thought it was pretty cool. I went to a few of the parties myself."

I tried not to show my surprise. This was a startling side of McKell I'd never suspected.

"Then one Saturday afternoon two young guys knocked at our door. Mom and Dad were away shopping or somewhere, and I was the only one home. I stood on the doorstep and talked to them because I thought the two of them were cute dressed in their white shirts and suits, with their short haircuts."

"Missionaries!" I blurted.

"Yup." McKell grinned at me. "Something inside me just knew the things they were saying were true."

"Wow. What happened after that?"

"They asked if they could come back when my parents were home and teach us about the gospel of Jesus Christ. I said sure."

I was taken back by her audacity. "What did your parents say when you told them about the missionaries?"

"They told me if I was interested in what the missionaries had to say, then they'd take an hour to listen to them with me."

"Your parents sound pretty open-minded," I observed.

"They are. They're wonderful people. I love them so much." McKell's eyes suddenly misted. "They invited the missionaries to our home and together we listened to the first discussion, which was about Joseph Smith and the restoration of the Church."

"And that was all it took? You joined the Church after that?" I asked, awed by the apparent simplicity of the process.

"Not right away. The missionaries gave us six discussions in all. Then we joined."

I leaned back into my chair. I could hardly believe a person, let alone a whole family, would change their entire lifestyle just because of six short conversations about religion.

"What are you thinking?" McKell grinned. "I can see the wheels turning."

I smiled at her. "I was wondering how you could so easily abandon your old way of life."

McKell rested her chin in her hand. "Maybe it's not as easy for some converts as it was for me and my family. The Spirit was just so strong when the missionaries were in our home. I wanted that feeling with me all the time."

"So you gave up your weekend parties," I concluded for her.

"And my new friends. And before very long I'd made other friends. Friends with the same goals and values I held."

"That's quite an experience, Kell. I'm impressed by how you stuck to your beliefs."

"Well, I had a lot of support from friends and ward members. I started attending Young Women. That's a Sunday meeting for girls age twelve to eighteen. That program really strengthened my testimony and provided me with some tremendous examples to follow. My Young Women leaders were incredible." McKell pulled a gold chain with a pendant from beneath her T-shirt. I'd noticed before that she wore a gold chain around her neck, but I'd never seen the medallion attached to it. She held it out for me to examine.

"I earned this medallion from completing goals and require-ments in the Young Women program. I worked hard to get it, and I'm very proud of it. I wear it often to remind me of the standards I need to keep."

I took the medallion from her fingers to inspect it closer. It was about the size of a quarter, oval shaped, and imprinted with the image of a slender young woman in a billowing skirt with a patch of flowers at her feet.

"It's a reminder to stand for truth and righteousness. That's the Young Women motto, and I try hard to live by it," she said simply.

I glanced from the medallion to McKell's face. Her soft brown eyes seemed peaceful, filled with serenity. I longed for that quality in my own life. I released the locket, and McKell slipped it back in place underneath her T-shirt.

"Ever since that day when the missionaries presented the first discussion about Joseph Smith, I've felt a deep love, respect, and appreciation for the man. That's why I came to Nauvoo, to be part of the City of Joseph for a little while."

I stared at McKell, envious of her faith and commitment to the principles she believed in.

She flashed me a sudden smile. "This place has such a spirit about it, doesn't it?"

I nodded, feeling a lump forming in my throat.

"Maybe that's the reason you're here, too. Because of the spirit of the place. It's hard to ignore the history and significance of this beautiful spot nestled on the shores of the Mississippi." She favored me with another bright smile, then rose from her chair. "And now . . . time to clean up this place."

I swept the kitchen floor while she vacuumed the carpet. Crumbs of food and bits of trash still remained on the floors from the party the night before. When I finished, I went to the bedroom McKell and I shared and sat down on the bed, mulling over all she'd told me. I could imagine the two handsome missionaries at her door, could hear her earnest discussion with her parents concerning them. I thought about the pair of missionaries I'd met a few days ago at the temple site and the gospel principles they'd explained to me. The doctrine was like a million pieces of a jigsaw puzzle floating in the air around my head, and no matter how hard I tried to fit the pieces together into one whole, I couldn't get a clear picture to emerge.

I remembered the book the missionaries had given me, urging me to read it. I had brought it back to the house and stuffed it in the bottom of my suitcase next to my abandoned camping gear. With barely a conscious decision, I got up and went to the closet where the suitcase lay. The case was scuffed at the corners from the rough handling I'd given it while camping with Carly. That camping trip now seemed like eons ago, rather than a mere few weeks. I wondered what Carly was doing and if she liked her new job in Wisconsin working at the advertising agency. *I should give her a call*, I thought, *to let her know I am spending the summer in Nauvoo.*

I grasped the suitcase, set it on the bed, and opened it. I scooted aside a mismatched pair of faded woolen socks and a tattered road map. Tucked in the bottom of the suitcase was the book, the title printed in gold letters. The Book of Mormon. I pulled the book from the case and traced the lettering with the tip of my finger. I knew if I opened the book, I'd be embarking on a journey that could lead me far from familiar territory—a trip into uncharted waters. I sat with the book in my hand and wrestled with the decision of what to do with it.

* * *

That afternoon McKell and I drove up Mulholland Street in Bridger's car, searching for possible employment. McKell had been the one to find Bridger at the stable site and had asked for permission to borrow his Paseo for a couple of hours. She'd wanted me to come along to ask him, but I'd made up some excuse for not being able to go. My feelings for Bridger were as jumbled and complex as my reasons for being in Nauvoo.

"What about that gift shop?" McKell asked me, slowing to a crawl as we drove past one of a half dozen small gift stores in the town.

"Let's go in and see if they're hiring," I said halfheartedly. I hadn't yet seen anything I was interested in pursuing in the way of a job.

McKell parked the car along the street outside the gift shop, and we went inside.

"May I help you?" an older lady with salt-and-pepper hair asked us from behind the counter.

McKell inquired about the possibility of summer employment.

"As a matter of fact, we are looking to hire a salesclerk. Would either of you be interested in that position?" the woman responded.

We both nodded our heads.

She walked to a desk at the back of the shop, opened a narrow desk drawer, and came back with two applications for us. "Just fill these out and return them to me, and I'll get in touch with you," she instructed.

"Thanks," we said simultaneously.

Back inside the Toyota, McKell asked, "What do you think? You interested in working there?"

My eyes flickered over the questions printed on the application. "I know I can't afford to be choosy, but I'm not really pumped about working in a gift shop. If you want to, why don't you fill out the application and submit it?"

McKell glanced over the paper in her hand. "I guess I wouldn't mind a job here. I like working with people. You sure you don't want to pursue it?"

I shook my head.

"Okay, I'll go ahead and apply. Let's keep looking for something you'd like."

We continued to slowly drive up Mulholland, hunting for a job opportunity. But nothing captured my attention. We were about to turn around and head back to the house when something caught my eye. "Hey, wait a minute, Kell. Is that an art gallery across the street?"

McKell turned to look toward the place I indicated. "Where?"

"Over there," I pointed. "Across the street and down a few doors. Turn the car around, will you?"

I kept my gaze fixed on the narrow shop sandwiched between an insurance company and a hardware store as McKell wheeled the Paseo back around and pulled to a stop in front of the door. Four paintings filled the small display window. I stared at the words lettered on the glass door. *Crandall's Art and Supply*, it read.

"Maybe it's only an art supply store and not a gallery," I said in disappointment as we climbed out of the car. We walked to the glass door and peeked inside. It looked as if the larger part of the room was stocked with brushes, paints, mats, and picture frames; a small area contained a display of framed photographs and paintings. "Let's go in," I suggested.

I pushed open the door. A couple of customers were browsing the shelves, and one person wandered among the photographs and paintings on exhibit. A middle-aged fellow with thick glasses stood behind the counter, counting change into a customer's hand.

While we waited to talk with him, I moved to where the paintings were arrayed on tall easels. There were perhaps a dozen, and some of the paintings were well crafted. I bent to read the signature appearing on the largest canvas. I wasn't familiar with the artist who signed his name as *M. Sobenski*. The colors on his canvas were bold and bright, and they depicted a peasant woman with a red babushka on her head gleaning golden wheat from a field.

I felt McKell elbow me in the ribs. "He's free," she whispered, nodding toward the counter.

McKell and I walked up to him. "Afternoon," I greeted him. "My name is Savannah Lawrence and I'm staying in Nauvoo for the summer. I just graduated from the university in Colorado Springs with a degree in art history and wondered if there might be a position available here."

The man peered at me from behind his glasses. The glass in them was so thick it made his eyes look protruding. "I hadn't planned on hiring anyone," he said after a pause. His voice was brusque.

I wasn't deterred by his response. "I noticed you have paintings and photographs on display for sale. I could be a real asset in helping you select future pieces of artwork."

The man slowly took off his glasses and wiped them methodically on the sleeve of his shirt. Without the glasses, his eyes were actually small and piercing, giving him a shrewd look. He stared sharply at me for a moment before replacing the glasses. "An asset, huh?" he said, rubbing his forehead with his hand. "You have any experience in retail?"

I swallowed. "Not actually in retail. But I do know art, and what people think is appealing. And I can recognize a good painting from a mediocre one."

"What did you say your name was?" the man asked after giving me a long, appraising stare.

"Savannah Lawrence. From Denver, Colorado." I'd felt relatively calm up to now, but I was beginning to realize how forward I must have seemed. I shifted nervously from one foot to the other. I heard McKell softly clear her throat at my side.

"Well, now, Savannah Lawrence from Denver, Colorado, I don't really need an art critic or a business partner. But I like your style. Forthright and confident. That kind of personality can sell a swimsuit to an Eskimo."

I didn't know whether to chuckle or thank him for the compliment.

"So I'm going to go out on a limb here and give you a try. You come in Tuesday morning, nine o'clock sharp, and I'll put you to work. The job pays $7.50 an hour."

As McKell and I left the shop, I was floating. I had landed a real job at a genuine art gallery, even though it was only a tiny one and a sideline to selling art supplies. "Oh my gosh. I'm excited!" I burst out after we'd closed the glass door behind us. "This is a perfect place to work."

"Congratulations," McKell grinned. "You were as bold as a lion in going after that job. I'm impressed."

"I really wanted it," I replied as I opened the car door and slid into the passenger seat. "I haven't seen anything else in town that appeals to me as much as this does."

"And you're going to be good at it. Lucky you, to be able to use your college degree."

"Yeah. I was afraid the best thing I was going to get in my field was developing photos at the drugstore."

McKell laughed at my remark. "Things are already going smoothly for us. You wait and see—we're going to have the most amazing summer of our lives."

CHAPTER 15

Good fortune must have truly been smiling down on us. McKell got the salesclerk job at the gift shop, and I came home from my first day of work feeling jubilant.

"How did it go?" McKell asked me as I walked through the front door late Tuesday afternoon.

"Super! I think I'm really going to like it. Mr. Crandall is kind of gruff, but I'll get used to him. He put me to work at the cash register."

"Are you going to get an opportunity to work with the art exhibits?"

"I hope so. After I've been there for a couple of weeks, I'll see if he'll let me have a hand in the art purchasing and displaying end of things. What'd you do today?" I asked, dropping onto the living room couch.

"I hung out around here," she replied. "I start at the gift shop day after tomorrow."

I nodded. "I hope you like it as much as I like my job. Now all we need is a car."

"I talked to Bridger about that, and he's going to take me car shopping in the morning for an hour before he goes into work. We'll see if we can find something for a good price."

I tried not to show the sudden twinge of jealousy I felt on hearing Bridger and McKell had made plans to hunt for a car—together. "Buy something that won't break down on us," I said, feigning a smile. "But one we can afford at the same time."

"I'll do my best."

"We'll have to pay for the whole thing on time. I haven't any money for a down payment. Do you?"

"Not a cent. I hope we can get a loan without too much problem."

I got up from the couch, intending to change out of my clothes. I'd borrowed slacks, a blouse, and a jacket from McKell because I had no clothing appropriate for the workplace with me; I'd packed only casual wear for the camping trip. A shopping excursion was an immediate priority. "Any mail come today?" I asked as I started toward the bedroom.

"Just some junk mail. Oh, I almost forgot. You got a telephone call this afternoon."

I stopped in my tracks and turned to her. "Yeah? Who was it?"

"Your guy friend, Jaden, from Colorado." She gave me a knowing grin.

"Jaden? What'd he say?"

"Not much. Just asked for you. I told him you'd be home around 5:30 or so. He wants you to call him."

"Uh-oh. I'm gonna have to tell him I'm not coming home yet. He'll be really mad at me." I frowned, imagining what Jaden's reaction would be when he learned I was staying in Nauvoo for the entire summer.

"Good luck. Maybe he can come out here to see you."

"I doubt it. He already did that once while I was in the hospital. He can't afford to take a flight out again."

McKell's expression was sympathetic. I went to the bedroom and changed into a comfortable pair of shorts and a sleeveless blouse, then headed for the kitchen to get something to eat. McKell and I talked as we ate supper together, then afterward I dialed Jaden's home number. His line rang several times. I was about to hang up and try again later when I heard his voice.

"Yeah, hello."

"Hey, Jaden. How're you doing?"

"Annie? Is that you?"

"Sure is. My roommate said you called earlier."

"Yeah. Hey, how you doin'? I'm missing you."

"I'm good. How are you?"

"Lonely. I can't wait 'til you get here. You haven't told me your flight plans yet. That's why I called you—so I can know when to pick you up from the airport."

I could hear the anticipation in his voice. I cleared my throat. "Hey, you know what, Jaden? I've been kicking around the idea of staying here for a while longer." I held my breath, bracing myself for his response.

There was a pause at the other end of the line. "What do you mean?"

"I'm just really liking it here, Jaden. One of the girls I've been living with has decided to stay for the summer. I thought I might stay, too."

"You're kidding," he shouted into the phone. "What are you talking about?"

"I know it sounds kind of crazy, but it just felt right. I'll be home in a few months and tell you all about it. I'm sure I'll have lots of news." I tried to sound nonchalant, hoping my tone would reassure him.

"A couple of months?" His voice sounded as if he were being strangled.

"It's not that long. Really. I'll be home at the end of August. The time will go by in a flash."

"I can't believe what you're saying," he sputtered. "We've had plans for months."

I heard the fury building in his voice. "Our plans don't have to change, Jaden. We can just postpone them for a bit. Okay?" I closed my eyes and gritted my teeth, waiting for his anger to cool.

Another lengthy pause filled the telephone. I could see a mental picture of Jaden running a hand through his cropped hair in exasperation. "You've already made up your mind about this, haven't you?" he snarled into the mouthpiece.

"Kind of," I hedged. I thought of telling him about my new job, but decided now would not be the best time to mention it.

"So—" he snapped. "Guess your decision's been made, hasn't it?"

"I hope you won't be mad about it," I said, trying to soothe him. "We can talk on the phone lots. And I'll write and send pictures. You do the same."

"Look," he interrupted me. "I'm freaked out about this at the moment. I gotta go."

"Wait a minute, Jaden," I pleaded. "Don't hang up yet. We can still—" I heard a click at the other end of the line.

I slammed down the receiver, anger sweeping through me. I knew Jaden was immature and had a jealous streak, but I hadn't anticipated the abrupt end to the conversation.

I sprawled out on the bed, thinking about him. I pictured his spiked and bleached hair, his narrow, ice-blue eyes, and his stocky build. I recalled the first time we met. It was at a party in some guy's apartment on campus. Carly and I knew a fellow who invited us to the party, and when we got there it was in full swing. Everyone was drinking, Jaden most of all. I probably wouldn't have given him a second glance except that he came over to me and introduced himself. We started talking, and as I got acquainted with him, I thought he was cute.

I should have been wary that very night of his jealous temper. One of the other guys at the party offered to give me a ride home, and Jaden ended up giving him a bloody nose. Our relationship since that time had been punctuated by Jaden's outbursts of temper followed by apologies and flowers. He was like two sides of a coin— funny, sweet, even tender; but also angry, sullen, and selfish. Sometimes I sensed a latent violence about him which frightened me, but his good qualities usually balanced out the bad.

I rolled onto my stomach, my chin resting on my arms. So why was I hesitant about marrying him? Had my feelings for him changed since being away? I didn't know the answer to either of those questions.

* * *

The next day at work proved to be more challenging than my first. I made a couple of mistakes at the cash register, and one customer was disgruntled with me for being unable to remember exactly where the picture hangers were shelved. At one point I caught Mr. Crandall eyeing me disapprovingly, and then I was late coming back from lunch, which caused him to comment on my punctuality. I returned home drained and upset.

"Kell?" I called as I walked through the front door. "Kell, you home?" The house was as quiet as a mouse hole. I walked into the kitchen and poured myself a glass of milk. Then I made a sandwich and sat down at the table to eat it.

As I slowly munched my sandwich, I reviewed the day in my mind. I chided myself for the mistakes I'd made at the store, and winced recalling the chastisement Mr. Crandall had given me for being tardy from lunch. That infraction was not altogether my fault, I thought, attempting to excuse myself. After eating lunch I'd hurried to the drugstore to drop off all the film I'd shot since starting the road trip with Carly. There'd been only one person behind the film counter and several customers ahead of me. I should have left at that point, rather than waiting in line, but I'd been anxious to get my film developed. By the time my turn at the counter arrived, I was already five minutes late.

My gloomy reflections were interrupted by the front door opening and footsteps sounding in the hall. I turned in my chair. "Kell? I'm in the kitchen."

McKell burst into the room, a wide grin on her face. She didn't say anything, just dangled a set of keys in front of her nose.

"You bought a car already?" I squealed.

She wiggled the keys and they made a little jingling sound.

"Where is it?" I cried, jumping to my feet.

"Right outside the door," she exclaimed. "Come on."

I followed her outside. Parked beside the curb in front of the house was a rusting, mud-colored, four-door Buick, its paint chipped and faded. I rushed to the passenger's side and threw open the door. "Holy cow," I breathed. "Not bad."

I surveyed the inside of the car from its worn brown upholstery to the small crack in the corner of the right rear window.

"What do you think?" McKell asked me.

"It's great. What year is it?" I asked, running my hand over the buckled skin of the dashboard.

"A 1980 Buick LeSabre. Fresh off the used-car lot."

"How much did you pay for it?"

"We got an incredibly good deal. Seven hundred dollars, with the first payment due in two weeks. And they handled the financing. Fantastic, huh?"

"Amazing. How did you ever swing that?"

"Bridger turned out to be some kind of bargain hunter."

I laughed. "No kidding? That's terrific."

"He wanted to stop by to see how you like it, but he had to get back to work 'cause he took time off this morning to go with me."

I was disappointed to have missed him. I hadn't seen Bridger since the party on Friday night, and we'd barely exchanged two words then. McKell had invited me to attend church with her on the following

Sunday, but I'd declined. I'd had mixed feelings when she'd mentioned Bridger would be at the meetings, and it occurred to me that she was seeing an awful lot of Bridger Caldwell lately.

"Hey," McKell said. I looked up and she tossed the keys to me. "Want to try it out?"

I snatched the car keys in midair. "Sure." We climbed in, and I put the key in the ignition and turned it. A low rumbling started up, then the engine coughed and died. I glanced at McKell.

"Try it again," she urged.

I pumped the gas pedal and turned the key again. This time the engine roared like a lion. McKell flashed me a triumphant look.

"We're off," I crowed, pulling away from the curb. We drove the nearby streets, then turned onto Mulholland and headed toward the center of town on the bluffs. The car handled fairly well, though it slowed to a crawl as we climbed uphill. Considering the price we'd paid for the car, I thought the plodding pace was excusable.

We drove the Buick around for about twenty minutes, McKell and I exalting in our newly found freedom, making plans for driving that would accommodate both of our work schedules so neither of us would be hoofing it to work. When we returned home, we were flying higher than clouds.

* * *

The rest of the work week skated by. We took the car to our jobs each day and afterward ran errands or entertained ourselves by driving someplace new in the Buick. On Saturday morning I drove the car to pick up my photographs from the drugstore. After paying for them and purchasing another roll of film, I sat in the car and opened the first envelope of photos. I smiled as one photo after another showed either Carly or me on the road during our trip, or an interesting scene I'd shot along the way.

The next two envelopes also contained pictures from our road trip, and I lingered over every one. At the tail end of the third packet of photos was a shot of the little blue cottage with white shutters and stone chimney, tucked beneath a shady tree, on the road into Nauvoo. The next packet of pictures was all shot in Nauvoo. I paused to study a photograph of Bridger perched on the split-rail fence bordering a grove of trees. I laughed at the following few photos where he'd clowned as a strongman, flexing his muscles and grimacing.

I thumbed through the rest, several of which were of Bridger— Bridger on the deck of the paddleboat, Bridger standing on the bank of the dapple-gray Mississippi in the morning sunlight, Bridger turning somersaults on the grass. The photos reminded me of how much I'd missed him over the past week. Since the party, I'd purposely avoided him; his attitude that night had hurt and confused me. I decided to drive by the stable site hoping he'd be there working, so I could thank him for helping us get the car—and try to make amends.

With the photos in the glove box, I drove to the restoration area. Bridger wasn't in sight, but I spotted his car parked in front of the trailer office. I glanced in the rearview mirror, smoothed my hair, and straightened my new blouse. McKell and I had gone to Keokuk with the Buick earlier in the week to do some shopping, and I'd purchased a couple of outfits. I exited the car and headed for the trailer. I swung open the door and stepped across the sill.

". . . ordered and paid for, and so you're mistaken about that," I heard James Baldwin say to Bridger. James sat at his desk with the computer behind him, and Bridger was towering in front of him.

"I saw the amount on the check, James. The balances don't jibe."

Color flooded the older man's face, and the veins in his thick neck bulged. "Look, Caldwell, what happens here doesn't concern you. Stick with doing your job, and only your job. Your presumptuousness is a dangerous commodity. It can get you dismissed from the project." James's voice rose incrementally until he was nearly shouting. He'd risen from his chair, his face beet red, and was stabbing a fat, stubby finger into Bridger's chest.

Engaged in their conversation, neither of them heard me open the door nor saw me standing just inside. I started to quietly back out the way I'd come in, since the two were obviously in the thick of a heated discussion, which I didn't wish to intrude upon.

"I'm not going to back off on this," Bridger retorted, "until I'm satisfied everything is above board. If it's not, then—"

I accidentally scuffed the door with the side of my shoe in trying to retreat. Both men jerked their heads in my direction.

"Uh, excuse me. I just dropped by for a second, but it looks like the two of you are busy. I'll come back later," I stumbled.

"No, wait a minute. We're through here." Bridger spat out the words as if they burned his tongue.

I glanced from Bridger to James. From the older man's expression, it didn't look as if the conversation was at all finished. James resumed his seat. "'Afternoon, Miss Lawrence," he said, glowering at me.

"Hello, Mr. Baldwin. I didn't mean to disturb you. I just came by to say hello to Bridger."

Bridger was at my side in a single stride. "Let's step outside to talk." He glanced at the scowling man behind the desk. "I'll be back in a couple of seconds."

Bridger pushed open the door. When we were both outside, I asked, "What was that all about? James looked as mad as a bull in a fighting arena."

"I questioned him about the discrepancy between the check I picked up for him, and what was recorded in the ledger as expenses. He's angry with me for prying into it."

"What's he going to do, now that he knows you're suspicious?" I asked, frowning.

"I don't know. I don't know yet what *I'm* going to do about it."

We were walking toward the Buick as we talked. When we reached it, Bridger brightened. "How do you like your car?"

"Kell and I are thrilled with it. I came by to thank you for your help in getting it."

"We made a sweet deal." Bridger's eyes swept the vehicle. He polished a spot with the tail of his shirt as if it were a shiny Mercedes.

"We've christened it *T. rex*," I informed him.

"As in *Tyrannosaurus rex*?"

"Exactly. 'Cause it's big and ancient."

He patted the hood of the car. "Let's hope old Rex here doesn't become extinct before his time."

I laughed. It felt good to be joking with Bridger again. He seemed more of his old self, although he was edgy because of his spat with James.

"Seriously, Bridger, what do you think James will do if you keep poking and prodding?"

"We're going to find out." Bridger's voice was grim and determined.

"What do you mean?" I asked, feeling a stirring of dread.

"I plan to get to the bottom of this."

I was almost afraid to ask the question poised on the tip of my tongue. "How are you going to do that?"

Bridger led me to the far side of the car, away from the trailer, and lowered his voice. "I can use your help, if you're interested in doing a little sleuthing."

"What do you have in mind?" I found myself lowering my own voice to match his. I glanced at the trailer, then back at Bridger's face.

"I want to spend some uninterrupted time at James's computer. And I could use someone to keep a lookout for me while I'm doing it. Interested?"

I gulped. "How are you going to get access to the computer? I thought you said that James changed the codes."

"He has. But I've been watching him when he boots up the computer. I think I know the password and can get into his financial files."

"Breaking and entering is against the law, isn't it?"

"Not if I'm working after hours."

"After hours?"

"Say . . . sometime after midnight."

"Bridger, you're joking," I exclaimed. "You can get into serious trouble if you're caught. And James is already annoyed with you. He'll send you packing in a heartbeat if he catches you. You could get kicked out of school."

"That's where you come in. To make sure there are no surprises."

"And just how do you expect me to ensure that?"

"I don't exactly know yet. But I'll figure out something."

I let out an exasperated sigh. "Just when did you come up with this crazy scheme?"

"About five minutes ago. But the more I think about it, the better I like it. I'd wager that something fraudulent is going on."

"Then contact the police and let them investigate it."

Bridger shook his head. "It would be too easy for James to cover his tracks if he got wind of some kind of official investigation gearing up. For now, I just want to see what he's up to."

"I think this whole idea is insane. I think you should forget about it. Or inform the company president and let him deal with James."

"I'll do that. But I need to have some sort of evidence to base an accusation of that kind on."

I shook my head, scowling.

"So what about it, Sherlock? Are you going to help me or not?"

CHAPTER 16

"Miss Lawrence, come here a minute."

I looked up from the colored cardboard mats I was returning to their slots after helping a customer choose a mat and frame for her picture. Mr. Crandall was at the rear of the store, speaking with a spare, slightly built man who looked to be in his early thirties. I saw the man's mousy brown hair was pulled back into a thin ponytail hanging down between his shoulders. I hurried over to the two of them, and my employer introduced me. "Mark, this is one of my employees, Savannah Lawrence. She has an eye for what sells. Savannah, meet Mark Sobenski."

"Wow, it's nice to meet you, Mr. Sobenski. I've noticed your paintings here at the store and like them very much. Especially the watercolor of the young girl gathering flowers with her mother. The colors are so vibrant, and I like the contrast in hues you've used." The words tumbled over themselves in my enthusiasm at meeting this particular artist. He wielded magic with his brush.

"Thank you for the kind words," he returned. His smile was brief and tight, as if he found smiling difficult. "I'm pleased you like my work."

"Miss Lawrence, I want you to take a look at these four paintings Mark has brought in and tell me which ones you think might be the most successful."

I turned to the first canvas laid out on the work table in front of us. It was a painting of a desert landscape done in greens, grays, and browns. "This is really beautiful," I murmured, bending closer to eye the details. "The desert looks as if it's breathing with life."

My boss lifted a second canvas onto the counter. This one was darker in mood and subject. Five uniformed soldiers poised in the heat of battle stood out starkly against a muted background. "I like the composition here," I remarked, tracing the outlines of the figures in the air with my finger. "This painting makes a bold statement, Mr. Sobenski," I said, turning to the artist.

He nodded, his eyes focused on the canvas.

"And what about this one?" Mr. Crandall asked, moving aside the two paintings to make room for a third on the table. This canvas was larger than the others, and every inch of it filled with motion and color. It depicted a teeming city street, tumultuous images clashing and clanging with one another.

The final canvas was as large as the previous one, but the feelings were very different. The lined face of an elderly Polish woman with a crimson scarf tied around her hair consumed the canvas. Her round face was faded and crisscrossed with deep lines, like an old quilt. Her eyes were dark and compelling, her mouth expressive. The scarlet scarf stood out boldly. The image demanded my attention, awakening strong emotions in me. The woman's expression told of personal struggle and loss, and the triumph of a resilient spirit.

"This one is my favorite," I said in awe. I stood back a pace to take in the whole. "It's brilliant. The experience of the world rests in this woman's eyes."

Sobenski stirred at my side.

I looked at the artist with renewed respect. "You've captured the human experience with this painting, Mr. Sobenski," I said in sincerity.

I turned to my employer. "You couldn't miss with this painting, Mr. Crandall. You could name your own price."

"I agree. And what would be your second choice?"

I moved the portrait of the old woman aside and stared in turn at the remaining three. "Though I very much like these other two, I think the desert scene would appeal to a wider audience. It evokes a feeling of serenity and peace, and the colors would complement nearly any décor."

Behind his glasses, Crandall's small, piercing eyes darted between the three canvasses. "I concur with that assessment." He turned to the artist. "Mark, I'll take the two we've mentioned. Though I like all four of the paintings, I don't have enough room to display them right now."

Sobenski nodded.

"When these sell, I'll be happy to take a second look at them. Now let's discuss a price."

While the art dealer and the artist hammered out a selling price, I gazed again at Sobenski's paintings. There was no doubt the artist possessed remarkable talent. I wondered that he chose this inconsequential little art shop, sandwiched between two buildings in a nondescript town far off the beaten path, to peddle his work. His talent deserved a broader audience and greater exposure. Perhaps he was a local artist, struggling to establish himself. And it was obvious, as I'd quickly learned, that Crandall possessed a shrewd eye for excellence. Perhaps Crandall's insignificant little art shop would eventually launch Mark Sobenski into celebrity.

When the two men finished with their discussion and the artist left the shop, I turned to my boss. "Have you ever given any thought to enlarging the gallery area of the shop, Mr. Crandall?" I asked him.

He removed his glasses and polished the lenses on his shirtsleeve. "What do you mean?"

"Well, uh, maybe phasing out the art supply end of the business and concentrating more on the gallery. There are a lot of wonderful artists who could use some exposure."

His beady, squirrel-like eyes narrowed to slits. "We're in business to make money, not to promote new artists."

"I know that. But you could do both at the same time," I said persuasively. "New artists are eager to show their work, and are more likely to settle for a smaller cut. You could expand the gallery to include several new artists and still make a profit."

"Most of our business here revolves around art supplies, not canvas and paint," he replied impatiently, waving his eyeglasses.

"That's true. But if you targeted a different customer base, you might be surprised how well you do."

He replaced his glasses. "Go on. I'm listening."

"Well, we could capitalize on the tourism here. Many visitors to a new city want to purchase something of lasting value to take home with them. We could make it available to them by selling quality art work."

Crandall pressed his palms together and rubbed them back and forth. The noise sounded like sandpaper on wood. "It's not a bad idea," he said grudgingly. "But I'm not convinced we could stay afloat. I don't believe we'd have a large enough customer base for such an enterprise here in Nauvoo."

"I understand thousands of tourists come to Nauvoo every summer. I'm starting to see that already in the few short weeks I've been here."

He peered intently at me. "Are you a Mormon, Miss Lawrence?"

I was startled by his question. "No. No, I'm not. Why?"

"It's mostly Mormon tourists who arrive in the summer. We have little here that would cater to their interests. No, I don't think it's a wise idea."

He turned back to his work, dismissing me with a wave of his hand. I returned to the front of the store to finish putting away the mats and frames. I hoped I hadn't been too outspoken. In spite of Mr. Crandall's objections, I still believed a sophisticated art gallery, even in this small town, could be successful.

* * *

When I got home from work that afternoon, I found McKell at the kitchen table hunched over a pile of papers. "What are you up to?" I asked her, dropping my combination purse and day planner on a chair. I glanced at the top sheet of paper on the stack. It appeared to be filled with names, dates, and places.

She looked up from her work. "Doing a little family history," she said.

"A little what?" I sat down on the chair next to her and picked up the top sheet of paper. "What is this for?"

She pointed at a name typed on the top of the page. "Andrew Charles Hunt. That's my great-great-grandfather, born in 1857, in Liverpool, England."

I followed her finger down the page as she went on.

"And this is his wife, Elizabeth Clawson. And their children." She ran her finger down the column of names, then turned the sheet over to the reverse side, where four more names were listed.

"Wow. A big family."

"Uh-huh. Four out of the eight children died before reaching adulthood, though."

"Oh. That's sad." I looked at the list of names and dates. "How do you know all this stuff?" I asked her.

"These are my mom's records. She's the one who's working on our family history. She has a bunch of old photographs of our ancestors displayed on a wall at home, and she spends hours searching out information on deceased relatives."

"That's an interesting hobby," I replied, glancing again at the paper in my hand.

"Actually, it's not just a hobby. She collects the names and dates so she can do temple work for our ancestors."

I looked up from the page. "Temple work?"

"Uh-huh. You know how you and I talked about the temple, and how members of our church get married there?" she began.

I nodded.

"Well, the temple is a place where marriages are performed as well for our ancestors who have died and didn't have the opportunity to do the work themselves. So we do it for them. By proxy."

"Let me understand this," I said, frowning in concentration. "You pretend to be your dead relatives and then get married in the temple."

She chuckled. "Sort of." She sorted through the pile of loose papers. "This is how far back Mom has extended the family line." She pointed to a date on the page. "Thomas Masters was born in 1720. But we don't know the names of his parents."

"How in the world does your mother find all this information?" I asked, thumbing through the several pages lying on the table.

"I don't know. Research at the Family History Library. Letter writing. Nosing around. She's like a bloodhound hot on the trail." McKell laughed. "Anyway, she sent me these Family Group Sheets because she wants me to check the names against records kept in Nauvoo to see if any of our ancestors ever lived here."

"You can find that out?" I asked in surprise.

"Yeah. At the Land and Records Office. It's the place where they keep land records and other stuff about the Saints who once lived here, and you can do a search of their holdings. I was supposed to do that for Mom when I first arrived here, but haven't gotten around to it."

I read through the names of the children born to Thomas Masters, noticing the blank spaces where his parents' names should be. "When are you going to the Land and Records Office to do it?" I asked McKell.

"Maybe tomorrow or the next day. I was just trying to get these records in order and become more familiar with them before I go. So I know what and who I'm looking for." She invited me to go with her, and I thought it would be interesting. "Maybe you can check on some names from your own family," she commented.

"Oh, my family's not from around here," I corrected her.

"What about your great-grandparents, and further on back? Any chance they might have lived in this part of the country?"

I thought about her question. "I have no idea. I don't even know my great-grandparents' names. Or where they're from."

"Now's a good time to find out. Would your mom or dad know that information?"

I shrugged my shoulders. "Maybe. Probably, I guess. I can't remember ever asking them, or them talking about it."

"It'd be fun if you had a name or two to look up while we're there," McKell responded.

"I suppose." I returned the paper to the pile. "Work go okay for you today?" I asked.

"Yeah. I'm starting to feel a little more confident about it. How about you? Any problems with Rex after you dropped me off at work?" she asked.

"None. He roared along at top speed, about thirty-five miles an hour."

McKell laughed. "That car is a genuine fossil."

"Yeah, well, I hope some day we can replace it with a little more modern specimen."

McKell chuckled a second time, then turned her attention to the papers on the table.

"I'm going to go change and then start supper. It's my turn to cook, right?"

She nodded.

"Okay. Then it's macaroni and cheese again tonight. That's all I know how to cook." I heard McKell chuckling as I left the kitchen.

As I changed out of my work clothes I kept thinking about McKell's project and the devotion her mother showed in tracing her ancestors. I wondered if my mother knew very much about her family who had passed on. While I was preparing supper, I couldn't get the topic out of my head. After I put the macaroni and cheese in the oven to bake, I resolved to give Mom a telephone call and ask her about it.

I went to the bedroom McKell and I shared and dialed my home number. It rang several times before I heard Mom pick it up. "Hello," she said in a flat voice.

"Hi, Mom. It's Savannah. How you doing?"

"Fine, Anne. And you?"

"Really well. Did you get the letter I sent you about my decision to stay here for the summer?"

"Yes, I got it." There was little in her voice to indicate her feelings on the matter.

"Did you tell Dad?"

"Uh-huh."

"Well, what did he say?" I was seeking some sort of validation, or at least acknowledgement of my situation.

"He didn't say too much."

"Oh."

A pause filled the distance between us. "Hey, have you heard from Brett? How's he doing?"

"I haven't talked to him since we returned from our trip. I'm planning to call him," Mom replied.

When? I thought. *Sometime next year?* My parents' apparent uninterest in my brother and me affected me like a festering sore that refused to heal. "When you do talk to him, tell him hello for me," I said, my voice laced with bitterness.

"I will, Anne."

"Anything new there at home?" I asked, trying harder to sound pleasant and cordial.

"No, not much. The Taylors' dog got hit by a car the day before yesterday."

The Taylors were my parents' next door neighbors. They owned a beautiful gold and white collie. "That's awful. Is it dead?"

"No. Duke suffered a broken leg, but the vet put a cast on it. How are you feeling from your accident, dear?"

The reference between the two incidents threw me momentarily. Was I no more important to Mom than the neighbor's dog? "I'm doing fine, Mom. I feel good. No ill effects. Not even a broken leg," I added caustically, but she didn't seem to notice.

"That's good to hear, Anne."

"Hey, Mom, one of the reasons I called was to ask you something." I went on hurriedly, stifling the urge to end the conversation and hang up. "My friend is putting together a list of her ancestors. Recording their names and dates and stuff. I wondered if you or Dad knew much about our relatives who have passed away."

"I'd have to think about that, Anne. Do you want information about your grandparents?"

"Yes. And my great-grandparents, and as far back as you can remember, or have any knowledge about."

"I'm afraid I don't know much."

"Can you send me what you do know, Mom? Can you think about it and check around a little bit?" I asked with an edge to my voice.

"Alright, Anne. I'll do that."

I could tell she was surprised by my sharpness. I softened my tone. "Is Dad there? I'd like to say hello to him."

"No. He had to work late. I'll tell him you called."

"Thanks, Mom. It's good to talk to you. And thanks for your help with the ancestor stuff."

"Alright, dear. I'll talk to you later."

"Okay. Bye, Mom." I hung up the phone, sorry that I had let my impatience and antagonism show through.

I tried to put hurt feelings out of mind as I set the table and finished the preparations for supper. My mood lightened when McKell and I sat down to eat, and then afterward put a video in the player and watched a lighthearted comedy. It was enjoyable, but I found myself nearly drifting off to sleep before it was over. McKell switched off the VCR while I stretched and yawned, too tired almost to get off the couch and into bed.

"I'll lock the front door and turn off the porch light," McKell said.

"Okay," I mumbled. I dragged myself off the couch, emptied into the trash the hard kernels of uncooked popcorn remaining in the bottom of the bowl and started toward the bedroom.

"Hey, Savannah. Come here a minute, will you?" McKell called softly from the living room.

I padded to her side. She stood by the living room window, her fingers pushed against a corner of the curtain. "What is it?"

"Look at that car parked across the street. Do you recognize it?"

I gazed out the window where she pulled aside the drapery a bit. A compact car was parked across the road and down the block. "Nope. I don't know whose car that is. Why?"

"I noticed it driving slowly past the house, and then back again, earlier this afternoon. I'm pretty sure it's the same car."

I glanced out the window again. "It's too dark to see the color of it. Are you sure it's the same one?"

"I think so." She let the curtain fall back into place. "It seems kind of strange to see a car parked here this late at night. There aren't many houses around."

"The car could belong to one of the staff here, or a tourist who was looking for an address earlier today," I said, covering a yawn with my hand.

"Yeah. You're probably right."

We turned away from the window. McKell switched off the porch light, and we headed for our room. I fell into bed and was asleep before I could say Rumpelstiltskin.

CHAPTER 17

The next day was Friday and the start of the first weekend in June. Though Crandall's Art and Supply remained opened on Saturdays, I hadn't yet been required to work a weekend, for which I was grateful. When I finished work and arrived at the house, I noticed Bridger's car parked in front at the curb. It had been McKell's day off, and I guessed she'd spent part of the day in Bridger's company. They'd been together a lot lately, I thought.

I tucked my day planner under my arm, juggled some papers Mr. Crandall had given me to take home to study, and started up the sidewalk to the front door. I turned as a car whizzed past on the street in front of the house. I caught a streak of green screeching by and frowned at the careless driver. A number of tourists were meandering about the grounds, some with children in tow, and the driver's speed was a menace to those on foot.

I reached for the door handle, thinking about how much busier the town had become in just the last few days. The tourist season was thick upon us, and people seemed to be arriving in droves.

"Hello," I said as I stepped through the door, loudly enough to give fair warning of my presence to McKell and Bridger in case they were engaged in more than conversation.

"We're in here," I heard McKell answer from the kitchen. I set my day planner and papers on a living room chair and went into the kitchen. McKell and Bridger were seated side by side at the table.

"Hey," I greeted them. "How's it going?" When Bridger saw me, a smile lit up his face. I forced a smile in return.

"Hi, Savannah," returned McKell. "How was your day?"

"Okay. Crandall sent me off with homework."

"Homework?" Bridger repeated. "What for?"

I leaned against the kitchen counter. "An inventory of the stock. He wants me to take a look at the sales for the last six months. I'm not sure why. But I'm supposed to have a report for him on Monday morning."

"Think you'll have any time to play over the weekend?" Bridger asked, leaning his chair backward until it balanced on two legs.

"I don't know. You guys have something planned?" I looked from Bridger to McKell.

"Bridger wants to drive to St. Louis tomorrow to spend the day," McKell answered.

I felt my face flame. First a trip to the fishing hole, and now a day in St. Louis, and I've been invited to tag along. "Sounds like fun," I said, trying to keep the bitterness from my voice. "Wish I could come, but I've got these papers to plow through for work."

"We can go another weekend if that's better for you," Bridger volunteered.

"No. You guys go ahead. Don't let me interfere with your plans."

"We want you to join us, Savannah," McKell protested.

I was about to embellish my excuse for not going when the phone rang. "I'll get it," McKell offered, rising from her chair. She picked up the cordless lying on the kitchen counter. "Hello," she said into the mouthpiece. "Hello?"

While she answered the phone, Bridger motioned for me to join him at the table. "Have a seat," he offered.

"Thanks, but you know what? I really want to change out of these clothes and into something cooler. I'll just be in my room," I said by way of excuse as I started toward the bedroom.

"That's strange," McKell commented as she replaced the receiver. "Whoever it was hung up when I answered."

"Probably a wrong number," Bridger suggested, pulling out the chair for her to sit on.

"I guess so. Savannah, where are you going? I haven't talked you into changing your mind yet?" She grinned.

"This weekend's really not good for me," I said lamely.

"But I don't want to go with just Bridger and Travis," McKell protested. "You have to come along or I won't go either."

"Travis? The guy who came with Bridger to the party?"

Bridger was the one to reply. "Yeah. He's obsessed with Kellie. He sent me to convince her into going out with him."

"I told Bridger I'd do it only if you two double-dated with us," McKell pleaded.

"I thought you and Bridger were the ones dating—" I caught myself in midsentence and felt my cheeks flame.

"You thought what?" McKell said, her eyes growing big. "You thought Bridger and I were dating?" She started to laugh. "Oh my gosh, Savannah. That thing between us was over months ago. I told you that."

"I know, but . . ." I bit my lip, forcing myself to stop before I stupidly said anything more.

"Is that why you've been avoiding me?" Bridger asked point-blank. "Because you thought Kellie and I were back together?"

"Avoiding you? Haven't you got that backward? You've been avoiding me." The hot words were said before I had a chance to temper them. I flushed with dismay.

Bridger leaned forward in his chair. "You and I need to talk."

"Look, Bridger, I really am busy with stuff from work at the moment. I'll talk to you later, okay?" As I turned to leave the room, I caught a glance of McKell's confused expression.

I hurried into the bedroom and shut the door before any more words could be exchanged. My head was reeling, and my heart pounded. I was ashamed and relieved all at the same time by what had transpired. I'd just started to change out of my work clothes when a knock sounded at the bedroom door.

"Savannah? Can I talk to you for a second?" It was Bridger's voice outside the door.

I quickly rebuttoned the blouse I was about to shed and opened the door with a shaky hand. "Everything's cool, Bridger. Really," I said before he had a chance to utter a word.

"Okay. How about going for a ride with me for a few minutes?"

"Why?" I blurted, for lack of anything else more appropriate to say.

"Because I've acted like a jerk. And I want to apologize."

"You have nothing to apologize for."

"I need to talk to you," he repeated. "I've been waiting for you to get home from work, so I could ask you about tomorrow."

"I can't go to St. Louis tomorrow, Bridger," I insisted, wishing he'd step away from the door. I felt my heart quivering, and the sensation made me weak.

"Then we won't go tomorrow. And Travis will have to do his own asking after this. Everything's gotten confused." He took my hand suddenly into his. "Come for a drive with me so we can talk. Please."

"Alright," I relented, feeling the breath go out of me as he pressed my hand in his. "Just for a few minutes, though. I'll be out as soon as I change my clothes."

Five minutes later we were seated in Bridger's red Paseo, driving in the direction of the river. We sat without speaking for a long, uncomfortable moment. "Thanks for coming with me," Bridger finally said. "Want to walk along the river?"

I nodded. In a short time we reached the water. Bridger parked the car, and we both climbed out. Without a word he took my hand, and together we started along the riverbank. My heart was doing cartwheels from his touch.

"How do you like your job?" he asked as we walked. I knew the question was an attempt to chip away at the silent barrier between us.

"I like it a lot. Especially the gallery side of it."

He gave me a sideward glance. "Any Rubens in the collection?"

I chuckled softly. "No, but there're one or two artists who have some nice paintings on display."

"Well, Rubens is my personal favorite," he joked.

I smiled, thinking it sweet of him to remember my partiality for the painter. We walked along for a time after that. I tried to think of a clever remark to make, as the silence between us was becoming uncomfortable. "You and Rubens have something in common," I ventured.

He looked at me. "Really? What is it?"

"Rubens studied architecture, among other things, when he wasn't busy painting."

"Architecture. No kidding?"

"It's true. His house in Antwerp was a remodeled palace complete with galleries for displaying his paintings and carvings, and the studio where he created his masterpieces. Outside were sweeping lawns, formal gardens, and a stable for his blooded Spanish horses."

"Sounds like an architectural playground," Bridger commented, his mouth twitching with a smile.

The exquisite painting of Peter Paul Rubens and his wife seated together beneath the honeysuckle bower in the garden, which I'd seen in the art book Bridger had given me, flashed into my mind. I remembered the silly daydream I'd concocted of Bridger and me transposed into that painting. "Rubens's pieces are like a dance—" I said aloud, "Warmth, color, and action moving in complicated rhythms."

I felt Bridger's grip on my hand tighten, and knew he wanted to talk about something more pertinent than Rubens's art. "Do you remember our conversation that day on the paddleboat," he began, taking a deep breath. "The part when you asked me why I wanted you to spend the summer in Nauvoo?"

My mind did a quick rerun of the conversation in question. "Yes. You said you'd enjoy getting to know me better." I chanced a glance at his expression, which was inscrutable. "Then the next time I saw you, at the party at our house, you didn't seem the least bit interested in getting to know me better."

Bridger paused in his stride. "I thought you weren't interested in getting to know me better."

"What gave you that idea?" I asked in surprise.

He shrugged. "Your refusal to even discuss the possibility of remaining in Nauvoo. That sounded pretty uninterested to me."

"I'm sorry. At the time, I really didn't see any way that I could stay."

"And then you did a complete reversal. Suddenly you're staying, and wildly enthusiastic about the idea."

I looked up at him with an apologetic expression.

"And your reasons for staying apparently had nothing to do with me. I figured you wanted me to back off." He let go of my hand as if emphasizing his point.

We continued walking in silence, our hands hanging at our sides.

"I don't know how to respond to that, Bridger," I began haltingly. "I was attracted to you, but I didn't realize it right away—not until I thought you were no longer attracted to me." I swallowed, wondering if my words sounded ridiculous.

He didn't reply for a moment. Then he said with a smile in his voice. "You thought I'd taken up with Kellie again, huh?"

I nodded miserably.

"When all the while I was just trying to hook her up with Travis. Kellie can be real stubborn at times."

"She's never said a word about Travis to me. Never even mentioned him."

"You'd have known how much Travis likes her if you'd gone fishing with us that night after the party. He was all red cheeks and sweating palms whenever she talked to him."

I laughed at his description. "Does she like him?"

"I don't know. I thought she'd confide in you if she did."

"Nope. Not a word." We continued walking along the shore of the river, though at a slower pace than before. I wished Bridger would take my hand again.

Bridger blew out his breath in an audible stream of air. "So. Are we attracted to one another or not?" He delivered the question in a lighthearted tone, but I knew my reply was important to him.

It took a moment to arrange my thoughts in order to answer him honestly. "I'm not Mormon, Bridger. That seems a pretty big deterrent to starting a serious relationship."

He remained silent for a few seconds. "I've given that a lot of thought," he said at last. "Normally, I don't date girls who aren't Latter-day Saints. There's no point, you know. I plan to marry my wife in the temple."

I tensed, vaguely annoyed by his intolerant attitude.

"On the other hand, I believe things eventually turn out for a person's best good. You have to exercise a little faith."

"What are you saying, Bridger?" I asked impatiently. All his talk about belief and faith seemed beside the point.

He stopped and turned to face me. "I'm saying the same thing as before—that I'd like us to get better acquainted."

I eyed him carefully. "In a romantic sort of way, or as friends?"

He grinned back at me. "Whatever develops."

"A romantic walk along the river. Some hand holding. Declarations of affection. And you end up saying you want to be friends with me." I laughed. "Do you know what the guys I used to hang with would be suggesting instead?"

Bridger took a step closer. "No, what?"

"Try figuring it out." I grinned at him.

"Would it be something like this?" He leaned toward me and gently pressed his lips against my forehead in a chaste kiss.

I closed my eyes, feeling tingles race through my body. I thought he might take me in his arms and give me a proper kiss, but he didn't. I opened my eyes to find him looking at me, a small smile on his lips.

"Yeah. Something like that," I said.

He chuckled, then confidently took my hand into his. We started back toward the car hand in hand. "I'm starving. Want to go into town and get something to eat?" he asked me.

"You mean at the one and only restaurant in Nauvoo?"

"You're forgetting about tourist season. It's arrived and now there are at least two restaurants open in town."

"Oh, no. For a moment I thought the choice was going to be easy."

We sauntered back to the car, comfortable with the easy bantering between us. He opened the door for me and I slid into the seat. When he came around to the driver's side, I saw him pause as he glanced off to one side. Then he settled into the seat and switched on the headlights. It was nearing dusk, and the sun spilled red onto the river. We pulled away from the riverside.

"Let's eat at the restaurant in the old Victorian hotel on Mulholland Street. I noticed the other day that it's open for business," he said.

"Sounds fine to me."

"I feel like a big meal. Maybe steak and baked potatoes. How about you?"

"Do they actually have steak and potatoes?" I asked jokingly.

"I hope so or my stomach is going to be awfully disappointed." He darted a glance in the rearview mirror, frowning slightly.

"Last time you promised me pecan pie, and then you didn't deliver," I teased.

"Hey, that wasn't my fault. There was no pecan pie on the menu." He turned the corner onto Mulholland.

"Then you promised you'd make one for me. I haven't seen it yet. You're all talk and no action, Bridger Caldwell."

He turned to offer me a grin. Before restoring his gaze to the road, he took another quick look in the rearview mirror. A frown quickly replaced the smile he'd been wearing.

"Something wrong?" I asked, noticing the change in his expression.

This time he stared into the mirror, taking his eyes off of it only long enough to make quick glimpses at the road up ahead. "I don't know. I think someone is tailing us."

"What?" I exclaimed. I jerked my head around to see a dark-colored car behind blinding headlights. "Why do you think so?" I asked, feeling a twinge of nervousness in the pit of my stomach.

"I heard his engine start up just as I was about to climb in the car. Then I noticed him behind us."

I craned my neck a second time, trying to determine the color and make of the vehicle. But it was rapidly growing dark, and the car had fallen back a fair piece as if the driver knew we'd spotted him.

"Let's see if he's really on our tail or not," Bridger muttered. When he came to the next intersection, he made a quick hard right without signaling his intention, then stepped on the accelerator. The Paseo shot forward.

Bridger kept an eye on the rearview mirror while I twisted in the seat to watch for the trailing car. Both of us were silent as we waited to see what would happen next.

CHAPTER 18

A second later, a pair of headlights whipped around the corner of the intersection and darted toward us. "That's him," Bridger hissed.

I stared at the oncoming lights. "Maybe it's just a coincidence that we're both headed in the same direction," I suggested hopefully.

"Let's test out your theory," he replied. Without warning, he spun into a U-turn and headed the opposite direction, stomping hard on the gas pedal. We passed the dark-colored car coming the opposite way before the driver could react to Bridger's offensive maneuver. The driver sped up, tearing down the road away from us.

"Did you get a chance to see the driver's face?" I asked breathlessly.

"No. It was too dark inside his car. Could you make out anything?"

I shook my head.

"But I got a better view of the car. It looks like a dark brown or blue. Or maybe deep green. A Honda or a Toyota, probably."

I stared at him, horrified by a sudden thought.

"I don't know why someone would be tailing me." He glanced into the rearview mirror. The street behind us was now deserted.

I grasped his arm and squeezed it. "Bridger, I don't think it's you he's following. I think it's me."

Bridger stared at me. "What?"

"You think the car might be green in color?"

"Maybe. I'm not sure. Why?"

"The day before yesterday Kell noticed a green car cruising slowly past our house. Then she thought she saw it later, only this time it was parked across the street late at night. Then today, when I returned from work, I saw a green compact car speed past. It went by just as I was getting out of my car to go in the house." The words caught in my throat.

Bridger couldn't hide the alarm that sprang to his eyes. "Are you sure about this?"

"Yes. Absolutely sure." My body started to tremble. "Why would this person, whoever he is, be following us?"

"I don't know," Bridger scowled. He hunkered down in the driver's seat, his body tense.

"Could the driver possibly be James?" I asked after a moment of thought.

"James? Why do you think it might be James?" Bridger glanced quickly at me. His eyes were a deep gray in the evening shadows.

"Remember my telling you about James's comment to me? The one about you tending to your end of the business. It was such a strange remark for him to make. Is he trying to scare us for some reason? Maybe try to persuade you to keep your nose out of his business when it comes to the company's financial affairs."

"Tailing us would be a strange way to get across his point. And James doesn't drive a dark-colored, compact car."

I put a hand to my forehead. "It doesn't make any sense, I know. But I can't think of anyone else who would remotely have a reason to be watching us."

Bridger turned left at the next intersection, and then right, back onto the street we'd been traveling to begin with. Both of us kept an eye out for the compact car, but we didn't see any sign of it. Bridger drove to the restaurant at the hotel. We had to wait in the lobby before being seated because the dining room was full, so we sat on a bench facing a window looking out onto the street. I kept glancing out at the road, afraid I'd see the compact car driving past.

"This town is beginning to give me the creeps," I said quietly to Bridger.

He covered my hand with his and gave it a reassuring pat. "Everything will be okay. That's probably the last we'll ever see of that guy in the green car."

I shook my head. "It's not just that. Other weird things have been happening ever since I got here."

Bridger stared into my face. "Like what?"

"First of all, the accident. I was nearly killed."

He nodded solemnly and squeezed my hand.

"Then I keep dreaming about this strange woman who pops out of nowhere and disappears in the blink of an eye."

"What?" He leaned over to look at me more closely. "What woman?"

"That's what I'd like to know. I've seen her in my mind's eye three times now. And there's this presence about her that I can't explain."

"An evil presence?"

"No. Almost a peaceful feeling. Peaceful, but with a purpose. As if she wants to tell me something. Or get me to do something for her." I shrugged. "So I have no clue what it all means."

"That is unusual," Bridger acknowledged.

A white-coated waiter came up to us. "Your table for two is ready, sir," he said to Bridger.

We got up from the bench and followed the waiter to a spot in the corner of the restaurant. The waiter pulled out a chair for me, then placed two menus on the table in front of us.

"Thanks," Bridger told him.

We settled down to the business of deciding what we wanted to eat. The menu featured several different cuts of steak, and Bridger ordered a filet mignon. I chose salmon. Indirectly, we were celebrating the cementing of our friendship. With our feelings for one another out in the open, we felt buoyant. We relished our meals and afterward ordered a rich chocolate mousse for dessert. With our stomachs full and our hearts light, we forgot all about the unsettling events that had plagued us.

* * *

I'd been in Nauvoo for three weeks and had seen just about everything there was to see at the restoration project. Bridger still wanted to take me to St. Louis for a day, so we planned the trip for the following Saturday. We intended to persuade McKell into going with us as Travis's date.

But first I had a whole week of work at the art shop to get through. On Saturday and Sunday I looked over the accounts Mr. Crandall had sent home with me, determining which products were selling best and ranking all the art supplies by the amount of income they'd generated. I had no idea why he wanted the information, but I was willing to oblige him because he offered to pay me overtime for my trouble.

Crandall didn't come into the shop until late in the afternoon on Monday. We were busy with customers nearly until closing, but a few minutes before five o'clock Crandall asked me for the results of my weekend labors.

"Here are the figures, Mr. Crandall. I've typed them up in a list for you, starting at the top with the best selling items down to the least."

I stood waiting, nervously chewing my lip while he pored over the items and accounts. When he finished, he removed his glasses and rubbed the lenses on his shirtsleeve. He set the paper down on the counter and looked at me with his razor sharp eyes. "I've been thinking about what you said on Friday." He replaced his glasses and slid the bridge up with the tip of his forefinger. "It may be a sound idea to enlarge the gallery."

"Really?" I squeaked.

"I'll have to look more closely at these figures, but on first glance it appears you may be right. We might be able to make a go of a gallery of paintings and sculpture, without the side products. If we were smart and chose our pieces wisely, we could just possibly make a successful venture of it."

I clapped my hands together. "Oh, I think it could be very successful! Just a small, intimate gallery with superior artwork, and some attractive backdrops and lighting to accent the pieces. Oh, and lots of promotional work and advertising would really draw the customers—"

Crandall put up a hand to stop my flow of chatter. "One thing at a time, Miss Lawrence. I said I was considering it. I'm not ready to put an ad in the *New York Times*."

I rocked on my heels, barely able to contain my excitement. Crandall had liked my suggestion for expanding the gallery, and I was bursting with ideas to help make it a success. "I understand, Mr. Crandall. But I think it's a wonderful idea, and I'd be willing to help in any way I can."

He gave me a crusty look. "I appreciate your enthusiasm, though it's a bit premature."

"Patience is not one of my virtues," I grinned.

He maintained his gruff demeanor, but when he turned away I saw a small smile curl his lips. I hurried to the front of the store, where I'd been restocking shelves, dancing on tiptoe. The remaining minutes of the work day dissolved away. At five o'clock, I grabbed my day planner and skipped out the door of the store. A voice interrupted my revelry.

"Are you up for a little detective work?"

Startled, I let out a gasp. Then I saw Bridger, with arms folded, leaning against the front of the building. "You scared me to death," I scolded him.

"I wanted to see how well you react under pressure." He grinned, not in the least chastened. "I need a partner with nerves of steel."

"What in the world are you babbling about, Bridger?" I asked, hiding a smile.

He fell in step with me as I headed toward my car. "James is going into Keokuk for the evening to a business meeting and dinner. He won't be back until after ten."

"So?"

"So it's the opportunity I've been waiting for to get a look at the accounts."

I stopped in my tracks. "Bridger, you can't be serious. I thought you'd abandoned the idea of breaking into James's computer."

He shook his head. "I've been keeping my eyes open. I think I know the password to get into the ledger accounts. It won't take me long to access the material and make copies of it. But I need a lookout. Just in case James comes home early."

"Me? You really want me to do it?"

"Who better than you? You like treading on the edge of danger, don't you?"

"Be serious, Bridger. Why don't you get Travis or your friend Bronson to keep watch? I'd have no idea what to do if James actually did show up while you were inside pilfering his files."

"That's why I want you there. It'll look more natural. You and me just spending a leisurely evening together. James knows we hang out."

"James also knows that I'm an accomplice of sorts. He gave me a message to deliver to you, remember?"

"I remember. But I'll be in and out of the office long before he's back."

"Good. Then you won't need me." I rummaged through my planner for my car keys.

Bridger lounged against the car as I fit the key in the lock. "You haven't seen the guy in the green car following you today, have you?"

My eyes darted up the street and back. "No. Why? You don't think he is, do you?"

"I hope not. Keep an eye out, anyway. Just in case."

I hadn't given the driver of the compact car a thought all afternoon, but Bridger's reminder sent a cold chill down my spine. I turned the key and opened the car door. "You be careful, too. We don't know which one of us he's interested in."

Bridger shut the car door after me as I slid into the driver's seat, then he leaned down to speak with me through the open window. "Are you going to have Rex at your disposal tonight?"

"Yes, I think so. I don't believe Kell has any plans that she needs to have the car."

"Okay. Why don't you pick me up at the motel at 9:00? I don't want James to get suspicious if he comes back early and sees my car. It will be dark by then."

"Bridger, I really don't think this is a good idea. Anything could go wrong, and you—"

In the middle of my sentence, Bridger pushed his head through the open window and without warning, planted a kiss on my mouth.

I was taken completely by surprise. "Bridger!" I sputtered. "What was that for?"

"To take your mind off your worries," he grinned.

I made a wry face at him, then rolled up the window. He stepped away from the car as I turned the key in the ignition.

"Nine," I saw him mouth through the glass. He lifted a hand in farewell as I pulled away from the curb.

It wasn't until I had turned the corner and Bridger was out of sight that my body reacted to his kiss. Suddenly my mouth felt hot and my hands sweaty. Bridger Caldwell had kissed me! I was stunned by it. And thrilled. My immediate reaction after that, however, was one of frustration. He'd done it so unexpectedly that I hadn't had time to prepare for or anticipate his kiss. I shook my head, a smile parting my lips. One of these days, I vowed, Bridger was going to kiss me in a way that was neither a token of friendship nor a means of diverting my attention.

I drove the few short blocks home. When I pulled up to the house, I was surprised to see two girls about my own age carrying suitcases from their car up the walk to the house. I parked the Buick and stepped out. "Hi," I said to one of the girls who was about to set foot on the front porch. The other had already gone inside the house. She turned to look at me, and a ready smile sprang to her face.

"Hello. You must be McKell or Savannah, right? I'm Sister Watson."

I walked up to her and took her proffered hand. She gave mine a sturdy shake. She was a tall girl, with chin-length red hair and a generous sprinkling of cinnamon-colored freckles across her nose. "I'm Savannah. Savannah Lawrence. McKell is probably inside."

My questioning look prompted a reply. "I'll bet you didn't know we were coming. We're missionaries, Sister Suafa'i and myself. We've both just been transferred here from a city farther north. It's awfully nice to meet you, Savannah."

Before I could respond, the front door burst open and McKell stood in the doorway shoulder to shoulder with the other girl, who was obviously of Polynesian descent with her glistening black hair and shining dark eyes.

"Savannah, guess what?" McKell announced. "A set of sister missionaries are going to be sharing the house with us. Won't that be awesome?"

I could see McKell was genuinely pleased by this new arrangement, though I didn't feel quite the same enthusiasm. "Yeah. That's great. Sister missionaries, huh? I didn't know girls could be missionaries. I thought only guys were."

Both missionaries giggled at my naiveté. "No, girls can be missionaries for the Church, too. Sister Suafa'i is from Samoa, and I'm from Michigan."

Sister Suafa'i stuck out her hand. She had as firm a handshake as her partner. "Nice to meet you," I said to her.

"Come in," McKell welcomed Sister Watson. "There are a pair of spare rooms, so you sisters can pick the one you want. Savannah and I have the room down the hall on the right."

"Thanks. We're thrilled to be serving here in Nauvoo," Sister Watson bubbled. "How long have you two been here?"

McKell briefly told her about our backgrounds and our reasons for being in Nauvoo. The other missionary, Sister Suafa'i, didn't say a lot. I wondered if she spoke much English, or if she was just more shy than her partner.

The girls put away their belongings in the room across from ours, and then we all gathered in the kitchen to get better acquainted. McKell brought out crackers and cheese to snack on, and soon the presence of the girls seated around our table seemed as natural as when Sierra, Hailee, and Kaitlyn were there. In all the excitement I nearly forgot about meeting Bridger.

"Oh, my gosh. It's almost nine," I exclaimed.

"What's happening at nine?" McKell asked innocently.

I wondered how much to divulge about Bridger's plan, then decided to confide in her. I got up from the table, made my excuses to the sister missionaries, and motioned for McKell to accompany me to our room. Once inside, and with the door closed for privacy, I told her about Bridger's scheme to get at the account records stored in James's computer and his reasons for wanting to do so.

"Wow. I had no idea," she responded, wide-eyed. "Be careful tonight. Do you want me to come with you?"

"No. I don't think anything is going to happen. James won't be back from Keokuk for another hour or so. But I'd better get on my way, or I'm going to be late picking up Bridger."

McKell walked with me to the door as we continued talking about the situation. She stood on the front porch nervously twisting the chain attached to her Young Women medallion while I got in the car. I waved to her as I pulled away from the curb.

My stomach started feeling queasy as I pulled up to Bridger's motel. He'd apparently been waiting in the shadows beside the building. I didn't spot him until he glided from the darkness to my car and quickly stepped inside.

"You gave me a start. I didn't even see you standing there," I said after he closed the car door.

"Let's get going," he said. I could sense the tension in his body. I pulled out of the parking stall and headed toward James's trailer, parked just inside the restoration site.

Bridger twisted in the seat to look behind him.

"What's wrong?" I asked quickly.

"Nothing. Just wanted to be sure you weren't followed." He turned back around, and I heard him take a deep breath.

I glanced in the rearview mirror myself, and not seeing anyone else on the road behind me, tried to relax. "Do you have a plan for me?" I asked, glancing at him.

"I thought we'd park the car a few blocks away, and cut across the grounds on foot. While I'm inside, you stand in the shadows by the window. If you hear or see anything unusual, rap on the window. I'll hear you and come out immediately."

"What if you hear my rap while you're in the middle of copying documentation?" I asked him.

"Then I'll have to scramble fast, won't I?" His tone was deliberately glib. "Nothing's going to happen. It'll all go like clockwork," he added, reaching over to pat my hand, which was clamped on the steering wheel.

I thrust him a sideways glance. His mouth was fixed in a tight line, and his jaw was rigid.

In a few moment's time we descended the curving hill leading to the restoration site. My hands on the wheel began to sweat, and perspiration formed along my brow.

"Pull over right there," Bridger directed in a low voice. He pointed to an abandoned building set back from the road. "There's a small place for parking behind the building," he said.

I steered the car in the direction he indicated. Then, when he said to turn off the headlights, I punched the button, and the car plunged into darkness.

CHAPTER 19

"I can't see anything," I whispered to Bridger.

"Pull forward a little bit more, up against the building," he returned in a low voice.

I slowly inched the car forward.

"That's good. Let's get out."

We left the car parked behind the building and wordlessly made our way across the grass of the restoration project to James's office. No one was about, and the night seemed perfectly still. A half moon gleamed overhead, shedding barely enough light to mark our way.

In a couple of minutes we were standing outside the trailer that doubled as James's architectural office and living quarters. A bare bulb above the door gave off a dull glow. Bridger reached in his pocket for keys to the office door. "You stand there," he pointed to the rear of the trailer, "by that back window and alert me if you see anything out of the ordinary."

I put a hand on his arm. "How long do you think you'll be inside?"

"Maybe fifteen or twenty minutes."

"That long?" I moaned. "Can't you hurry it up?"

I could sense his grin in the darkness. "Why? Are you going to get tired of waiting?"

"Very funny," I whispered. "Just get in and get out again as fast as you can."

"That's my intention," he snickered. I heard the soft click of the key in the lock, and the quiet swish of the door opening.

I tiptoed to the rear of the trailer and took up my post. From the office window gleamed a faint patch of light as Bridger switched on his flashlight. I watched the little beam of light bounce off the walls of the room, then settle into a stationary position. I stared out into the darkness, biting my nails in trepidation. As my eyes adjusted to the inky blackness, I was able to see vague shapes in the dark. I peered at a shrub growing nearby. In the blackness it looked like a human crouched on his haunches, ready to spring at me. The leaves of the trees rustling in the slight breeze sounded like creeping footsteps. I shifted my gaze to the window where the circular beam of light emanating from Bridger's flashlight illuminated a corner of the room.

I chewed on my nails, poised for any sight or sound that seemed out of place. I glanced at my watch. The glowing hands pointed to 9:20. What if James decided to come back earlier than expected? I felt my breathing speed up with the thought. *Relax*, I told myself. *Everything will be fine, like Bridger said.*

I'd been watching and waiting about ten minutes when a sudden noise, like the cracking of a twig, sounded to my right. I stared hard into the darkness where the sound originated, my ears tuned for the slightest disturbance. I thought I saw a shadow of movement in the bushes off to my right. I licked my parched lips, my eyes transfixed on the spot.

"Savannah!" I heard my name called in a loud whisper. I whirled in the opposite direction. Nothing moved in the blackness. Then an inky form stepped from behind a tree a few yards to my left. I felt a shriek building in my throat. "Savannah, it's me," the figure swathed in shadows whispered.

"McKell?"

"Yes. I have to talk to you." She stepped out a pace from the protection of the tree and gestured for me to come to her.

"What are you doing here?" I sputtered as I moved toward her.

"Savannah, listen to me." She pulled me into the shelter of the wide, branching tree and put an icy hand on my forearm. "When you pulled away from the house, I started to go back inside. But something out in the street caught my attention. A car was parked there, with the motor running. And the headlights off."

"What? What are you talking about?" I felt my pulse quicken.

Her hand clamped down tighter on my arm. "The driver began to follow you without turning on the headlights. Savannah," her grasp felt like a claw on my arm, "it was the same car we saw parked in front of the house the other night."

I started to speak, but McKell placed a finger over her lips. We pressed tighter against the rough bark of the tree.

"I knew something was wrong when I saw the car following yours from a distance. I panicked. I didn't know what to do. I had to warn you, but you were already gone and the car was right behind you."

I gripped McKell's cold hand. "How did you get here so fast?"

"Sister Watson let me borrow the mission car. She misplaced her car keys in all the confusion of unpacking and it took some time to find them or I would have been here sooner to warn you."

"You made a big mistake coming at all." It was a man's voice, low and menacing, and with the words a lightning fast arm from behind snaked around McKell's neck. The other hand covered her mouth.

I blinked in astonishment and terror, too stunned to move a muscle, too shocked by the identity of the assailant to even draw a breath. "Jaden?" I gasped.

"Surprise, hon."

The chilling words drove the breath from my throat. I uttered a strangled cry, but the sound didn't reach past my lips. I could see McKell's eyes in the thin beam of light coming from the trailer porch. They looked like huge round saucers staring out of a ghostly face.

"Don't scream, Annie. Or make a sound," Jaden warned. A glimmer of moonlight shone on the silver hoops in his ears. His baseball cap, black in the darkness, was pulled low on his forehead.

I watched him raise a hand that held a gleaming metallic object. My head reeled as I realized the shiny object was a pistol.

"I'm afraid this gathering is only for three of us," Jaden hissed in McKell's ear. "And you're not invited." With a quick motion, he struck McKell on the back of the head with the gun. McKell groaned and slumped to the ground.

"Jaden, what are you doing?" I cried out in stunned disbelief. As I took a step toward McKell's motionless body, Jaden swore and aimed the pistol directly at my chest.

"Don't make me shoot you, Annie. It's not you I came for. Though you deserve killing along with that sneaking architect."

I froze. My mind couldn't get a fix on his meaning. It made no sense. I stared at the gun gleaming in the moonlight. Jaden's arm remained rigid, with the pistol held point-blank against my chest. My eyes darted from the wild, savage look in his eyes to McKell's limp form on the ground in front of me. "Jaden, I don't understand—"

Before I could say another word, he grabbed me and slammed me against him. I felt his hot breath on my face. "You've been cheating on me, Annie. All along. That's why you're still here in this place. Cheating and lying to me." His words were spoken in my ear in a venomous whisper. He yanked me tighter against him, and I felt the sudden cold pressure of metal against my temple.

My heart was thrashing so hard in my chest I could scarcely stand. "Let me go, Jaden! Let go!" I gasped. He was crushing the breath out of my lungs. I had never seen him so enraged, so bereft of his senses. His eyes were two burning nuggets of fury, and his mouth was a mere slash in a contorted face.

With the gun in hand, he held me fast by the roots of my hair. My head throbbed from his cruel grasp, and I was nauseated by the stench of alcohol on his breath. "Maybe I shouldn't let you live, either," he ranted.

I was desperate to get away from him, but my mind refused to function, to think of a plan for escape. Then a terrible thought struck with such force that my knees buckled underneath me. Bridger was inside the trailer a few yards away, oblivious to the fact that Jaden intended him harm. I had to warn him! But I didn't know how. If I screamed or struggled, Jaden would surely mete out the same punishment to me as he had to McKell, or worse. "Jaden, let me talk to you," I said, nearly choking on my words.

I felt the pressure of his grip ease slightly, though the hand with the gun remained tangled in my hair.

"Let me go, Jaden, so I can breathe. I want to talk to you."

He released his hold on me. I could hear his heavy breathing in the quiet night. I chanced a quick glance at McKell. She hadn't moved.

Jaden lowered the gun. "Go ahead. You have thirty seconds."

My breathing came in ragged gasps, and my heart was bounding inside my chest like a spooked jack rabbit. "Jaden, this isn't what you think. Bridger and I are just friends. I swear it."

His mouth curled into an ugly sneer. "Don't lie to me, Annie," he snarled. "I've seen you with him. The two of you at your house. Walking along the riverbank together." His eyes burned with fury. "I saw him kiss you."

"No! It's not what you think," I cried. I shook with the jolting realization that he'd been following us. Stalking us. I broke out into a sweat. "This is all a misunderstanding. Please, Jaden. Please, put away the gun and we'll talk about it."

He raised the pistol again, pointing it at me. "Not until I do what I came here to do, hon." The term of endearment took on a twisted, malevolent meaning. Beneath his dark cap, Jaden's eyes smoldered like hot black coals.

From the periphery of my vision, I caught a glimpse of a shadow stealing forward. A hand shot out, straining for the gun.

"Bridger! Watch out!" I screeched. My fists flew to my mouth as Bridger tried to wrench the pistol free of Jaden's grip. He grunted as Jaden's elbow rammed into his belly. Cursing, Jaden twisted toward his attacker and struck him a hard blow to the face.

I stared, mute with horror, as the two men fought for possession of the gun. They wrestled one another to the ground and rolled in a tangled heap on the grass. The baseball cap Jaden wore slid off his head and disappeared between the two struggling bodies. Jaden cursed and raged as Bridger attained the advantage and pinned him against the ground. I saw Jaden's knee come up and slam into Bridger's back, throwing him off balance. Jaden still gripped the pistol. He whipped it against Bridger's forehead, opening a gash along his brow.

"Jaden, stop it!" I screamed hysterically.

Suddenly, a loud crack filled the air. I jerked, my teeth clamping together. With the sound of the gunshot, both Bridger and Jaden lay abruptly still. A scream curdled in my throat, and tears streamed from my eyes. I didn't know if, or who, had taken a bullet.

I darted toward the two men. Then I heard Jaden grunt. He sat up, swaying dizzily. Bridger remained motionless on the ground.

"Oh, Bridger! No!" I shrieked, tears flowing down my cheeks.

Jaden stumbled to his feet. He stood, his body wobbling, then took a step and bent down to reach for something in the grass. Just as I got to Bridger's side, Jaden scooped the pistol from the grass and pointed it at my head.

From somewhere among the houses on the flats, a porch light flickered on, the residents aroused by the sound of the gunshot. Jaden grabbed me by the wrist and started to yank me away with him.

"No! Jaden, stop! I have to help Bridger."

Jaden lifted me off my feet, half carrying, half dragging me away. I kicked and fought him, struggling against his hold. When I tried to cry out, he clamped a foul-smelling hand over my mouth.

"You let out one more sound, Annie, and I'll put a bullet into you. I swear it," Jaden growled, leveling the gun at me. I had no choice but to obey him. With a last desperate glance at my friends, who lay unmoving on the ground, I allowed Jaden to lead me away.

He broke into a trot, breathing heavily and heading in the direction of the road outside the restoration property. He didn't say another word. I was silently crying, tears tumbling down my face. Sick to my stomach with the fear that Bridger was dead and McKell gravely injured, and unable to do anything for them, I prayed that someone would find them and administer aid. I clung to that hope. It was the only thing that was saving me from dissolving into hysteria.

Jaden dragged me along after him. I stumbled once in our haste, and he paused barely long enough for me to regain my footing. The next moment, I spotted a car parked off the side of the road. It looked black under the cover of night, but I knew with sickening assurety that it was green. Jaden stopped alongside of it, fumbled in his pocket for keys, and swore furiously as he tried to ram the key into the lock of the trunk in the darkness.

At last the key slid into place and the trunk lifted. "You're going home with me," Jaden spat. With those words, he picked me up off my feet to dump me inside the trunk.

"No!" I cried out. "Don't do this! Jaden, please!" I fought him, scratching and flailing, crying out for him to let me go. He flung me over his shoulder as if I were nothing more than a rag doll, then tossed me into the trunk of the car. I hit my head on the side of the trunk as I tumbled inside. For an instant, a hundred glowing stars flickered in front of my eyes. The blow stunned me just long enough for Jaden to shove my legs into the trunk and slam the lid down tight.

CHAPTER 20

Suffocating blackness enveloped me. The sudden impact of total darkness frightened me almost out of my senses. I opened my eyes wide, straining to see any glimmer of light. Panic swelled inside me. I couldn't see! I couldn't breathe! I had to get away from the dark!

A scream started in my throat. I lunged against the lid of the trunk, but it didn't give an inch. I rammed it again and again with my shoulder, throwing all my strength into it. "Jaden," I screamed. "Let me out!"

The blackness was closing in around me. I coughed, sputtered for breath. Something deep inside me urged calmness, and I drew in several mouthfuls of air, trying to steady myself. Though it was as black as pitch, if I kept control of myself, I might be able to survive the darkness, the smothering closeness of the trunk.

I realized suddenly that Jaden had not started the engine of the car. We weren't moving, and I couldn't hear any sound outside of my black prison. What was he doing? Had he gone back to make certain that Bridger was dead? "Jaden?" I called. "Jaden, open the trunk. For pity's sake, open the trunk!" I shouted.

Nothing but silence greeted my pleas. If he was anywhere near the car, he wasn't letting me know it. I banged on the lid of the trunk and screamed his name. I pounded my heels against the floor. In the cramped, confined space of the trunk, I was nearly bent over double. Frantically, I started running my hands over the walls of the enclosure, seeking an avenue of escape. I dug my fingernails into the crack where the trunk door fit against the frame. I clawed at the rubber lining separating the two. I tried to tear the lining away, to get at the metal where the door fit into the frame. I felt my fingernails rip and was almost glad for the pain—it meant that I was still conscious and lucid.

With a desperate cry, I gave up trying to pry loose the snug-fitting rubber liner and returned to searching with my fingers for any kind of crack or opening, knowing I couldn't keep my sanity much longer locked in the unforgiving blackness.

I alternated between quiet whimpering and shouting myself hoarse for help. It seemed as if I'd been imprisoned for an eternity, though I guessed it had been only moments. My head was pounding from the blow I'd sustained when Jaden threw me into the trunk. And I couldn't stop thinking it was my fault that my two dearest friends lay injured or dead in the grass. I felt as if I were sinking into a deep, black abyss from which there was no escape. Panic and recrimination threatened to overwhelm me.

Savannah Marie.

My fingers froze from their frantic search. I held my breath, listening. Had I actually heard a sound? A voice? Perhaps I was slipping closer to the brink of that bottomless black hole of insanity.

Savannah Marie. Grasp the handle and raise the floor of the trunk.

This time I heard the voice distinctly. I glanced wildly in every direction. Nothing but blackness. Yet it was as if someone were next to me, speaking softly in my ear.

Find the handle, Savannah Marie.

My hands reached wildly. At first I felt nothing but smooth metal as my hands groped along the floor of the trunk. Where was the handle? I howled in frenzy. My fingers pressed into the edge where the floor met the walls of the trunk, and I felt something sharp slice the tip of my finger. Crying out in pain and frustration, I kept hunting for a handle.

There! There it was at last. A small, rectangular piece set in the floor of the trunk. I yanked up on it. Nothing happened. I yanked again with all my strength and felt the floor beneath me quiver. I realized I was crouched on top of the plate that needed to be raised. I scooted backward, feeling for the ridge where the plate ended. Locating it, I scrunched into a ball at the very rear of the trunk, my head nearly resting on my knees in the confined space, and heaved on the handle. My angle for lifting it was all wrong, and I couldn't get the leverage I needed to raise it. I kept at it, twisting and turning my hand to get a firm grip on the handle.

I tugged at it with all my might, and the plate lifted just enough for me to slip a hand inside the well underneath it. I scoured the recesses with my hand, groping and fumbling for anything inside. My fingers came into contact with something cool and hard. I latched onto it, dragging it out of the space beneath the plate.

I took several labored breaths; I felt the contours of the metal piece in my hands. A tire iron! Of course! Why hadn't it occurred to me before? In the space beneath the trunk was where the spare tire was usually stored, along with tools for changing the tires.

I nearly laughed out loud with relief. At last I had something solid to use to batter my way out of the trunk. I immediately swung the tire iron against the lid of the trunk. The sound of metal striking against metal rang in my ears. I struck it a second time with more force. I pounded again and again, aiming for what I estimated was partway up on the trunk door, where the lock might be located.

Would the noise draw Jaden's attention? The car still hadn't been started, but I had no idea where Jaden was. Did he intend to just leave me inside the trunk while he disappeared? That thought made me as angry as a bee in a bottle. I slammed the tire iron against the trunk door, using all the strength I could muster in my scrunched position.

Without warning, the trunk lid flew open! I blinked, stunned by the sudden rush of cool air onto my face. "Oh!" I cried. "I'm free!" I scrambled out of the trunk, falling onto the ground with a grunt in my haste. I picked myself up, and stood for an instant without moving, trying to get my bearings in the darkness. My knees and hands were bruised and hurting, my shoulder sore from thrusting it against the trunk, my back throbbing from my cramped position.

Before I even had a moment to consider which direction I should take, I heard footsteps racing toward me. Then Jaden burst into view, heading for the car. My heart nearly stopped beating as he halted suddenly on seeing the trunk standing wide open and me hovering beside it. I saw his hand come up, and the gleaming of metal in the faint moonlight.

I poised myself for flight, but before I could take a single step I saw a figure hurl from the shadowy darkness. The figure lunged at Jaden, tackling him around the ankles and knocking him to the ground.

"Bridger!" I cried out in astonishment.

Bridger threw himself crosswise over Jaden's body and pinned him to the ground with his weight. I could hear him grunt with the effort of it as Jaden cursed him and struggled to free himself.

Quick as lightning I knew what I had to do. I sprang toward Jaden and tore the pistol from his hand while Bridger held him fast. Panting and heaving for breath, I threw the gun as far from me as I could. As I turned back, I saw Bridger plunge a fist into Jaden's face. A second blow rendered Jaden immobile. He lay motionless with his arms outstretched on the grass.

I dropped down beside Bridger as he rolled off of Jaden's limp body, his breath coming in spasms. "Bridger!" I sobbed.

Without speaking, he drew me to him. I buried my face in his chest. "Did he hurt you?" Bridger asked between ragged breaths. His arm tightened around my shoulders.

I tried to gain control of my emotions before I completely fell apart. It took more than one attempt before I could speak without sobbing. "I'm okay. Oh, Bridger, I'm so sorry. I had no idea Jaden would do something like this. You're hurt," I whimpered.

"I'm all right," Bridger grunted as I helped him to his feet. "The gun went off and the bullet must have grazed my head. I lost consciousness for a few seconds. When I came to, Jaden was there. I think he was looking for his hat, and as soon as he found it, he took off again for the car. I got up and followed him."

In the dim flow of light from the moon, I saw him nudge Jaden's still form with the toe of his shoe. "Check Jaden's car for some rope, will you? Or anything to tie his hands with. I don't want him moving until we get the police here."

I hurried the few steps to Jaden's car and with shaking hands opened the door. In the gleam of light coming from the bulb in the ceiling, I glanced inside. I could see nothing lying on the front seat except a crumpled road map. I checked the glove box. Nothing there but registration papers and paperwork in connection with the car rental in Jaden's name. In the backseat I found a sack with a bundle of rope, still in its plastic wrapper. He apparently brought it to tie me up with when he abducted me, but in his deranged fury, forgot to get it. Or maybe he'd planned to use it later. I shuddered and took the rope to Bridger.

"I have to go to Kell," I said quickly, after handing him the rope. In a few seconds, I was kneeling at her side. She was conscious, but inert. She looked up at me out of glazed eyes, and her lips moved but no sound came out. I cradled her head in my arms and brushed her short brown curls out of her eyes. As I knelt on the grass, I felt something hard and solid pressing into my knee. I glanced down and saw McKell's Young Women medallion glimmering in the faint glow of moonlight. The chain was broken in two, and the medallion lay trodden in the grass. With tears filling my eyes, I picked up the ruined necklace and put it into the pocket of my jeans for safekeeping.

Bridger joined me moments later. "What did he do to her?" he said in anguish.

"I didn't know he had the gun until he hit Kell with it," I moaned, feeling myself losing control again. "He hit her, and she fell."

Bridger put a comforting arm around me. "She's going to be all right. Can you get your car and bring it up here? We'll drive Kellie to the hospital."

I nodded. I started off in a sprint across the lawn, my legs feeling as weak as jelly. I forced myself to concentrate on reaching the car without collapsing. Finally, I stood panting against the car door. Slipping inside, I twisted the key in the ignition, and for once, the car sprang instantly to life. I quickly drove the few blocks to where Bridger waited with McKell.

As I pulled up and threw open the back door, Bridger carried McKell to the car and gently laid her in the seat.

"I'll call the police to come for Jaden. You get Kellie to the hospital."

I bit my lip to hold back the tears, appalled by the whole horrifying turn of events. Then my mind latched onto something else. "Bridger, what about your files?" I rasped.

"What?" he said, poised to help me back into the car.

"The files. You couldn't have had time to finish. They must be open in plain view on the computer screen," I said breathlessly.

"That doesn't matter now," Bridger replied quickly.

I put a hand on his arm. "But James will know you broke into his computer. It will mean the end of your job here. And maybe even the end of everything you've worked for in your training as an architect. Bridger, you have to finish your work inside that office tonight. Before James returns."

He glanced at me and I could sense his hesitation. "The only thing that's important now is getting Kellie to the hospital," he answered.

"I know that. Don't you think I know that?" I fairly shouted. "I'll drive her. You clean up inside."

Our eyes looked up simultaneously as a pair of headlights appeared over a rise on the bluffs near town. We watched the car descend the sloping road and head toward the flats. We stood speechless as we stared at the oncoming lights.

"What did you do with Jaden's gun?" asked Bridger sharply.

"I threw it across the lawn," I answered in a choking voice. "It was purely a reflex. I didn't want to touch it."

I heard Bridger's breath escape in a hissing rush of air. "Alright. You get in the car and go." His eyes followed the headlights of the car coming swiftly down the road toward the flats. "I'll stay here and deal with whoever it is."

"It's James's car, isn't it?" I wheezed, gripping his arm. "You still have time to get inside and turn off the computer."

He practically shoved me inside the car. "Get going. Keep your lights off until you reach the main road, so James won't know you've been here with me. I don't want him starting any trouble with you."

I turned the key in the ignition. "He's going to find Jaden. How will you explain that to him? And the cuts and bruises on yourself?"

"You let me worry about that." He slammed the car door shut. "I'll meet you at the hospital as soon as I can."

I shifted into first gear. "Shut down the computer, Bridger. You don't have much time left before he gets here," I said desperately, stomping on the gas pedal. The tires screeched as I peeled away.

* * *

I sat hunched in my chair in the hallway of the hospital, waiting for the doctor to complete his examination of McKell. She had regained full consciousness while I drove to the hospital in Keokuk and insisted that she was fine. But I wouldn't be dissuaded. She needed to be checked by a doctor. It was nearly midnight, and I was emotionally and physically drained. It was nerve-racking, also, to be sitting in the same hospital where I had been treated after my bicycle accident only one month before. Those thoughts led me again for the hundredth time to wonder what was happening between James and Bridger at the trailer office. I gnawed at my thumbnail, which was already chewed down to the quick. All of my nails were broken and torn from clawing at the trunk.

A pair of double doors to my left opened, and a white-coated doctor stepped out into the hallway. I leaped from my chair. "How is she, Doctor?"

"You can relax. Your friend is going to be fine. She's suffered a concussion, but a couple of days' rest should take care of it."

I let out my breath in a noisy rush of air. "Thank goodness. I'm so relieved to hear that."

"I want to keep her overnight for observation. But she's free to go home first thing in the morning if nothing more develops."

"Thank you so much, Doctor. I really appreciate your help," I said, grabbing his hand and pumping it up and down.

He smiled at me. "You're welcome. Good night."

I sank back down on the chair as he walked away. Relief flooded over me like a rushing wave. I closed my eyes and leaned my head back in the chair.

I must have dozed after that because my next conscious awareness was of a hand gently rubbing my shoulder. I opened my eyes to find Bridger crouched in front of me. I threw my arms around his neck.

"How's Kellie?" he asked as I clung to him.

In the glare of the hospital lights I saw clearly for the first time the bloody gash on his forehead and an ugly purple bruise marring his cheek. Tears surged to my eyes. "She's going to be fine. The doctor has seen her." I put out trembling fingers and gently touched his forehead. "Oh, Bridger," I lamented. "I'm so sorry."

He captured my hand in his. "It's not your fault," he said. "You're not responsible for Jaden's actions."

The tears trickled down my cheeks. "This all seems like some horrible nightmare."

Bridger wiped away my tears with his thumb. Still holding fast to my hand, he pulled a nearby chair next to mine and sat down on it. "It's all over now and everything is going to be fine."

I squeezed his hand, trying to absorb some of his strength and confidence. "What happened with James?" I asked in a quivering voice.

"He figured Jaden was an intruder trying to break into the office, and I'd stopped him from doing it. Which was pretty much the truth."

"And the files? Were you able to get the computer shut down in time?"

"Yes, and I have the disk outside in my car."

I leaned forward in surprise. "You had time to copy the files?"

"I had already started to download the files onto a disk when I heard voices outside the trailer. When I got back inside after you left with Kellie, the downloading was completed, so I grabbed my disk and shut down the computer."

"And Jaden?" I asked in a hushed voice.

"In police custody. And they've impounded his rental car."

I shivered and huddled closer to Bridger.

"Is McKell being released from the hospital tonight?" he asked.

I shook my head. "The doctor wants to keep her overnight for observation. I'll come back in the morning to get her."

"So, are you ready to leave now?"

I disengaged my hand from his and leaned forward in my chair. "Not until a doctor has looked at that ghastly cut on your forehead. It's split wide open."

He put his hands on his knees, preparing to stand up. "No way. I'm afraid of needles."

I ignored his glib excuse. "I'm serious, Bridger. You might require stitches. And that cut on your chin needs disinfectant."

"I'll put a Band-Aid on it when I get home." He rose to his feet and reached for my hand.

"There's a nurse down the hallway at the nurse's station. We're not going anywhere until we see her."

He protested as I dragged him to the nurse's station. He ended up with five stitches in his forehead and a sterile strip covering the cut on his chin. We decided to leave my car in the parking lot and drove back to Nauvoo together in his Paseo. It was nearly two in the morning by the time we arrived at the Weeks's home.

"Oh my gosh!" I exclaimed as we pulled up.

Bridger glided to a stop and turned off the ignition. "What's the matter?" he asked in concern.

"The sister missionaries will be worried sick about us."

"The sister missionaries? What are you talking about?"

"I forgot to tell you with all the stuff that's been happening tonight. A pair of sister missionaries just moved into the house this afternoon."

A grin settled on his face. "No kidding. Where are they from?"

"Sister Watson is from Detroit, and Sister Suafa'i is Samoan. Kell and I have to keep LDS standards if we want to continue living in the Weeks's home while the missionaries are there," I explained all in one breath.

He let out a low whistle in the darkness of the car. "Well, what do you know about that?" he said as if to himself.

My thoughts didn't linger long on the sister missionaries. I put a hand on Bridger's arm. "What will happen to Jaden?" I asked him quietly.

"It depends."

"On what?"

"On what the authorities decide to do."

I stared into his face. The expression in his eyes was concealed in shadowy darkness. "He tried to kill you," I replied, shivering.

He covered my hand with his. "Let's not talk about it anymore for tonight," he said. He brought my hand up to his lips and gently kissed it. The soft touch of his lips sent my head spinning.

He drew me close and smiled into my eyes. I could smell the faint scent of his cologne, and it set my whole body tingling. "What are you doing?" I asked with a nervous laugh.

"I'm about to kiss you, Savannah Lawrence."

"Oh." I squeaked. My breath was trapped somewhere in my throat. I closed my eyes as Bridger leaned closer, my heart pounding. I felt his breath on my cheek, and then the gentle press of his lips on mine. The kiss was not one of friendship or comfort, and I quivered with the thrill of it.

.

CHAPTER 21

That night my sleep was punctuated with terrible nightmares of Jaden firing his pistol. Though I managed only a few hours' rest, I was relieved to see the sun come in my window and chase away the bad dreams. Bridger drove me to the hospital in Keokuk to get my car and collect McKell.

On the way back we stopped at the gift shop where McKell worked to inform her boss she'd be taking the day off under doctor's orders. She had a knot on her head the size of an ostrich egg. Then I drove her to the edge of the restoration property where she'd parked the sister missionaries' car the night before. She took the car home, and I went to the art shop.

The day dragged in spite of the good news Mr. Crandall had for me. He'd decided to sell out the existing stock of art supplies and begin to enlarge the gallery area. Though I was pleased about the change, I couldn't get out of my mind the terrifying incidents of last night, and Jaden's twisted behavior. It was horrifying to think I had nearly shared my life with him, or that I'd chosen such a monster to be my boyfriend. How could I have so misjudged his character?

By five o'clock I was exhausted. I couldn't wait to get home. McKell had dinner already prepared, and we talked about mundane things as we ate, not mentioning the events of the previous night. Just as we finished washing the last dish, the doorbell rang.

"I'll get it," I said to McKell. When I opened the front door, all I saw at first was a huge bouquet of bright flowers. Then Travis Perry poked his blonde head over the top of them.

"Hello, Savannah. How's McKell feeling? Is she here?"

"She seems to be doing fine. Come in."

Travis stepped nervously across the threshold.

"Have a seat in the living room, Travis. I'll go get her." I started for the kitchen, then paused to turn around. "Those are really beautiful flowers. She'll love them." I had to chuckle as I left the room. Travis was perched stiffly on the edge of the couch, his hands gripping the bouquet so hard that his knuckles were white, and his lips the color of paste. *He's as nervous as a kitten in a thunderstorm,* I thought, grinning.

"Hey, Kell. There's someone to see you," I announced as I entered the kitchen.

She was just folding the dishcloth and putting it away in the drawer. "Who is it? I'm not expecting anyone."

I leaned against the counter. "Someone bearing gifts."

Her brows flicked together in question.

"Travis." I grinned broadly.

"Travis Perry? What's he doing here?" Her hand glided through her hair, smoothing it.

"He wants to see you. Bridger must have told him you'd been hurt."

"Oh!" she said in exasperation, rolling her eyes skyward. "I'm fine. Bridger should use a little discretion."

I laughed. "Get going before the flowers start to wilt."

"Flowers?" She couldn't hide the spark of pleasure that crept into her eyes. She tucked in her T-shirt. "Do I look all right?"

"You could be wearing a flour sack and still look all right. Especially to him," I said, jerking my thumb toward the living room.

She giggled.

"I'll be in my room," I said.

On my way down the hall I heard McKell's exclamation of delight as Travis handed her the bouquet, and his anxious queries about her state of health.

I closed the bedroom door behind me and flopped down on the bed, smiling at the mental image of McKell and Travis together in the living room. Travis had apparently liked her for quite a while, suffering long in silence while she and Bridger dated. It had never occurred to McKell that he might be fond of her, since he'd not given any indication of it until recently. I knew she wasn't sure whether she liked him in a romantic sort of way or not. In her mind, Travis was just one of the guys she and her friends hung out with.

I sat on the bed, swinging my legs, content to be doing nothing at all after the trauma of the night before. After about ten minutes, however, I began looking for something to occupy my time. I needed to sew a button on my yellow blouse, and the dresser and nightstand needed dusting, but I didn't feel like doing either. I stood up and went to the dresser where a small stack of books lay next to my Nauvoo red brick. I picked up the brick, feeling its grainy surface and remembering the day Bridger and I had viewed the brick making exhibit. It seemed like such a long time ago, though it was only a few short weeks. How my life had changed in those few weeks.

I returned the brick to the top of the dresser and reached for one of the books. I glanced at the title, but its contents didn't interest me. Then I thought about the book stashed in the bottom of my suitcase. It took a moment for me to locate the book among the array of clothing, shoes, and socks still packed inside the case. I grasped the book and opened the dark blue, hardback cover. Across the title page were printed the words *The Book of Mormon*. I had considered reading the book once before, but had decided against it. Maybe now was the time. The examples set by my new friends in Nauvoo, and all I had learned about The Church of Jesus Christ of Latter-day Saints, had definitely left an impression on me. I decided to retreat to a cozy swing on the back porch.

I must have been reading for about twenty minutes or so when I heard a soft rap on the screen door, and then the word, "Savannah?"

I scrambled to my feet, my heart quickening.

Bridger stepped out onto the porch. "Hi."

"Hi, yourself," I replied. Just seeing him brought a blush to my cheeks. The kiss he'd given me in the car the night before still lingered on my lips.

"Kell told me you were back here. My presence seems unwanted in the living room at the moment."

"Sure. How are those two getting along?"

"Well, Kellie has a red rose tucked behind her ear and Travis is on one knee serenading her."

"You're kidding, right?"

He chuckled.

I couldn't help stealing a glance through the screen door and into the living room, just to make sure. McKell and Travis were sitting on the couch in conversation. "When did you get here?" I asked Bridger.

"Just a couple of minutes ago. Mind if I sit?"

Bridger eased into the cushions of the porch swing, and I sat down in a chair opposite him.

"So. How are you doing?" he asked me. His lips were smiling, but his eyes revealed the strain I knew he must be feeling.

"Okay, I guess. I didn't sleep much. How about you?"

"The same." He glanced at the cushion beside him. There lay my Book of Mormon, open to 1 Nephi, where I'd been reading. He reached over and picked up the book. "What's this?" he asked me.

I took it out of his hand. "Don't jump to any conclusions, Bridger. I was browsing through it. That's all." I placed the book behind me, not wanting Bridger to suspect the interest it had aroused in me—at least not yet. Not until I'd had a chance to read more of it.

Bridger gave me a long, steady look without saying anything.

"McKell seems to be feeling a lot better today," I said to him, wanting to change the subject before he could question me about my motives for reading the book.

He leaned back. "That's good. I was worried about her."

"Me too." I stared at the stitches in his forehead and the bandage across his chin, and shivered. "I'm glad you came over. I wanted to talk to you about Jaden."

"That's what I want to talk to you about," he returned, shifting his position. "The detective at the police station stopped by the trailer this morning to question me further about last night's events. He said that Jaden will be charged with attempted murder, or a lesser count of assault and battery, depending on the district attorney's decision. He also said that we might be able to influence that decision, to press for a stiff penalty if we feel so inclined."

I looked down at my hands, not wanting Bridger to see my quivering lips. "What do you think we should do?"

"I've been going over it all day in my mind. Do you think he actually intended to kill one of us?"

I stared at Bridger. His gray eyes were hard, and his jaw clenched.

"I have no idea. I would never have thought Jaden was capable of doing what he did."

"It's possible he was bluffing with the gun. Trying to scare you into going back with him." Bridger took a deep breath and let it out slowly.

"It's possible, I guess. But he was acting so completely crazy. I've never seen him like that before."

Bridger steepled his fingers and blew softly through them, intent in his thoughts. "Do you suppose he might have been high on drugs?"

I avoided his gaze. "Perhaps. I know he'd been drinking because I smelled it on his breath."

Bridger let out a low sigh. "Have you discussed this at all with McKell?"

"Yes. She'd prefer to see the authorities be more lenient toward Jaden, rather than punishing him with the harshest penalty." I drew a shaky breath. "I'm not sure I feel as charitable."

"Our input might be a factor in the punishment meted out to him. Why don't we go talk to Kellie some more about it?"

"Now?" I asked, wanting to avoid this painful subject.

"The sooner the better, I think. Travis won't mind if we discuss it in front of him. He's upset already that Kellie got hurt. He'd be glad to be included in our discussion."

I could tell Bridger was trying to keep his anger in check. He spoke with deliberate slowness and softness, but I knew he was infuriated with Jaden for attacking us. My anger was more visible. I was sure Bridger saw it in the flash of my eyes and heard it in the ring in my voice.

"Alright." I got to my feet and Bridger followed suit. Then he bent down to retrieve the book I'd inadvertently left lying on the cushion and handed it to me. "This will be the most important book you will ever read, Savannah," he said, his hand on the cover. "It's a narrative about rebelliousness and righteousness."

I stared in earnest at him. "Will it help me find charity and forgiveness in my heart?"

Bridger looked at me thoughtfully before he spoke. "It will set forth Christ's perfect example to follow."

* * *

The four of us talked until nine o'clock, when the sister missionaries returned from their teaching. McKell and I introduced them to
Bridger and Travis, who soon left. We had decided to give Jaden the
benefit of the doubt and to encourage the authorities to charge him
only with assault. I hoped I wouldn't have to testify against him, or
ever see him again. Any tender feelings I might have harbored for
Jaden before last night were completely destroyed now.

The next morning I awoke feeling rested and refreshed. I determined to put Jaden and the awful events of the other night out of my
mind, to concentrate on my job and my friendships. My most important friendship was the one I was cultivating with Bridger Caldwell. I
found myself thinking of him often throughout the day, and wanting
to be with him. I also thought about the book resting on my nightstand. What I had read in the first few chapters of the book of 1
Nephi had sparked a desire to read more. I could hardly wait to get
home from work to pick up the book again.

When I did arrive home, I found a note from McKell telling me
she'd gone out to dinner with Travis. I smiled as I read over the hastily
scribbled lines a second time. I fixed myself a cold supper, then
guessing McKell would be away for the rest of the evening and not
wanting to stay at home alone, I decided to take my Book of
Mormon to the temple site to read.

It was a cozy June evening, with soft breezes caressing my hair and
the fragrant scent of flowers filling the air with perfume. I strolled
leisurely across the broad green lawns of the restoration property and
out onto the road leading to the temple site, where a stream of
tourists visited. The missionaries serving there rarely had an absence
of listeners.

Scores of people milled around the depression in the ground
where the temple had once stood; several more lingered in conversation with the missionaries. I caught a glimpse of Elders Gardner and
Witt through the crowd and smiled to myself. The enthusiasm and
devotion to duty I had noticed in them was the same kind exhibited
by the sister missionaries living with us at the Weeks's home. I
admired their spirit, and their eagerness to serve. They carried a
certain glow about them which was hard to describe, but which I
recognized as genuine. I imagined Bridger in his dark suit, white

shirt, and tie, teaching the people in Argentina about the gospel of Jesus Christ. I was certain he must have been every bit as effective in his calling as the missionaries I saw here.

I thought also about Bridger's brother, Lincoln. He had given his life in service to God and his religion. If he had known he would never return home from his mission, would he have still chosen to serve? I wondered. Somehow, from what Bridger had told me about his brother, I suspected that he would. What was it about this religion that caused people to sacrifice their time, their means, their very lives if required? I wanted to discover the answer for myself.

I chose a quiet spot at the edge of the temple grounds, away from the crowd, to open my Book of Mormon. Soon I was immersed in the story of Nephi and his family, and their desires to choose good or evil, obedience or disobedience to God's commandments. It didn't take long to discover the central theme of the book was Jesus Christ and His mission. Nephi testified of the reality of the Savior and His work among men, as his father, Lehi, did. This testimony of the Lord Jesus Christ, delivered by ancient prophets living on the American continent, penetrated deep into my heart. As I continued to read Nephi's account, a feeling of peace and comfort took root in my soul.

Desiring to mark a particular verse, I reached into my jeans pocket in search of a pen or pencil. They were the same jeans I'd been wearing two evenings before, and instead of finding something to write with, I felt an object cool and solid against my fingertips. I dug deeper into my pocket and latched onto a smooth, thin, oval-shaped piece of metal. Puzzled, I drew it out into the sunlight and stared at it. McKell's Young Women medallion, which I'd thrust in my pocket during Jaden's attack and then forgotten about, glimmered in the fading sunlight. The necklace had been ripped from her neck when Jaden accosted her.

I stared at the piece of jewelry. The sun glinted off of its shiny surface, creating cascades of light which danced and shimmered. I knew what the medallion meant to my friend, what it represented, and how hard she'd worked to earn it. As I studied it, I remembered McKell's words about the goals, values, and standards she strived to live by.

I retrieved the severed chain from my pocket and carefully laid the gold medallion and chain across the cover of my Book of Mormon. The medallion and chain gleamed in the fast fading light. The contrast between the sparkling gold of the necklace and the deep blue of the book's cover was striking, like a master artist's painting. As I contemplated the two emblems of Latter-day Saint belief, I knew within my heart that I wanted to embrace those same gospel standards and principles.

It was nearing dusk now, and becoming too dark to read. Soon the gate to the temple grounds would be closed for the night. People were beginning to disperse, though some still remained at the site, reluctant to leave. I put McKell's necklace back in my pocket to give to her at home, and then sat quietly for a moment, savoring the feeling of peace that surrounded me.

I closed my eyes and breathed in the delicate scent of flowers lingering in the air. With my eyes closed, my senses were heightened and I could feel the cool prickles of grass beneath ne, and the gentle breeze. I seemed to recall a wisp of a memory—a warm smile, a soft voice, intelligent blue eyes. And now I remembered something new—a tall, majestic-looking man standing before a congregation of people, speaking to them, and his words created a tremendous excitement and joy among the listeners. I sensed that their cause for jubilation had something to do with this very place where I was sitting, and the building that would soon be restored to its original beauty and sacred purpose.

Even as I tried to grasp a firm hold on the memory, it slipped away, fading like the last golden rays of light at sunset. With my Book of Mormon clutched in my hand, I reluctantly left the temple site. The breeze rustled the leaves of the trees and gently caressed my cheek. I thought I heard, floating on the wings of the breeze, a strange refrain—*Be faithful to your trust.*

CHAPTER 22

It was Friday after work, and Bridger and I were sitting outside on the lawn in front of the Weeks's home waiting for McKell and Travis so the four of us could spend the evening together. The June sun felt warm and soothing on our backs. Bridger sucked on a blade of grass, listening as I described what I had felt at the temple site. I'd already told him about my visit to the garden behind the Visitors' Center and of the strange impressions I'd experienced there, as well as at the riverside. I did not mention the dream I'd had right after my accident. I wasn't ready to share that with anyone, though fragments had begun to surface in my memory. I had become convinced that these things were not a product of my imagination or a result of my accident.

"The first time it happened was at the wooded lot while I was with you," I told him, remembering my impressions of a beautiful woman with the smile of an angel.

Bridger stretched out on the soft grass. "Is there any significance attached to the places where you felt these promptings?"

"I can't think of any. No connections come to mind."

"That is puzzling," Bridger responded. "Maybe it will eventually end up making sense to you."

"I hope so."

Bridger tossed aside the blade of grass he'd been nibbling. "So, where is Kellie? I thought she and Travis were going with us tonight."

"They are. As soon as Kell gets back from rehearsal. She's practicing for her role in the *City of Joseph* play," I replied.

Bridger folded his long legs into a bow. "She has a speaking part, right?"

"Speaking and singing. Did you know Kell has a fabulous singing voice?"

"I know she likes the theater and stuff."

"She does. She performed in plays at her high school and college, and she sings with a trio back home. She's been pestering Sister Watson and Sister Suafa'i to ask the mission president if she can join the performing missionaries for their shows down at the river."

Bridger plucked a blade of grass and tickled my cheek with it. "What kind of thing do they do at the river?" he asked, his eyes teasing.

"It's like a musical revue. Singing, dancing, playing instruments. The Nauvoo Brass Band performs old tunes from the Nauvoo period. It runs most every night all summer."

"Why didn't I know about this?" he said, leaning over to kiss the tip of my nose. "We'll have to go see it."

"You know all about the revue, don't you?" I said accusingly. "Yet you just let me ramble on." I punched his shoulder for teasing me. He retaliated by pinning my arms and tickling my face with the stalk of grass until I shrieked for mercy. Then he released me, both of us laughing.

We talked about our plans for the weekend, and about Bridger's job at the stable site. "Have you had a chance to look at the copies you made of James's accounts?" I asked him.

"I spent an hour on it last night after work. It's pretty plain that he's been jockeying the numbers."

"Are you sure? How'd you figure it out?"

"The architectural firm in Omaha sends him a check every month for expenses related to the work here. He's entered the amount of the check into his ledgers and then listed the expenses."

"Go on."

"The trouble is, he's entering expenses where none have been made. For example, I found a notation for $250 to Reynolds Engineering, Inc., for purchase of a drafting table. There is no drafting table in our inventory, and I'll bet when I check further into it, there isn't even such a place as Reynolds Engineering, Inc. He's concocted the whole entry."

"What about a bill of sale for the goods? Wouldn't he be required to keep a record of that?"

"He has a bill of sale, all right. Scribbled out by a fake employee of a bogus company."

"How would he dare do such a thing? And what's he doing with the money that has supposedly been paid out to expenses?"

"He's pocketing it. That's the only clear answer I can come up with."

"Now that you know, what are you going to do about it?"

"I haven't decided yet. I don't know whether to confront James about it first, or contact the company president. I have to be sure that I'm right before I start making accusations."

While we were discussing the discrepancy in James's account ledgers, McKell drove up in the Buick. Bridger and I climbed in the backseat, then we picked up Travis and the four of us drove to Fort Madison, across the river, to watch a movie. Afterward, we went out for pizza. At the end of the evening we dropped Travis off at his home and Bridger at his motel. Bridger gave me a good-night kiss before getting out of the car.

McKell parked the car in the street in front of the Weeks's home. I noticed she was wearing the Young Women necklace which I'd returned to her; she was toying with the mended chain at her throat as we started up the walk.

"Did you get the mail I left on the kitchen table for you?" she asked as we climbed the porch steps.

"No. I guess I didn't notice it. What did I get?" I opened the front door and we went inside. The house was dark and quiet. The sister missionaries were home and apparently in bed for the night.

"A package."

"A package? Who sent it, did you notice?"

"I think it's from your mom."

I hurried into the kitchen and flipped on the overhead light. On the table lay a letter addressed to Sister Watson and a large padded envelope for me. I picked it up and glanced at the return address. Sure enough, it was from home and written in Mom's cramped hand.

McKell came to my side. "What's in it?"

"I have no idea. Mom's not in the habit of sending me packages." I tore open the envelope and slipped my hand inside. "What's this?" I murmured, withdrawing a single page covered with Mom's handwriting, and a small, hardbound notebook with a blank cover.

I looked at the page of writing first. Mom had penned a brief, explanatory paragraph, and then scrawled half a dozen names on the page. "Oh my gosh," I exclaimed. "It's my genealogy!"

"What?" McKell leaned closer to see the page for herself.

"Look at this. My grandfather's name was Clayton Lawrence, and his wife's name was Marie. His father's name was Jacob Lawrence." I pointed to the short column of names, then looked up at McKell. "This is so exciting! I didn't think Mom would know any of this stuff. Especially on my dad's line."

McKell's eyes widened. "What's the book?" she asked me.

I put down the letter and opened the book to the first page. It was filled with faded handwriting, from the top of the page to the bottom, the letters compact and closely spaced. My eyes scanned the page.

While I glanced over the next few pages, McKell picked up the letter and turned it over to the other side. "Wow, Savannah. Did you read this?" she said to me, her eyes never leaving the page. "Your mom says she sent you an old diary."

"What?" I squealed. I took the paper from McKell's hand and quickly read aloud the few words penned on the reverse side. *I'm sending you a journal that belonged to one of my ancestors. I found it in an old trunk in the basement. Mother.*

McKell and I exchanged a look of astonishment. "Whose journal is it?" she asked breathlessly.

"I don't know. Mom didn't say." I rifled quickly through the pages of the diary. "There's no author's name that I can see," I said in disappointment.

"Maybe you can figure out who it belonged to when you read it. Wow, Savannah, what a treasure."

I closed the journal and softly stroked the cover. No printing of any kind adorned the plain beige cover of the notebook. It was about a half inch thick, and the last third of the pages were blank.

"I know what you'll be doing for the rest of the evening," McKell declared, smiling at me.

I looked at her with shining eyes. "Can you believe this? It's really the first time I've ever even thought about my ancestors." I glanced at the letter again. "Mom has listed my dad's parents and grandparents, but I don't see the names of her parents anywhere."

"Do you know your mother's maiden name?"

"It's Bolton. I think her father's name was Richard, and her mother's was Susannah. That's one of the reasons she named me Savannah, because it reminded her of her mother's name."

"That's a nice legacy for you."

"It is, isn't it? I never gave it much thought until now."

McKell stretched her arms over her head and yawned. "I'm going to leave you to your diary and go to bed. I'm tired, and tomorrow we'll be getting up early to spend the day in St. Louis with the guys. So try not to stay up all night reading," she said, grinning.

"I won't. I'll just browse through the journal for a few minutes, then I'll come to bed. I won't turn on the light and wake you."

As soon as McKell closed the bedroom door behind her, I went into the living room and snuggled into the corner of the couch with Mom's letter and the diary. I reread the letter, then set it aside and carefully opened the journal to the first page.

I was born the twentieth day of May, eighteen hundred and seven, in Greenbrier County, Virginia. My father's name was Benjamin. He was also born in Virginia and died when I was nine years old. His father's name was John. Father had several brothers, some of whose names I remember: William, James, Jeremiah, and Samuel.

I blinked in amazement. In just a few short sentences, I'd learned more about my forebearers than I'd ever hoped to imagine. I read on eagerly.

My mother's name was Mary Lucas, daughter of Charles and Margaret Lucas. Her sisters were Betsy, Margaret, and Hannah. Her family lived near a place called Locust Creek in Kentucky.

As my father died when I was very young, my recollection of him is dim. But folks tell me that he was honest and hardworking, and had the confidence and goodwill of his associates. When he died, he left Mother with the house and farm. Mother was very affectionate to her four children: myself, Elizabeth, Warren, and Elijah. She was attached to the Baptist denomination in the early years of her life, but in process of time, none of her own society being near and a Methodist society being in the vicinity, she united with them. My mother always taught me good principles and especially to have implicit faith in the Bible.

I switched on the lamp sitting on the table beside the couch to better see the writing. Whoever had written this account had a fine hand, the words clear and legible, though a bit faded with time. But he still had not revealed his name, nor had I yet figured out his exact relationship to me. I held the book closer and read on.

When my sister Elizabeth was sixteen years old, we removed to Montgomery County. In a few years more we removed to the state of Indiana, Monroe City, two hundred miles north. I was then thirteen years old. My mother was not neglectful in sending me to school when opportunity offered, which was generally in the winter season. In the summer we were employed on the farm.

I turned the page, hardly taking the time to draw a breath so immersed was I in the account.

About the year 1825 or 1826, the family, all except Warren and myself, joined the Methodists, who were quite numerous and also very zealous at that time. My sister Elizabeth, in particular, was very much devoted to the cause of religion. She was struck with the palsy and after being bled in her right arm she recovered the use of that arm, but her left hand and arm and also her left leg remained almost useless. A second attack about two years afterwards proved fatal. She lived but a few hours.

I found my eyes welling with tears, and my heart sorrowing for Elizabeth's death. How strange, I thought, that I should be so affected by the misfortune of someone I never knew.

I continued to read, taking no note of the passing time. The author told of his family's move to Owen County in the year 1826, and how he was attacked by a bear one afternoon while in the woods and barely escaped with his life. At age twenty-one he took a wife, Abigail Squires, the daughter of Thomas and Polly Squires. The young couple purchased a farm, and in the winter he taught school in a one-room log schoolhouse.

At last, several pages into the narrative, the author revealed himself to me. *We called our firstborn son, born on the twentieth day of February, after my own name, Jeremiah Bolton, and these were, I think, the happiest days of my life as nothing seemed to cross my path, and my course seemed to be onward to prosperity and happiness.*

"Jeremiah Bolton." I tried out the words on my tongue. The name tasted sweet. Jeremiah Bolton. I finally had a name to attach to my relative. I'd need to put a pencil to figure out how many generations removed he was from me. I smiled, whispering his name again. I liked the sound of it. Solid. Unpretentious. A no-nonsense kind of name. I grinned, almost giddy with the revelation. Jeremiah and Abigail Bolton were real people, with actual experiences. And somewhere along the family chain their son had a son, and his son had a son, and on down to the birth of my mother and then to me. I was a link in that great chain. A whole new view of the continuity of family opened to my mind. And with it I felt more connected to my mother than I ever had before.

It was an incredible feeling to be staring at words set down on paper by my own grandparent. Smiling with satisfaction, I again took up the story.

I concluded to try to better my condition by removing some thirty miles west where there was good timber as well as soil. I here purchased land, set out an orchard, fenced and cleared sixteen acres, and prepared two acres of bluegrass for my sheep. I had four or five milk cows, three horses, and a fine stock of hogs, and ten or twelve beehives. I raised flax, provided a wheel and loom for my wife, both of which she used to good advantage. Fortune still smiled on our mutual exertions to get the comforts of life, and what added still more to our happiness, we had, while living in this vicinity, three more children added to our family: Mary Eleanor, born the twenty-sixth of August, 1831; Elizabeth, born the twelfth of March, 1833; and William, born the seventh of May, 1835.

I turned the page and read on.

There was in the settlement Baptists, Presbyterians, Methodists, and Campbellites. In reading the Bible I discovered that baptism was required of the believers, as one of the foremost duties. Hence, my object was to receive baptism. I began to attend the meetings of the Campbellites. My wife and I were baptized in a little muddy stream called Black Creek. We lived a year or two with this people, enjoying ourselves very well according to the light which we had received, when George M. Hinkle came along preaching Mormonism.

My jaw dropped open. Mormonism? This wasn't possible! I reread the last sentence, thinking my eyes had deceived me. But there it was, plain and bold in Jeremiah's firm handwriting. I was stupefied. Had I an actual ancestor who was exposed to Mormonism? I blinked in amazement. With a heightened sense of interest, I plunged on.

George M. Hinkle was, at that time, a good man, and preached with a spirit and power that waked up every one that heard him. He set all to reading their Bibles, and Mormonism was the interesting topic. Many believed his testimony, but to obey required sacrifice that but few were willing to make. The testimony delivered fastened itself upon my mind with such weight that I could not, nor dared not, shake it off.

My wife also believed the doctrine, but, oh, the cost! We had so many endearing associations, and it seemed that everything that makes life desirable must be torn from us if we obey this gospel. But after much reading, reflection, and prayer, I went forward and gave my hand as a candidate for baptism, the only one at that time. My wife hesitated a few days, but finally consented and we both went forward and were baptized in the same little stream we had been in before, so the saying went out that Bolton and his wife had been in every hole in Black Creek. This was in 1835.

I was utterly astonished by what I just read. Never would I have suspected that a relative of mine had been baptized into the Mormon Church. It was almost more than I could comprehend. I closed the journal, stunned, and filled with disbelief. I sat on the couch, my mind trying to make sense out of something I couldn't understand. If Jeremiah and Abigail Bolton joined themselves with The Church of Jesus Christ of Latter-day Saints, why didn't their descendants have any inkling of it? What happened to Jeremiah's posterity to make them wander so far from the faith?

CHAPTER 23

The following morning Bridger, Travis, McKell, and I drove to St. Louis to spend the day shopping and sightseeing. I had stayed up late the night before reading Jeremiah's diary, and his words still swirled in my head. On the drive to St. Louis I told the others about what I'd read in the journal. They were as amazed as I in learning Jeremiah and his wife had joined the Church, and we spent most of the ride discussing it.

We had a great time in the city seeing the sights. The sky was overcast and a sprinkle of rain fell throughout the day, but that didn't dampen our enthusiasm. Bridger and I had our picture taken standing beside the famous St. Louis arch. It stretched into the clouds like a silver rainbow. Bridger insisted on buying me a soft lavender sweater that he caught me eyeing, and Travis and McKell purchased matching T-shirts with a rendition of the arch pictured on the back.

We didn't get home until after midnight, but I couldn't rest until I'd read a few more lines in Jeremiah's journal. After McKell retired to bed, I sat at the kitchen table munching on a cheese sandwich and reading from the slim volume.

In the fall of 1835 I made preparations for moving. The Saints were living all over the upper Missouri, but chiefly in Clay County. Little William came down with the sickness which hindered us from moving for another year, and in all that time our relatives used their influence to persuade us from going. When they could not turn me aside, they tried to influence my wife to stay behind, but they could not prevail. We set out with our sick child, a pair of horses and a light old wagon which broke down before we got twelve miles from home. When we arrived, the

Church was leaving Clay County and settling in Caldwell and Daviess Counties, so we followed on and stopped in Caldwell near Far West.

I bit my lip in thought, wishing I knew better the early history of the Church. Today in the car while traveling, Bridger had explained to me the beginnings of the Church and its movements from place to place. Settling originally in Kirtland, Ohio, and Jackson County, Missouri, the Church was driven from those places by mobs who robbed and persecuted the Saints. Did Jeremiah and his little family experience the persecution of this period? I wondered. I leaned my elbows on the table, and my chin in my hands, and read on.

I bought land and commenced farming in Caldwell County, four miles from Far West. I cleared land, fenced and put in eight acres of corn, built a good white oak log cabin the first season, and also dug a well some thirty-five feet deep, but got no water. The next spring I commenced making rails and fencing for another field in the prairies. I enclosed, broke and planted in corn, potatoes, pumpkins, and squash ten acres more.

On the nineteenth of April, 1838, we had another son added to our family who we named James. The health of the family was good, except little William who was still afflicted. It was in this year that our persecutions and troubles commenced in upper Missouri. The mobs plundered my corn, fodder, potatoes, chickens, and hogs, and a company of Missouri militia ran us off our property, using my fine oak house as a headquarters.

I swallowed hard, and my eyes burned as I continued reading the narrative.

I sent my family ahead to Diahman in Daviess County, and when I arrived a few weeks later I found them camped out in the snow and cold. My wife was considerably cast down in spirits, and our baby was quite sick, having been so much exposed to the cold. Hundreds of our brethren were here camped out in the cold, which was truly a melancholy sight.

I shivered, and hugged my arms to my body.

Within the next two weeks, we were told we must remove to Caldwell County for the winter, and then we must leave the state. Two or three days before the time set for us to go, our little James died on the fifteenth of November. We had sat up and watched him night after night, and he died in my arms when we were alone.

Tears trickled from my eyes, and I felt a portion of the pain and suffering Jeremiah and his wife must have endured with the death of their little son. I turned to the next page of the journal, hoping to find happier tidings.

We picked up what we could and went over to Brush Creek, and made a log shanty. My horses stood out in the cold all winter when I had a good stable at home near Far West.

I read Jeremiah's account for another half hour, his words creating vivid pictures in my mind.

While here I had an attack of typhus fever, and my wife's health was very poor indeed, being confined to her bed many times. We had added to our family a daughter, Margaret Ann, born on the twenty-second day of May, 1839, named after my wife's sister. Though we had to contend with poverty and sickness while in Missouri, the privileges I there enjoyed seemed a rich compensation. I have many times sat at the feet of Joseph and others to hear them preach, and it was a perfect feast to me. I felt thankful that I ever enjoyed the privilege of seeing and hearing the prophet of God, whose calling it was to lay the foundation of this church. I passed through the persecutions which were heaped upon the Saints while in Missouri, feeling grateful to be counted worthy to suffer for Christ's sake.

Though it was very late by this time, I couldn't stop reading. There were only four or five more pages left in the journal written in Jeremiah's hand. I almost hated to read it, immersed though I was in the story, because in a few short pages the lives of Jeremiah Bolton and his family would disappear from history. I stood up and got myself another glass of milk, postponing the inevitable.

At last I settled back in my chair and bent over the open book. The few pages did not take long to read. To my great disappointment, the journal ceased abruptly with Jeremiah's removal from Caldwell County. The end of the narrative caught me by surprise, for it seemed Jeremiah quit the history at a critical point in his life. Driven from Missouri with the rest of the Saints, he failed to record where he and his family next settled, and their fortunes afterward.

Not wanting to believe I had read the last word of his journal, I thumbed through the next few blank pages in the notebook. Ten or twelve pages beyond the close of Jeremiah's narrative, I came across a brief insert. I held the book close, eager to see what he'd written.

My dearest Abigail, who stood faithfully by my side through all the persecutions heaped upon us because of our religion, and the frailties of this existence, continued to sink in strength. Her hair, sweet as brown sugar, lost its sheen and a deathly pallor settled on her cheeks. At the last, as she lay upon her cot, too weak to speak, she closed eyes the very shade of heaven for the last time. She was a good companion to me, and an affectionate and tender mother to her children. She had the confidence and esteem of all who knew her. She was ever faithful to the gospel of Christ, unwavering in her devotion to duty. How I miss her, the wife of my youth and the desire of my heart.

The poignant description of Abigail Bolton's passing moved me to tears. What a tragedy, I thought, after all she'd suffered and sacrificed for her family and her church. I leaned back in the chair, the journal open before me on the table, and tried to picture Abigail and her husband. They seemed so real to me, so close at hand.

At last I closed the slim volume and caressed the cover with my hand. How extraordinary to catch a glimpse into the lives of these people, my own ancestors. I yearned to know what happened to Jeremiah and his children, and where I fit into his posterity. When I finally went to bed, sleep evaded me. I lay awake for a long time thinking about Jeremiah and Abigail.

* * *

On Sunday, McKell quietly dressed for her church meetings without waking me. Usually she asked if I wanted to accompany her to church, but this morning I was still sleeping when she left. I got up about ten o'clock and dragged myself into the kitchen to make some breakfast. Sister Watson and Sister Suafa'i were sitting at the table, with their open books of scripture.

"'Morning," I mumbled to them. This was one morning I would have enjoyed a cup of strong coffee to perk me up, but Latter-day Saints didn't drink coffee, and so there was none in the cupboard.

"Good morning," Sister Watson greeted me brightly. "Did you sleep well?"

I glanced at her as I pulled a pitcher of orange juice from the fridge. "Yes, I slept well. I just didn't get enough of it."

Sister Suafa'i pulled out a chair for me at the table and I sat down on it. "You girls are studying, huh?" I asked, as I poured the orange juice into my glass.

"Uh-huh. We don't have any appointments until after our church meetings, which aren't for another two hours," Sister Watson told me.

"Have you had breakfast?" I asked them.

Both of the sister missionaries nodded, then Sister Suafa'i spoke. "You didn't feel like going to church with McKell?"

I smiled to myself. Both missionaries knew I wasn't a member of the Church, but they never failed to invite me to every Church activity. "I'm afraid I was asleep when she left," I responded.

"How would you like to go with us to sacrament meeting? We meet in the same building, just at a different hour. You'd have plenty of time to get ready."

I took another drink of my juice, then set the glass back on the table. "Okay. Maybe I will," I said.

The looks on their faces were worth a million dollars. "Really? That would be terrific," Sister Watson exclaimed.

"Yes, terrific," her companion echoed.

I leaned my elbows on the table. "Before I do, though, there's a couple of things I'd like to ask you."

"Absolutely. We'll try to answer your questions," Sister Watson replied, leaning forward.

I was silent for a moment, trying to figure out how to capture the jumble of puzzle pieces floating in my head enough to phrase an intelligent question. "I have some questions about the temple your church is going to rebuild here in Nauvoo. Everyone seems so excited about it."

The sister missionaries both nodded eagerly.

"I understand a little bit about temple marriage because McKell told me about it. And I know the members perform some kind of rituals for their dead at the temple. But what's it all for? How does it fit together in the end? That's the part that confuses me."

Sister Watson didn't bat an eye. She seemed to know exactly what to say. "Let's look in the Bible for an answer to that question." She closed the Book of Mormon she'd been reading, and thumbed through the pages of her Bible. "Here it is, in Romans, chapter 8, verses 16 and 17." She turned the book around and pushed it across the table to me. "Why don't you read it," she said.

I wanted to decline because I hadn't read the Bible in a long, long time, but the smile of encouragement on her face persuaded me to give it a try. "The Spirit itself beareth witness with our spirit, that we are the children of God," I started hesitantly. "And if children, then heirs; heirs of God, and joint-heirs with Christ; if so be that we suffer with him, that we may be also glorified together."

"Good. What do you think that means?" Sister Watson asked me.

I looked from her to her companion, hoping to get some help to answer the question. Both of them sat smiling confidently at me. "Well, I don't know for sure." I silently reread the scripture. "I guess it means that we are children of God, and as such, will be heirs of God."

"That's exactly right," Sister Watson replied. "Do you know what it means to be an heir?"

I shrugged. "It means we receive all the possessions our father has after he dies."

"Correct. Only in this instance the scripture is referring to our Heavenly Father, who is immortal. The scripture tells us that we will receive all that the Father has if we are faithful to His commandments."

"I never thought about it in those terms," I said, trying to take it all in. "I guess I never gave it much thought at all, about God being our father, literally speaking."

"God is the father of our spirits," Sister Watson went on, "and as such has a plan for us, His children, to enable us to return to Him after this life and live with Him again. A very integral part of that plan, however, is the divine mission of His son, Jesus Christ."

I listened closely as Sister Watson explained how we need help to overcome sin and death, and consequently our Father in Heaven sent His Son, Jesus Christ, to show us the way and to fulfill the plan. We read from John, chapter 3, verse 16, which explained how God so loved the world that He gave His only begotten Son, that whosoever believed in Him should have everlasting life. And we turned to another scripture in John where we read that Jesus Christ is "the way, the truth, and the life;" and no man can come to the Father, except through Christ. Sister Watson talked about faith, and developing the faith to do what Christ taught and to follow His example.

Then Sister Suafa'i spoke about Joseph Smith, and how he was confused about religion and went to a grove of trees to pray and ask God which church was right. She explained how God the Father and His son, Jesus Christ, appeared to young Joseph, telling him not to join any of the churches because they were all wrong. She even had pictures to help illustrate what she was teaching me about the Prophet Joseph and the coming forth of the Book of Mormon. She talked about witnesses and the prophets who testified of Christ, and Joseph Smith's role as a witness of Christ; and how the Book of Mormon contains the writings of the prophets. Then she explained how the Book of Mormon prophets taught of Christ and testified of Him.

I listened, amazed at the understanding they had and their ability to open my mind to things of a spiritual nature. I was like a sponge, absorbing every drop of information. I asked few questions; mostly I just listened.

"You can know for yourself that Joseph Smith was and is a prophet of God," Sister Suafa'i said to me. "The Holy Ghost will witness that truth to you if you pray with a sincere heart and ask God with real intent."

"I haven't prayed since I was a child," I confessed to her. "I don't think I'd know how to offer a sincere prayer."

"Would you like one of us to offer a prayer on your behalf?" Sister Watson asked me.

"Now?"

She nodded her head. "There's no better time than the present to start communicating with our Heavenly Father."

"Alright," I replied with a tremor in my voice.

The sister missionaries folded their arms and bowed their heads, and I followed suit. Sister Watson gave the prayer, and she uttered the most incredible prayer I'd ever heard. She spoke with God as if He were standing in the room with us. She asked Heavenly Father to help me understand the things I'd been taught, to soften my heart to the word of the gospel, and to send the Holy Ghost to bear witness to me of the truth of the message I'd received that morning.

Then she paused for an instant. I opened one eye to catch a glimpse of her expression. She appeared deep in concentration. When she resumed her prayer a second later, she petitioned God to grant me all the blessings of the temple that I might receive the ordinances for myself, and accomplish the work for my kindred dead.

I felt my heart soar with her words, and joy swelled through me. She concluded her prayer by thanking God for all her blessings, and she expressed her appreciation for the gospel and the opportunity to serve a mission. When I opened my eyes at the conclusion of the prayer, I knew God's great plan of happiness made provision for me, and that knowledge was the first step on the path toward changing my life.

CHAPTER 24

McKell was already home when I got back from church with the sister missionaries. She saw me come in the door with them, and a perplexed expression crossed her face. "Where have you been?" she asked.

"You're not going to believe it," I replied.

She glanced from me to the sister missionaries with a questioning look.

"Sacrament meeting, then Sunday School, and then Relief Association," I announced with a grin.

Sister Watson nudged me in the shoulder. "Relief *Society*," she whispered, emphasizing the last word.

"Oh, yeah. Relief Society. With all the women."

McKell let out a shriek. "Are you serious? That's so awesome, Savannah." She rushed toward me and enfolded me in a big hug. "How did you like it?"

"I liked it a lot. How come you never invited me to go?" I teased her.

"Oh, you. I invited you every single week." She hugged me again, then turned to Sister Watson and Sister Suafa'i. "How in the world did you persuade her to go to church with you? I've been trying for weeks."

"It was her idea," Sister Watson answered. "She was ready."

The sister missionaries left McKell and me to talk while they went into the kitchen. I grasped McKell's hand and pulled her down to the couch to sit with me. "Kell, I hope it doesn't hurt your feelings that I went for the first time to meetings with the sister missionaries, rather than you."

McKell squeezed my hand. "Of course not. I'm just thrilled you decided to go. What made you change your mind?"

"A combination of things—getting acquainted with the sister missionaries, reading my ancestor's journal, listening to you and Bridger talk about your feelings for the gospel."

"That's terrific, Savannah. I'm so pleased to hear that."

"I sat down at the breakfast table this morning with Sister Watson and Sister Suafa'i, and decided to ask them a few questions about the Church. We spent nearly two hours talking about stuff."

"You did? What did they talk to you about?"

I leaned back into the cushion of the couch. "Lots of things. God's plan for His children. The mission of Jesus Christ. Joseph Smith's vision in the grove where he saw God the Father and Jesus Christ. It was remarkable, the things they explained to me. And they even had pictures to show me what happened to go along with what they were saying."

"Did they talk to you about the origin of the Book of Mormon, and how the Holy Ghost can testify to you of its truthfulness?"

I looked at her in surprise. "Yeah. How did you know that?"

McKell chuckled. "The sister missionaries just gave you the first discussion."

"What?" I said in surprise. "The first discussion? Like you and I talked about when you were converted to the Church?"

"One and the same," McKell grinned.

"Well, what do you know. And I thought it was absurd that someone could be converted after six conversations about the Church." I reflected on the discussion I'd had with the sisters, and the implications it held for me. "The first discussion, huh?" I repeated.

"Absolutely."

I shook my head, smiling.

"Are you going to have the sister missionaries give you the rest of the discussions?"

"I suppose I will."

McKell gave me another hug. "Congratulations, Savannah. I know you've made a wise decision."

"Hey, Kell," I said as we stood up from the couch to join Sister Watson and Sister Suafa'i in the kitchen for lunch.

"Yeah?"

"Don't mention anything to Bridger about me taking the missionary discussions, alright?"

"Okay. I won't say a thing to him about it if you don't want me to."

"Thanks. I think I want to surprise him, you know, later on."

"Good idea," McKell said, winking at me.

* * *

On Tuesday night Bridger, Travis, and I drove down Parley Street to the river where we watched McKell participate in *Sunset on the Mississippi* with the young performing missionaries. The group put on a lively show of singing and dancing, stories and jokes, and played an assortment of instruments emphasizing the music from the old Nauvoo period. McKell sang a solo, a sprightly piece with an accordion for accompaniment, and danced in several numbers. My favorite part was listening to the Nauvoo Brass Band play selections popular in the 1840s. Bridger and I locked arms and swayed to the old-fashioned melodies of "Tittery-Irie-Aye" and "Lilly Dale." Travis enjoyed himself just watching McKell. The grin never left his face whenever she was on stage. I was impressed by her talents too. She sang beautifully and had a flair for dance. The finale included audience participation in a rousing sing-a-long under a full silvery moon, its reflection shimmering on the water.

When the evening's fun concluded, the three of us crowded around McKell. "You were fantastic!" I exclaimed.

"Yeah, isn't she great?" Travis beamed.

"Congratulations. That was really good," agreed Bridger.

"Thanks," McKell laughed. "I'm glad you liked the program." Travis slipped his arm around her and gave her cheek a kiss. She flushed with pleasure. "What are you guys going to do now?" she asked Bridger and me.

"Just hang out," I replied.

Bridger took hold of my hand. "Why don't we meet you two back at the Weeks's house in a while, okay?"

Travis nodded. "Alright. See you later." He stood with McKell while she accepted congratulations from those who'd watched the show. Bridger and I slipped away from the crowd.

Bridger kept hold of my hand as we sauntered toward his car. "What would you like to do?" he asked me.

"I'm starving. I'd like a big piece of pecan pie."

He put a hand to his forehead in mock pain. "You're not going to start with the pie issue again, are you?" he moaned dramatically.

"You promised me a piece of homemade pecan pie ages ago."

"I swear I'll get it for you. Soon."

"Yeah, yeah. That's what you always say," I answered playfully.

He bent to kiss me as we walked. A shivery feeling shot through me when Bridger's lips met mine. I smiled up at him, and returned his kiss. When we were seated inside the car, I scooted close to him and tucked my hand in the crook of his arm.

"Are you hungry, really?" he asked as he started the engine.

"Yes. But only for pecan pie."

He smiled at my teasing as he pulled away from the curb and out onto the road. "There's nothing open this late at night in Nauvoo. Want to drive to Fort Madison and try to find a restaurant there?"

We drove north and crossed the river into Fort Madison ten or so miles away where we found a little hamburger stand still open. We ate hamburgers and fries in the car and shared a strawberry malt. As we started back to Nauvoo, under the full moon, Bridger reached for my hand. "I spoke with Jaden's defense attorney today," he began quietly.

I tensed. "You did? What did he say?"

"He's arranged bail for Jaden's release from jail. The trial is set for six weeks from now. McKell, you, and I will probably have to testify."

I swallowed, and flicked my tongue across dry lips. "I was hoping we wouldn't have to do that. I don't want to see Jaden. Not even for a minute. We can't just talk to the judge?"

"No. But it might be possible to forego a trial. The defense attorney is willing to talk to the prosecutors about working out a plea bargain. Right now Jaden is being charged with attempted murder, attempted kidnapping, and assault with a deadly weapon. But the prosecutors might be persuaded to seek a lesser charge to which Jaden could plead guilty and avoid trial."

I let out my breath. "What penalty does a lesser charge carry with it?"

"I don't know. That's up to the judge. The prosecutors recommend the plea bargain to the judge, who will take it under advisement. Then Jaden goes to court for an arraignment and pleads guilty to the lesser charge of assault and battery. If he's lucky, Jaden might not get any jail time at all. The judge might grant him probation."

I sat silently, recalling the horrifying events of a week ago. The memory of it was still just as fresh in my mind as if it had happened last night. And just as terrifying. "I knew he had a vile temper," I said, close to tears, "I just didn't think . . ."

Bridger pressed my hand. "Soon we'll have the whole thing behind us, and we can try to forget about it."

"I don't think I'll ever forget about it," I replied, shaking my head. "I feel like such an idiot, a dupe, for ever having anything to do with him."

"You misjudged him. That's all," Bridger replied. It was obvious that he was trying to harness his own angry emotions concerning Jaden.

We came to the bridge overlooking the river and started across. Below us the waters of the Mississippi gleamed in the moonlight. I looked out the car window at the river, running silent in the night. I wanted to put Jaden and the awful events of that night out of my mind. I couldn't bear to think about it anymore. "It's amazing, isn't it?" I said almost to myself.

"What is?"

"The river at night. Except for the moon shining on it, you'd never know it was there in the darkness. There in all of its strength and beauty, flowing for miles to the sea. A quiet giant."

Bridger leaned over and kissed me. I put my arm around his neck and cuddled against him.

He kissed me again as we came off the bridge and headed toward Nauvoo. Few cars traveled the road. Everything around us seemed wrapped in a soft veil of darkness. Quiet and serene. I felt my body relax, the tension flowing out of it like the waters of the Mississippi gently rolling out to sea.

"Savannah?"

"Umm?" I replied, laying my head on Bridger's shoulder. I smelled the scent of his cologne; sweet, yet masculine. I inhaled deeply, drawing in the intoxicating smell of him.

"What do you foresee for the two of us? Together, I mean," he said quietly.

I lifted my head and looked at him. "What do you want to see happen?"

A smile twitched at his lips. "I asked you first."

I stroked his cheek with my fingertips, feeling the little hollow that was his dimple. "I don't want the summer to end," I said, in answer to his question.

He glanced at me. "Neither do I."

"I've never met anyone like you, Bridger," I said. "I can't tell you how much I admire your strength and determination to live by the standards you've set for yourself. It's been an incredible example to me." I was tempted to tell him about my conversation with the sister missionaries, about my growing desire to embrace the principles I'd been taught in so many ways since coming to Nauvoo, but I decided to wait until my feelings on that subject were more settled.

He let go of my hand and put both of his on the wheel, staring straight ahead in silence. I couldn't read his expression in the darkness.

"What? Did I say something wrong?" I asked, sensing his withdrawal.

"No. No, not at all. That's just not what I thought you were going to say." He gave a forced laugh.

I wrapped an arm around his neck. "You didn't let me finish."

He looked at me without speaking.

"I do admire your many fine qualities, it's true," I said almost teasingly. "But in addition to that . . ." I paused, my tone turning serious. "I'm afraid I'm in love with you."

I heard his quick intake of breath. "That wouldn't be so bad, would it?"

"It presents a few problems for you," I replied.

He chuckled softly. "I'm way ahead of you. I started to fall in love with you the first day I met you."

"You did? Honestly?"

He gave me a sideways kiss, keeping his eyes on the road. "Honestly. Would I lie about a thing like that?"

"Have you ever lied about anything in your whole life, Bridger Caldwell?" I grinned.

"Never. Absolutely never."

* * *

The next evening after I arrived home from work I sat down with McKell and the sister missionaries to hear the second discussion about the gospel. Sister Watson and Sister Suafa'i explained to me about the importance of faith in Jesus Christ, repentance for sins, baptism, and the gift of the Holy Ghost. We talked about obedience to the commandments of God, and Sister Watson asked me if I would make a commitment to obey the commandments as they had explained them to me. I said I would. But I was deeply concerned about the sins I'd committed throughout my life. Many of them were grievous to the Lord, as I now had come to understand, and I felt a deep regret and sorrow for what I'd done.

I asked the sisters to continue with the next discussion right then. They had no other appointments for the evening, and so they obliged me. Sister Suafa'i took the lead in teaching me about the apostasy and the restoration of the gospel. We discussed ideas about truth and error, and revelation from God, as well as the restoration of the Aaronic and Melchizedek Priesthoods. By the end of the evening, I was nearly overwhelmed with the amount of information I'd received, but my heart was lifted. I began to feel deep within my soul that these things being related to me were the truth and I should take hold of them.

I went to bed that night suffering from a jumble of emotions— sorrow for my sins, joy in the possibility of being forgiven for them, and reverent awe for the love Heavenly Father had for His children. I understood more fully now about the role of the priesthood, and priesthood blessings, and gained a greater appreciation for Bridger's opportunity in having such a gift. I pondered long over the subject of the Holy Ghost as Sister Watson had explained it to me. I remembered an earlier conversation with Bridger on that same topic, and Bridger had promised me that the Holy Spirit would testify of the truthfulness of the gospel. I wanted that testimony to flood my heart. I wanted to know without a doubt that this was Christ's true church.

My mind was racing, and I found it impossible to sleep. After a time I quietly got up from bed, reached over for my copy of the Book of Mormon, and slipped out of the bedroom so as not to wake McKell. I flipped on a lamp beside the couch, and curled up there with my book. Soon I was completely immersed in the story of Nephi and his brothers in the promised land.

The following day at work I could hardly wait to get home to hear the next discussion. I was disappointed, however, to find the sister missionaries gone when I arrived.

"Did Sister Watson say when she'd be back?" I asked McKell who was fixing supper for us.

"About nine. They had an appointment set up to teach tonight."

"Oh," I said, trying not to let my disappointment show.

"But I have a great idea for something we can do while we're waiting for them to return," McKell said.

"What is it?"

"Let's pay a visit to the Land and Records Office."

"To check on our family names?"

McKell nodded.

"That is a good idea. You can research the names for your mom, and now I know a few of my ancestors' names, too." My thoughts turned to the journal Jeremiah Bolton had kept. I wished I had more information on him and his family.

McKell put the casserole she'd prepared into the oven to bake, and we left, hurrying to reach the Land and Records Office before it closed for the day. We drove Rex to the corner of Parley and Partridge Streets where a single-story, red brick building housed the office. McKell showed the woman at the counter the names we wanted, and then we waited. The room was taken up with shelves of books. McKell and I browsed through a few of them to fill the time. After about ten minutes, the woman returned with a single manila file folder in hand. She motioned to us.

"I found reference to only one of the names you girls wanted researched." She opened the file to glance at the name. "Jeremiah Bolton."

CHAPTER 25

With trembling hands.I took the folder from the woman. McKell and I sat down at a table, and I held my breath as I opened the slim file folder.

"Savannah, this is so exciting," McKell whispered.

I exchanged a glance with her, hardly daring to draw a breath as I lifted the top sheet of paper to look at it.

"What is it?" McKell asked, leaning closer to inspect the paper in my hands.

"Some sort of drawing or map," I answered, turning the page sideways to see a different angle of it.

"It's a plat map, Savannah. Look, it has a red X here, on this plot or lot of ground."

I zeroed in to where McKell pointed with her finger on the map. Sure enough, a small X, drawn in red ink, identified a specific place on the plat map. "What does it stand for?" I murmured.

McKell picked up the next sheet of paper lying in the folder. "Look at this," she said excitedly. "Property tax records for the years 1841 through 1843 with Jeremiah Bolton's name underlined for you."

I set the map down and took the second page from McKell's hand. "This means he owned property here in Nauvoo," I said breathlessly. "If you paid taxes, wouldn't you have to own property?"

McKell nodded. "I'm sure of it. Wow, Savannah. Look, he owned seven acres." Her finger followed across the page opposite Jeremiah Bolton's name to the amount of taxes he paid each year, and the size of his lot.

"He must have owned a farm, like he did near Far West," I said in amazement. McKell's and my eyes met in wonder. "I have an ancestor who actually lived in Nauvoo."

McKell squeezed my arm. "Can you believe it?" she squeaked.

I set the tax record aside and picked up the last sheet of paper in the file. I read aloud the few lines handwritten on the page. "Nauvoo Burial Record. Buried, on the twenty-sixth of February, in the year of our Lord eighteen hundred and forty-five, Abigail Lucretia Bolton, wife of Jeremiah Bolton."

It felt as if a lightning bolt had passed through me. My insides quivered, my hands trembled and my mouth went dry. The date recorded on the page provided the missing data in Jeremiah's diary. His wife had died, and after that Jeremiah must have lost all motivation for continuing the journal. How long after Abigail's death did he survive? I wondered. Did he keep his farm in Nauvoo? Did he go west with the Saints, and if so, where did he settle? The questions swirled in my head.

"Gosh, she's probably buried in the old cemetery," McKell said. "Maybe you can find her grave."

"Where is the cemetery?" I asked hastily.

"On the outskirts of town. About two miles east, up on the bluffs."

"Does it have grave markers?"

"A few. But they're badly worn and faded. When I was there to see the cemetery, I could make out only a few names on the markers."

I bit my lip, a sense of anticipation building inside me. "Will the cemetery have records of where persons are buried?"

"I don't know. You may be looking at the only record of Abigail's burial," she replied, tapping the page with her forefinger.

"But we can try to find it, right?"

She nodded. "But look at this, Savannah," she said, picking up the first page we'd examined. "The land your ancestor owned is marked clearly on the map. It looks like it's southeast of the city. We ought to be able to find that easily enough."

I stared at the red X on the plat map. The feelings in my heart were nearly overwhelming.

A few minutes later we closed the file folder and after getting the clerk's assurance that the copies were mine to keep, we left the Land and Records Office. McKell drove us to the area, as near as we could determine, which was marked on the map. It was unclear where the exact plot of land began or ended. Farmland and fertile fields occupied the general area. I was disappointed that the plot was not more easily defined, but McKell suggested we visit the County Recorder's Office the following day to see a modern map of the spot.

We returned home to eat our supper, but I was so excited I could hardly swallow a bite. After the meal, I brought out Jeremiah's journal and McKell and I pored through some of it together before McKell had to leave for her performance at the river. When the sister missionaries came home, I told them about my discoveries. I spent the rest of the evening in conversation with Sister Watson and Sister Suafa'i as they instructed me further in the gospel. They explained to me about our premortal existence where we lived as spirits with God the Father, the purpose of our mortal life on earth, and insights concerning life after death that I'd never heard before. I was eager to learn about the spirit world, the resurrection and judgment, and the degrees of glory to which we might attain. The topic, which was part of the fourth discussion, flowed into a discourse on saving ordinances for the dead.

"Millions of people have died without a knowledge of the gospel of Jesus Christ, or without receiving the necessary ordinances of the gospel," Sister Suafa'i was saying. She posed a question to me. "If obedience to God's commandments is essential for exaltation, then how can these people be judged and condemned when they did not possess a knowledge?"

I chewed on my lip in thought. "It doesn't seem fair, does it? Surely God will provide some way for them to enter His kingdom."

"That's exactly right. For those who didn't have an opportunity to receive the gospel while on earth, it will be taught to them in the spirit world."

"Wow. Missionaries in the spirit world as well as here, huh?"

"Yes. But the way is straight and narrow, and the entrance is baptism into Christ's Church."

"Then I suppose the dead must be baptized. But how is that possible after they've already left this world? Can they be baptized in the spirit world?"

Sister Watson took up the discussion. "No. Baptism is an earthly ordinance that needs to be done while in the flesh. But God has made provision for those who did not have the opportunity while on earth. Baptisms can be performed for the dead by proxy, in the holy temples."

Sister Suafa'i turned in her scriptures to 1 Corinthians, chapter 15, verse 29, and read the passage aloud. "Else what shall they do which are baptized for the dead, if the dead rise not at all? why are they then baptized for the dead?"

"I guess I've never read that particular verse before," I remarked, astonished by the new information I was learning.

"Work for the dead is an important service that members of the Church can perform. Sacred ordinances and covenants necessary for our salvation are made in the holy temple. We have an opportunity to go to the temple on behalf of the dead where we can perform by proxy the ordinances necessary for their exaltation."

I felt as if I were teetering on the brink of a marvelous discovery, balancing between knowledge and ignorance, and I knew the doctrines being taught had something vital to do with my ancestors and temple work for the dead. I couldn't assemble the information into a clear pattern yet, but many of the puzzle pieces were coming into focus and taking shape to create a unified, whole picture. Once that picture was complete, it was going to be beautiful.

* * *

"He's gone."

"What?" I exclaimed, turning to face Bridger who was seated behind the wheel of the car. "What do you mean, gone?"

"Gone. Fled. Disappeared. When I got to the office this morning, the door was unlocked, and James was nowhere in sight. All the files, statements, and records have been removed from the office."

"You're kidding," I said in disbelief.

Bridger shook his head. "James has apparently taken all the files and fled with them."

"Why would he do that?"

"I know exactly why. Yesterday afternoon I confronted him with all the evidence I'd gathered. There's no doubt that he's been embezzling funds from his company. I have copies of the bank statements and copies of the figures James entered in the computer accounts.

There's a big discrepancy between the billing statements and the actual goods or services received."

"Oh my gosh. What did he say when you showed him the evidence?"

"He denied any wrongdoing. Told me he'd see that I got thrown out of school for making such a wild accusation, and that I'd never get another job in the field."

I put a nervous hand on Bridger's arm. "Can he do that?"

Bridger only laughed. "Not now."

"Are you going to call the company and report everything?"

"I already have. I talked to the project manager. He asked me to send copies of all the documents I have."

A chill crept over my skin as a sudden thought struck me. "Bridger, what if James tries to pin the whole scheme on you. Intends to set you up. Frame you."

Bridger slowed to make a turn on the road. "That's possible, I suppose. But I don't think it's very likely. I think James has dropped out of sight. And the company knows I'll cooperate with the investigation a hundred percent."

I let out a whistling breath. "I never would have expected James to do a thing like that."

"Me either. I'm pretty stunned by it all."

Neither of us said anything more for a moment as Bridger drove the curving road east of town. It was nearly noon on a hot, cloudless day in late June, and I had arranged with Bridger to take the lunch hour to show him the plot of ground my ancestor, Jeremiah Bolton, had once owned and farmed. My camera hung around my neck, and I was eager to walk the field with Bridger and take some pictures of it. But this news about James unsettled me.

"How's everything going at your job?" Bridger asked, taking my hand.

I sensed that the actuality of James's flight upset Bridger more than he was willing to let on, so I didn't return to the subject of his former boss. "Mr. Crandall is letting me choose the paintings we'll be taking on contract, subject to his final approval, of course. I'm really excited about it. I've seen some terrific pieces of artwork so far."

"He must have total confidence in your abilities," Bridger said, giving me a smile.

"Crandall comes across as gruff and stubborn, but in truth he's a shrewd and hard-nosed businessman. If anyone can, he should be able to make the gallery a success." We were coming up on the plot of ground now. I pointed out the car window. "There it is, Bridger. About halfway up that field. That's where the property starts."

"Okay," he replied, slowing the car. "Where should I park?"

"A few feet up ahead, just on the side of the road." I bit my thumbnail in anticipation as the car rolled to a stop and Bridger parked.

"Is this the spot?" he asked.

"Yes. All this ground on both sides of the street once belonged to Jeremiah and Abigail. The clerk at the County Recorder's Office marked the boundaries for me."

We climbed out of the car and walked to the edge of the road where a field of ripening wheat glistened in the afternoon sun. The wheat was knee high, golden in the sunlight. Bridger took my hand and we entered the field. I relished the feel of the wheat brushing against my legs as we walked.

"You're strolling the very spot of ground where your ancestors walked," Bridger said to me. "How does that make you feel?"

"Incredible. It's totally incredible." I was grinning hard enough to stretch my face all out of shape, savoring this amazing moment. "Look how beautiful it is here, Bridger. I could stay right here forever."

"Let me get your picture." Bridger reached for my camera. I took the strap from my neck and handed the camera to him. He stepped back a few paces, jockeyed for a good angle to take the shot, and placed his finger on the button. "Ready?" he asked.

"Wait a second." I spread my hands over the heads of wheat, and assumed a reflective pose, gazing off into the distance. "Now I'm ready," I told him.

Bridger snapped several pictures of me in the field standing in different poses. The last one made him laugh when I plucked a blade of wheat and put it between my teeth like a Spanish dancer with her rose.

"Now you're getting punchy," he grinned, handing me the camera. We walked together hand in hand for a ways, enjoying the solitude of the isolated field and the pleasure of being together.

"Do you know what I'd like, Bridger?" I said to him wistfully.

"No. What?"

"I'd like to build an old Nauvoo-style, red brick house right in the middle of this field, and live the rest of my days in it."

"The current owner probably wouldn't be real thrilled with that idea," he joked.

"Then I'll just have to buy the field from him."

"A perfect solution," Bridger responded, planting a kiss on my lips. "And I'll draw the plans for the house. According to your strict specifications, of course."

I laughed. "Can't you just picture Jeremiah and his family living here? Working their farm, rearing their children, experiencing life's joys and sorrows." I looked out over the scene. "Do you think they lived in a log house or a red-brick one like the restored homes on the flats?"

"I think they were prosperous farmers and built a handsome two-story brick home, out of the same Nauvoo red clay as the brick you have."

My thoughts went back to the brick making exhibit Bridger had taken me to see on my first full day in Nauvoo and the small red brick I'd been given as a souvenir. That day seemed like ages ago, though it was less than two short months. I wondered why it felt like such a long span of time and decided it was because of how much I had personally changed since coming to Nauvoo. I was not the same person now as when I had arrived here. It seemed an ideal time for me to tell Bridger that I was taking the missionary discussions and entertaining serious thoughts about joining the Church. The setting was perfect—private and peaceful. But still I hesitated.

"Want any more pictures?" Bridger asked me.

"No. I think that's enough." I consulted my watch. "I should be getting back to work. What are you going to do for a job now?" I asked half jokingly.

We started back through the field of wheat toward Bridger's car. "I'm right in the middle of work on my project at the stable site. I'd like to finish it and that's going to take a few weeks to do. I'll be talking to someone else at the company headquarters in Omaha later this afternoon. So for a while, I'll still be hanging out at the office."

We reached the car, and I slipped into the seat. "And after that? Will you be going back to Salt Lake City before the summer is over?"

He grinned at me as if I'd made some sort of humorous remark, then he leaned over and kissed me. "Not a chance, Savannah. Not a chance."

* * *

On the second Saturday in July, Travis, McKell, Bridger, and I spent the afternoon in Carthage, Illinois, touring the jail where Joseph Smith and his brother Hyrum were killed in 1844. The place held a somber feeling. Standing in the room where the Prophet and his brother were shot affected us all deeply. On the grounds outside rested a bronze statue of Joseph and Hyrum. I stood staring at it for a long time, thinking about the Prophet and all he'd sacrificed to bring about the restoration of the gospel.

All of us were in a reflective and melancholy mood as we drove the few miles back to Nauvoo. The guys didn't come into the house when we arrived because the sister missionaries were there, a mission rule we all kept if McKell and I wanted to continue living in the Weeks's home. The guys kissed us good night on the porch steps and then drove away.

McKell opened the door softly so as not to wake the sister missionaries. We tiptoed into the bedroom we shared and quietly changed our clothes and got into bed. In the darkness I heard McKell let out a soft sigh.

"You okay?" I whispered to her.

"Yeah. I'm fine. I was just thinking about Travis."

I chuckled softly.

She raised up on one elbow in her bed. I could see her inky outline in the moonlight splashing through the window. "What do you think of Travis?" she asked me.

"I like him a lot. Why?" I answered quietly, so as not to disturb Sister Watson or Sister Suafa'i who were sleeping across the hall.

McKell remained perched on her elbow. "I think I'm in love with him, Savannah."

"What?" I practically shouted. "You're kidding, right?"

McKell put a finger to her lips. "Shh. You'll wake the missionaries."

"You're joking with me, aren't you?" I whispered. "You two have only been dating a few weeks."

"A month, to be exact."

"You're serious, aren't you?" I asked incredulously. "You're really serious about this?"

"Yes. I am."

She lay back down on the bed. I peered at her through the darkness, wishing I could see her expression. "Well, he ought to be happy to hear that. Bridger says he's crazy about you."

"I haven't told him yet how I feel, though he's hinted at his feelings for me."

"Hinted?" I snorted. "It's obvious the boy is turned inside out over you."

I heard McKell giggle in the blackness of the room.

"So are you going to tell him how you feel?"

"I guess I will."

"When? When are you going to tell him?"

"Soon."

We lapsed into silence after that, each of us following our own thoughts. McKell and Travis. Yes, I should have seen it coming. They made a perfect couple. My meditations turned to Bridger. In my mind's eye I assembled his face—his bright and inquisitive eyes the color of blue smoke, a mouth quick to smile, and the dimple marking one cheek. I turned onto my side toward the window, letting the rich golden moonlight bathe my face. I drifted off to sleep with thoughts of Bridger lingering sweetly on my mind.

CHAPTER 26

The summer was half over before we received word on the resolution of Jaden's case. The plea bargain for a lesser charge was successfully worked out and when Jaden appeared in court for sentencing on the appointed day, Bridger was in attendance. He told me afterward that the judge sentenced Jaden to five years' probation. Jaden, who had been required to remain in Illinois until the outcome of the case, was free to return home, though the requirements of his probation were strict. I suspected that Jaden would go back to school in spite of the fact that he was not much of a scholar. I hoped our paths would never cross again.

In the meanwhile, McKell won the role of Emma Smith in the summer performance of *The City of Joseph*, held on the lawn east of the Visitors' Center. The play was to run seven nights, including the last weekend in July and the first week in August. Bridger and I went to see it on opening night, and a second time during the following week. Travis was in attendance at the performance all seven nights. We teased him about his devotion to watching McKell on stage, and his only reply was a sheepish grin.

While McKell was away performing in the play, I spent most of my evenings receiving the remainder of the missionary lessons from Sister Watson and Sister Suafa'i. The last half of the fourth discussion addressed chastity and the Word of Wisdom, both of which I listened to with a burning conscience. The fifth discussion detailed the requirements for living a Christlike life. On the closing night of the performance of the play, Sister Watson taught me the last discussion.

"The mission of the Church is threefold, Savannah," she said to me as we sat on the couch together in the living room of the Weeks's home. "The first is perfecting the Saints. What do you think that means?"

I scratched my chin. "I suppose it has to do with keeping the commandments."

"That's right," Sister Watson said. "And receiving gospel ordinances. We gain fellowship and strength from one another, and grow when we serve others."

The three of us talked about the subjects of exaltation and immortality until I had a clear understanding of the requirements and blessings associated with each.

"The second point is proclaiming the gospel. That means we share the gospel with others, like McKell and her friends from BYU did with you. After we have an understanding of gospel principles ourselves, we should invite our friends and others to learn more about the Church. One doesn't have to be a missionary called and set apart like Sister Suafa'i and I have been, in order to share the gospel with others."

I thought about what she was saying, and felt a strong sense of gratitude for McKell and the others for having the courage to share their beliefs with me.

"The third important mission of the Church we should be anxiously engaged in is redeeming the dead. We do this by seeking out our kindred dead and then performing temple ordinances for our ancestors who didn't have the opportunity to do the work for themselves."

As Sister Watson went on to explain about our role in redeeming our dead ancestors, I felt a flame ignite in my soul. The flame grew brighter and brighter until it seemed to fill my whole body with warmth and light. I felt such an outpouring of the Spirit testifying to me of the correctness of this principle that tears flooded my eyes.

As I struggled to control my emotions, Sister Watson invited me to set foot on the straight and narrow path that leads to exaltation by accepting baptism in The Church of Jesus Christ of Latter-day Saints. I was too overcome to speak. All I could do was nod my head in acceptance.

* * *

The following day was Sunday, and I went to church meetings with McKell. I was so filled with emotion that it was hard to hold back the tears during the entire three-hour block of meetings. McKell sensed something dramatic was happening to me; but she kept her peace, not wanting to intrude on my private thoughts. I had slept little the night before, pondering all that the missionaries had taught me. Little by little the pieces of the gospel began to fit together into a comprehensive whole, and as I lay in my bed I had for the first time a clear picture of what I wanted to achieve, both here in this life and throughout eternity. I had slipped from the covers onto my knees to utter my first sincere prayer. At the beginning, it had been difficult framing the words in my mind into utterance. But as I persisted in trying to express my feelings and my gratitude to my Father in Heaven, it became easier to pour out my heart to Him.

I spent the rest of the day after church alone in my room, reading the pages of my Book of Mormon. The more I read, the greater the testimony I gained of the book's authenticity and truthfulness. I believed with my whole heart and soul that Joseph Smith had translated the book from ancient plates, just as he'd said. I knew that the purpose of the book was to testify of the Savior, and the most powerful thing I gained from reading it was the assurance and testimony that Jesus is the Christ, my Savior and Redeemer.

* * *

I sat close to Bridger in the front seat of the car. He had one hand clasped in mine and the other on the wheel. We were driving home after spending an evening with Travis, McKell, and Travis's family, at their home on the bluffs in Nauvoo. Mr. and Mrs. Perry had moved their family to Nauvoo from West Virginia shortly after President Hinckley's announcement in April conference concerning the rebuilding of the Nauvoo Temple. Travis's father was a structural engineer, and he'd volunteered his expertise to work on the temple alongside other engineers, carpenters, sculptors, and architects, without pay. Travis had still been on his mission in Peru when his family moved to Nauvoo, and he was excited when he returned shortly thereafter to get the opportunity to spend a few months in the City of Joseph.

"It was so cool to talk to Travis's dad about the plans for reconstructing the temple," Bridger said enthusiastically. "Especially the architectural end of it."

"I know. You had a running conversation with him throughout dinner," I ribbed Bridger.

"I didn't commandeer the conversation at the table, did I?" he asked, looking regretful.

"No, of course not. I was only teasing you." Travis's mom had invited us to dinner and Monday night family home evening. The home evening discussion had centered around the temple, and Mr. Perry had explained about the research taking place in order to restore the temple as it was originally. It had been a fascinating topic, especially for Bridger.

"Wasn't it amazing to hear how the Temple Construction Department has prepared preliminary drawings showing how the edifice can be rebuilt to function like a modern-day temple? I'd sure like to see those drawings," Bridger said.

"I bet you would."

"I'd also like to be a member of the committee doing the historical research on the structure."

"Didn't Mr. Perry say they had access to a list of construction materials kept by the original builders? It's extraordinary that something like that could have survived all these years."

"Yeah, it is," Bridger said. "As well as journal accounts written by the builders themselves. Who would have thought that stuff would ever be available?"

"Quite incredible," I agreed. I leaned my head on Bridger's shoulder. His thoughts were so fixed on the evening's conversation that I doubted he even noticed my small gesture of affection.

"The committee will probably study past photographs of the temple, look at diaries, old letters, newspaper accounts, and any other original sources to get all the information they can about how the temple looked, and what materials were used to construct it. The archaeological excavation will tell them a lot."

I was surprised to learn from Mr. Perry that there were few existing photographs of the old temple, and no known photograph of one whole side of the building's exterior, or the interior of the temple.

Mr. Perry also told us how the original architectural drawings done by William Weeks had survived and fallen into Church hands. He related the story of how two Mormon missionaries in 1948 knocked on the door of a man who turned out to be the grandson of William Weeks. The man, who had possession of the drawings, showed them to the missionaries and later offered them to the Church, where they were kept in Church archives until the present time. "The whole thing is remarkable," I said to Bridger.

Bridger thumped the steering wheel with the heel of his hand. "I'd give a million bucks to be a part of that architectural team. They'll have to sketch out plans to incorporate fixtures and designs into the building that weren't there originally, and make it look true to the period. Probably one of their biggest challenges will be the lighting. The building would have had scant lighting back then, but it'll have to be up to standard today. Electrical circuitry, heating and cooling systems, and plumbing and duct work, too, will have to be incorporated where there was once none. It's going to be some project."

"I think it's awesome how Mr. Perry is donating his time and labor to the project."

"Absolutely," Bridger agreed. "The reconstruction of the temple is so emotionally tied to the history of the early Church that many members want to be a part of it."

I understood what he was saying. The almost mystical pull of the temple was the thing that had initially interested me about the Church.

"Savannah, I know I made a promise not to discuss the Church with you," Bridger began, his voice like dry husks rustling in the breeze. "But if you could only understand the majesty of the gospel, and the importance of it in . . ."

I put my fingers to Bridger's lips. "Shh, shh," I said softly. "I can't talk to you about this. Not now." My faith was so new and so fragile that I couldn't share it yet with Bridger. He didn't know I'd been receiving the missionary lessons, though I felt guilty about withholding that information from him. I could see the pain cloud his eyes. He so wanted me to gain a testimony of the gospel for myself. I could feel his heart reaching out to mine, yearning to share the gospel's good news with me.

He put his arm around my shoulder and drew me close. "I love you, Savannah. I want you with me, always," he said. "Nothing is right in my life without you."

We completed the rest of the drive home in tender silence. When we reached the Weeks's home, Bridger turned off the ignition.

"You can't come inside, Bridger, because it's late and the sister missionaries will be home," I said regretfully.

"I know." We cuddled together, hand in hand. I wished I didn't have to go inside and leave him. I hated being apart from him. "Got any plans for this Saturday afternoon?" he whispered in my ear.

"Yeah. I have a date with an artist I met at the gallery," I kidded him.

"Then you'll have to cancel it. I'm going to take you on a picnic."

I turned my head to look up at him in the darkness of the car. "A picnic? That sounds inviting. Where are we having it?"

"It's a surprise. So cancel your date with the artist and I'll pick you up at noon on Saturday."

"I'm going to see you again before then, aren't I?"

"What do you think?" He brushed aside a strand of hair from my cheek, and put a kiss there in its place.

* * *

On Saturday, Bridger came for me in his shiny red Paseo at twelve o'clock sharp. He looked incredibly handsome in his khakis and midnight blue dress shirt. He'd let his dark hair grow longer during the summer, and his skin was bronzed from working outside in the sun. Tall and muscular, he could have been mistaken for Adonis himself. As he ushered me into the car, he still wouldn't say where we were going for the picnic. He headed east, away from the flats and the river, toward the town on the bluffs.

I twisted around to steal a look at the brown paper sack resting on the back seat of the car. "What do you have in there to eat?" I asked him.

"You'll have to wait and see."

"Come on. Give me a little hint."

"Nope. No way."

"What's in the box sitting beside the lunch sack?" I asked, snuggling up against him.

"You ask way too many questions. Do you know that?"

I leaned over to kiss him. "I remember saying that same thing to you when we first met."

His brows rose in response.

"No more questions. Instead, I think I have some answers," I said.

"Answers to what?" Bridger asked.

I put my hand in my lap and drew a shaky breath. "I believe I know the identity of the woman whose image keeps coming to my mind. I think she's my ancestor. Abigail Bolton."

Bridger looked at me, startled. "What makes you think that?"

I began by telling him what I could remember of my dream after my accident. I could only recall certain fragments, but it was then that I had first seen Abigail Bolton, although I hadn't known who she was. Later, as I became acquainted with Nauvoo, I began to feel her presence here," I explained. "I sensed her close by first in the wooded lot, as if she wanted to let me know that she had once lived in Nauvoo. The second time was beside the river when I thought I saw a woman standing on the river-bank. Perhaps she was trying to tell me that she hadn't left with the rest of the Saints at the exodus in 1846. The third time occurred at the temple site, where I felt her near, as though she wanted me to under-stand the importance of the temple and its sacred purposes."

Bridger stared at me a moment before his eyes returned to the road.

"And that's not all," I said. "In his journal, Jeremiah Bolton mentioned that his wife had hair the shade of brown sugar, and eyes the color of heaven. That description exactly fits the woman I saw—light brown hair and eyes a sky blue."

Bridger remained silent, listening to my explanations. "I believe it was Abigail's voice I heard telling me to lift the handle on the floor of the trunk when I was locked inside Jaden's rental car. Getting into the spare tire compartment and then using the tire iron to batter my way out of the trunk was something I'd never have thought of on my own, especially at that moment when I was practically out of my mind with fear."

I'd come to a conclusion about who the woman was, and the reasons for where I'd sensed her presence, but I hadn't yet figured out why she was trying to get my attention.

Bridger covered my hand with his, and I continued. "I can't explain the reasons for it, but I know that something extraordinary

happened to me after I was knocked unconscious from my bike accident. I have a memory of it, though fuzzy and indistinct. Some kind
of exchange took place between Abigail and me, but I can't remember
much about it. I only have this vague feeling that she and I are not
strangers." I stared into Bridger's face. "Does all of this sound
completely crazy?"

His face had lost some of its color, and when he spoke his voice
was subdued. "No, I don't think it's crazy at all. I think something
very special has been happening to you."

I folded my arms and nestled deeper into the seat. "Yes, I think
so, too."

I felt Bridger's gaze on my face. I wished I could have explained
more fully to him about my feelings concerning Abigail, but I
couldn't frame the feelings into words enough to even satisfy myself. I
trusted Bridger enough to reveal the innermost stirrings of my heart.
That's why I'd decided to tell him this afternoon, after our picnic,
about my conversion to the gospel of Jesus Christ and my desire to be
baptized into the Church.

It was then I noticed Bridger slowing as we came upon a large field
full of ripening wheat. "Bridger, this is Jeremiah and Abigail's farmland," I exclaimed as he pulled to a stop along the side of the road.

"I know. I figured this would be an ideal place for us to have a picnic."

I straightened in my seat. "You're kidding. We can't just go spread
out a blanket in someone's wheat field and sit down to eat," I sputtered.

Bridger stepped out of the car and reached for the brown paper
sack and box on the back seat. "That's why I had a visit with Mr.
Thornton."

I climbed out of the car, too, and joined Bridger at the side of the
road. A couple of cars passed by, one of the drivers staring curiously at
us. "Who in the world is Mr. Thornton?" I asked as Bridger pulled a
fluffy blanket from the trunk and thrust it into my arms to carry.

"The owner of this wheat field. I explained to him that I wanted to
take my girlfriend on a picnic in his field, and he gave me permission."

I stared incredulously at Bridger's beaming face.

"Come on. I'm starving."

CHAPTER 27

I trudged alongside Bridger with the blanket tucked under my arm through a field of growing wheat. The August sun cast a brilliant golden glow across the field. Once I got used to the idea that we were having a picnic in the middle of some stranger's wheat field, I felt excited. What a sweet and clever idea of Bridger's to treat me to a picnic on the very ground that had once belonged to my ancestors.

We walked for several yards into the field of ripening wheat, enjoying the feel of the sun on our backs. Finally, Bridger stopped in a small clearing in what seemed the very heart of the field. "This is a good spot. Let's spread out the blanket here," he suggested.

I grinned with pleasure, aware that he had scouted out the spot previously. I obediently set out the fuzzy blanket Bridger had brought and sat down on it.

"Hungry?" he asked as he started pulling items from the sack. He handed me a sandwich.

I peered at the contents of the sandwich. "Did you make this?" I asked, pleased with his choice of lunch meats and dressings.

"With my own two hands." He took from the sack another sandwich for himself, and then a bag of potato chips and two bottles of soda.

"I'm impressed," I said, laughing.

He flashed me a wide smile, revealing the dimple in his cheek. "You should be. I even remembered to bring napkins." He withdrew from the sack two white paper napkins, smoothly rolled and held in place with silver napkin rings.

"Pretty fancy," I conceded. I took the napkin from his hand and removed the napkin ring. It was made of shiny metal, rubbed to a lustrous glow. I shook out the napkin and jokingly tucked it into the neck of my T-shirt, letting it drape down the front of me.

We ate our sandwiches and chips in the natural beauty of the field of tall, waving wheat amid laughter and cozy conversation. He questioned me more about my thoughts concerning Abigail and the vision I'd had of her while unconscious, and I told him everything I could about the encounter, which wasn't much, as the whole memory was only a fleeting, fractured picture in my mind.

After we'd eaten our sandwiches, Bridger cleared away our litter, stuffing it in the brown sack. "Now for dessert," he announced mischievously, a gleam in his eyes. He reached for the square, plain cardboard box. "Close your eyes."

"What?" I laughed.

"Do it. Close your eyes. I want you to be surprised by this."

I shook my head in amusement, but closed my eyes as he directed. A moment later he told me to open them. "Oh my gosh!" I squealed.

Sitting on the blanket before me was a lovely little bouquet of wildflowers tied with a green ribbon, and a luscious pecan pie. The fluted edges of crust were perfectly formed, and the pecan halves shimmered in the dark golden brown custard.

"Where did you get this gorgeous pie?" I asked.

"I made it," Bridger said, puffing out his chest.

"You did? You sweet thing." I leaned over and kissed him soundly.

"I promised you a pecan pie, and I always keep my promises," he added, kissing me back.

"Bridger, I love the flowers," I told him, picking up the bouquet to smell the delicate fragrance. "And this is the most delicious looking pie I've ever set eyes on. You made this all by yourself?"

"Truthfully? Mrs. Perry, Travis's mom, gave me a smidgen of help."

I laughed. "You are incredible. Do you realize that?"

"Sure."

I sat smelling the flowers while Bridger cut two slices of pie for us. "Let me give you a clean napkin before you eat that," he said.

"The napkin I have is fine," I replied. "I've barely used it." I set the flowers on the blanket. When I looked up, I was surprised to see a tense line creasing his brow.

"No. I brought more."

In his voice I heard a tremor, and as he reached into the lunch sack I thought I saw his hands tremble. I cast him a quizzical look.

He took from the sack another white napkin, rolled and tucked like the first inside a napkin ring, only this napkin was made of soft white linen. "Thanks," I said, taking the napkin from his hand and wondering why he was suddenly acting so nervous.

"You're welcome." His gray eyes seemed full of warmth and light.

"Now can I eat my pie?" I quipped. As I started to remove the napkin holder, my eye was drawn to its shiny, glimmering surface. I raised the circular holder for a closer look. To my astonishment, I realized the circlet was not a shiny silver napkin holder at all, but a diamond-studded ring, sparkling and glittering with light.

My breath clotted in my throat. "What is this?" I wheezed, staring at the ring encircling the linen napkin. The wide silver band held a single large diamond, with two smaller diamonds planted on either side of it.

Bridger gently took the napkin and ring from my hand. He removed the ring and holding it between his thumb and forefinger, scooted onto one knee. "I promise to fill the rest of your life with sunshine and flowers. And all the pecan pie you can eat," Bridger said, his eyes gleaming as brightly as the ring he held in his hand. "I love you, Savannah. I want you with me always. I'm asking you to marry me."

The shimmering stones mounted on the band wavered as my eyes filled with tears. "Oh, Bridger," I whispered. "Nothing would make me happier. But I can't. Not yet." I stared at him imploringly with tears gliding down my cheeks.

He didn't seem surprised by my refusal. It was almost as if he expected it. Leaning toward me, he embraced and kissed me, reaching up a tender hand to smooth my brow.

"My life is turned upside down right now, Bridger," I said, trying to hold back a sob. "Will you be patient with me for just a little while longer?"

"I love you. I'd wait until the end of time for you if you asked me to," he answered softly in my ear.

I slipped from his embrace. "This is the most exquisite, the most glorious ring I have ever seen," I said in a shaking voice.

Bridger sat back on his heels and pressed the ring into my hand. "It's yours. Whenever you'll accept it," he said simply.

I stared at the beauty of the stones, the attractiveness of the setting. I turned the ring this way and that to catch the rays of sunlight and watch how the stones sparkled and danced.

He wrapped his hand around mine and together we admired the glittering ring. "The band is platinum. I thought you might like it better than gold."

"Yes. Yes, I do. It's incredibly beautiful, Bridger. I love it." My eyes filled again with tears. "You keep it for me. For a little while." I placed the ring in his hand.

"Don't you at least want to try it on?" I heard the hurt in his voice.

I shook my head. "Not until I'm ready to leave it on my finger permanently."

Bridger looked at me, unable for an instant to disguise his disappointment. I felt like crying all the more, seeing the expression on his face.

We ate our pieces of pecan pie with subdued spirits, and then Bridger gathered up the blanket and we left the field. We rode home mostly in silence, with Bridger's arm wrapped tightly around my shoulder.

* * *

Bridger left Nauvoo the next week for Omaha to speak with the board of the architectural firm where James had been employed. They wanted to talk directly to him about James's activities and explore the possibility of recovering the embezzled funds. Neither Bridger nor the company officials had heard from James since he'd disappeared.

I missed Bridger terribly. It was late August, hot and muggy, and I felt miserably alone. McKell was spending most of her free time with Travis, and Sister Watson and Sister Suafa'i were continually busy with their missionary labors. I spent my evenings after work reading in the Book of Mormon and studying pamphlets about the Church which the sister missionaries had given me. Though I believed in the doctrines and principles of the Church, and wanted to embrace the gospel, I felt uncertain whether I could actually abide by the strict standards expected of Church members. I wished I'd told Bridger about my desires and concerns regarding membership in the Church, but I'd been so taken back by his unexpected proposal of marriage on the day of the picnic that every other thought had fled my mind.

I wanted to marry Bridger. But I knew I was unable, and unworthy, to marry him in the temple at the present time. And I knew full well how important a temple marriage was to him. How he must have wrestled with the decision to ask me, knowing I might never join his faith. I suspected that he'd spent a great deal of time on his knees in prayer before deciding to ask for my hand. He must have felt an affirming influence or he would never have carried through with the proposal, even though he loved me. I was in anguish, knowing I had disappointed him, and had conducted my life in a way that prevented me from receiving the blessings of the temple.

Two days after Bridger left, I went to the old Nauvoo cemetery east of town to wander the grounds. I had been there twice before, the first time with McKell when we spent an hour searching for the grave of Abigail Bolton, and then again by myself to look further for her grave marker. As I walked into the shadowy graveyard, shrouded with ancient, bent trees and decaying moss, I had no illusions about finding Abigail's grave. Many of the graves of the early Saints were unmarked, or the headstones had toppled. Even when the headstone was still in place, the writing chiseled on it was often too faded to read.

I walked the dim graveyard, gloomy with overhanging branches and upturned roots. Sitting down on a hollow log, I pictured Abigail Bolton as I had seen her in my mind—her calm blue eyes, her smile radiant and loving. Her body likely lay somewhere in this cemetery crumbled to dust, but her legacy lived on. It lived in her children, and her children's children, and on down the chain until it laid claim even on me. A legacy of faith . . . of hope . . . of love.

As I sat in the shadowy stillness of the cemetery, a memory skittered across my mind of Abigail standing beside me in a field of exquisite flowers, her heart reaching out to mine. I caught a brief, mental glimpse of a crowded room, a congregation presided over by a prophet of God imparting the joyous news of a temple restored. Abigail and I were somehow connected to that roomful of people, in a way I could not yet comprehend. But I knew that in some future day, I would understand, would grasp the full meaning of that remarkable fragment of memory.

The impression was fleeting, but powerful. As I sat by myself in that silent and solemn graveyard, I realized the circumstances that brought me to Nauvoo were not happenstance. A plan was in effect. A plan that transcended my limited understanding. A stream of sunlight suddenly broke through the leafy roof of the cemetery, chasing away the gloom. In the sparkling glow of light, the graveyard yielded its hopelessness and awakened into a beautiful place of promise. The old gnarled trees looked majestic in the ancient grove, their branches stretching heavenward. The carpet of moss under my feet felt velvety soft and luxuriant. The scene spoke peace to my mind, lightening my heart and swelling my soul with joy.

* * *

The afternoon before Bridger was to return to Nauvoo, I visited the department store in Keokuk where I made a special purchase. I came home and wrapped the item in silver paper and ribbon, and set it on my bedside table beside my scriptures to await Bridger's company. He called the gallery the next day while I was at work to tell me he was back, and how much he'd missed me while he was away. He wanted to pick me up from work and take me to dinner.

"Bridger, I can't wait to see you. But could you meet me at the temple site around six, instead? I have something I want to show you."

"Sure. I love you, Savannah."

"I love you, too."

My heart was pounding as we hung up. I still had three hours before getting off work, and I could hardly bear waiting for the day to end. At 5:30 I dashed out the door of the gallery, jumped in the Buick, and pressed the pedal to the floor. I said a hasty hello to McKell who was already home from her job at the gift shop, grabbed my wrapped package, and drove Rex the few blocks to the temple site.

Bridger was there waiting for me. He folded me in his arms, hugged and kissed me. "I missed you so much," he said emphatically.

"I missed you, too." I inquired about his trip to the corporate office in Nebraska.

"They asked me a lot of questions which I answered the best I could, and took the documents I'd brought for them. From what was said, I gathered that James has probably embezzled thousands of dollars."

"Do they know how he did it?" I asked.

"They're guessing he fraudulently wrote and endorsed checks, set up a secret bank account for the laundered funds, and systematically skimmed money from the firm."

"That's crazy," I exclaimed. "Did James think he could get away with a scheme like that?"

"Apparently so. He'll be facing a prison term when he's found. The company has hired a private investigator to go after him. And guess what else they said to me?"

We were still standing close together, hand in hand. "What?"

"They're going to send me a check as a sort of reward for reporting the incident to them."

"Alright!" I squealed. "How much do you think you'll get?"

"I have no idea. But I'll be happy with whatever they decide to give me."

"Bridger, that's great. Everything turned out all right after all."

"Yes, it did." He bent to kiss me. "Everything is going to be fine."

After another kiss, I tugged at Bridger's hand. "Come with me. I have something for you."

"You do? What is it?" he grinned as he trailed alongside me to where Rex was parked beside the curb.

"Patience, my love," I smiled back at him. When we reached the car, I opened the door and took the silver wrapped package from the seat. "Let's go sit under that tree," I suggested, pointing to a shady maple not far from the temple foundation.

He pretended to try to snatch the gift from my hand as we walked to the spot. We sat down together under the leafy canopy, cross-legged on the grass. I held out the gift to him. "This is my answer to your proposal of marriage," I said softly.

His gaze lingered on my face for a moment, as if trying to determine whether I was joking with him or not. Then he took the box from my hand. He didn't speak as he unwrapped the silver paper. I held my breath, knowing my whole future hinged on this moment.

He paused an instant to glance at me before lifting the lid of the box.

"Go ahead," I said breathlessly.

He removed the lid, pushed aside the tissue paper cradling the item inside, and lifted out a bottle filled with emerald-colored liquid. "Cologne? A bottle of cologne is your answer?"

"It's not just *any* cologne," I replied quietly.

He glanced at the bottle again. "Eternity," he said slowly. He looked up at me, his eyes suddenly registering comprehension.

All the words I'd kept huddled inside rushed out in a whirl of emotion. "I couldn't accept your proposal before because I wasn't sure if I could commit to a life of living gospel standards. But now I know I can, Bridger. I can." I took his hands into mine. "Now I know that Heavenly Father believes in me, trusts me. I know He loves me and will give me the strength I need to be a good Latter-day Saint."

Bridger was silent, letting me speak.

"I've decided to be baptized, Bridger. I've been taking the missionary discussions from Sister Watson and Sister Suafa'i for the last several weeks, and read most of the Book of Mormon. The Holy Ghost has borne witness to me of the truthfulness of all I've been taught."

"Why didn't you tell me this before?" Bridger asked in a voice husky with emotion.

"I just couldn't." My eyes welled up with tears. "Not until I was sure of my decision to embrace the gospel." I melted into Bridger's arms, and my tears bathed his cheeks. "I love you, Bridger. I will always love you. I want to live throughout eternity with you by my side."

I felt his tears mingle with mine. We clung to one another under the shade of the tall, leafy maple, beside the foundation of the temple at Nauvoo.

* * *

With the glittering diamond engagement ring on my finger, I smoothed a clean sheet of paper and picked up my pen. I held it poised over the paper an instant, gathering my thoughts, and then began to write.

Dear Carly,

I feel the need—the need for speed—to tell you about the incredible things that have happened to me while here in Nauvoo. In all seriousness, Carly, my life has taken a whole different course in these last few months.

First, and most important, I have become a member of The Church of Jesus Christ of Latter-day Saints; maybe you know them better by the name of "Mormons." I can't explain adequately to you the joy I feel, the peace and assurance, since coming to a knowledge of the purposes of God, and the mission of His Son, Jesus Christ.

I went on to briefly explain to Carly about the restoration of the gospel, and a short overview of a few of the basic principles.

Carly, I'm enclosing a very special book that I want you to read. It's called the Book of Mormon. I promise you it will change your life, just as it changed mine. Then I want you to do one more thing for me. Seek out the Mormon missionaries in your area and listen with your heart to what they have to say.

I filled the whole second page of the letter telling her about my romance with Bridger Caldwell and our plans to marry in January of the new millennial year. We would both be leaving Nauvoo, I wrote, in just a few days; Bridger to return to his home and schooling in Utah, and me to Denver. When I got home, I told her, I intended to start rebuilding my relationship with my parents and my brother, Brett, for I'd come to a clearer understanding of the eternal nature of families. Then after visiting with them for a few weeks, I planned to fly out to Salt Lake City to stay until we were married by Bridger's bishop. We would have our marriage sealed in the temple, I explained to Carly, as soon afterward as my standing in the Church as a new member would allow.

I hastily described the ugly situation that had happened with Jaden and then closed my letter to Carly with the wish that we might see one another soon. McKell accompanied me to the post office to mail the letter and pick up some packing boxes.

It was with bittersweet feelings that we packed our belongings in preparation to leave Nauvoo.

EPILOGUE

The walls of the temple glistened in the morning sunlight. Rising five stories high, built of concrete and steel covered with gray limestone, the sight of the completed temple set my heart soaring. I clutched Bridger's hand and we exchanged a breathless glance as we stood together outside the majestic edifice in Nauvoo, Illinois.

We stood speechless, our eyes trying to take in all at once the beauty of the workmanship that had gone into the building. The exquisite stone carvings of sun, moon, and stars, the shimmering airy windows, the stately tower capped by a gold-gilded angel, all combined to create an extraordinary picture reminiscent of the original temple. Spacious grounds provided a setting for the gleaming jewel. Sweeping green lawns, shady trees, and flowers in all colors of the rainbow designated this as a place of rest and peace.

"Annie!" I heard a voice shriek from the direction of the parking lot. I turned, looking for the source of the sound. A second later, Carly burst into view.

"Oh, Carly!" I cried. I met her halfway as she came dashing toward me. We came together in a bear hug, both of us laughing and trying to talk at once.

"Look at you!" she exclaimed. She put her hand on my swollen belly. "You and Bridger are pregnant!"

"A girl," I informed her, grinning. "Due in eight weeks."

"Where's the proud papa?" Carly asked, her eyes darting like fireflies for a glimpse of him.

"Right here," Bridger said, coming forward to give Carly a hug. "How are you doing, Carly?"

"Wonderful. Great to see you again, Bridger. And congratulations on the little one," she bubbled. She turned when a young man with wavy brown hair and blue eyes stepped to her side. "Oh, I nearly forgot to introduce you in all the excitement," she giggled to her handsome companion. "Brantley, this is Savannah and her husband, Bridger Caldwell. Guys, meet Brantley Moore."

We shook hands with Carly's friend. "It's nice to meet you," I said. "How long have you known Carly?"

He and Carly exchanged a private smile. "I met her on my mission."

I could see Carly was bursting to tell me the story and she launched right into it. "I followed the advice in your letter to seek out the missionaries, and there was Elder Moore, serving right in Madison, Wisconsin." She laughed and caught his arm and gave it a squeeze. "Of course, I thought he was an absolute babe. I started taking the missionary lessons because he was so cute and I wanted to date him."

I saw the former Elder Moore roll his eyes.

"But then the things he and his companion were teaching me began to sink in. Even though he was transferred shortly after that, I kept seeing the missionaries. When he finished his mission, he looked me up. And voilà, here we are." Carly held out her left hand, and I beheld a beautiful diamond ring sparkling on her finger.

"Carly!" I gasped, grabbing her for a squeeze. "You're engaged! That's terrific."

"Engaged and baptized, both," she grinned. "Courtesy of Brantley, here." The two of them joined in a tender kiss.

I smiled at the blissful couple. Carly had written me about her boyfriend, but she had never mentioned how they met, or that he was a returned missionary. And I had no idea they'd decided to marry. She'd apparently kept her news to share in person.

"Can you believe this gorgeous temple?" Carly said, slipping her arm through her fiancé's. "Brantley and I arrived yesterday from Madison and saw it for the first time then. It's incredibly beautiful, isn't it?"

Our gazes swept the lofty structure in reverent awe.

"I'm so glad you called me about meeting you here," Carly said. "It worked out great for us to take a couple of days off from our jobs, for both Brantley and me."

"What line of work are you in, Brantley?" asked Bridger.

"Marketing. I work for a marketing firm in Madison. How about yourself?"

"I'm an architect. I just recently landed a job with the Church's Temple Construction Department as part of the committee to draw up plans for the construction of new temples."

"Sounds interesting," Brantley responded. "Are you working out of Salt Lake?"

"At the moment, yeah. But Savannah and I have purchased a piece of ground northeast of town here. A spot, in fact, once owned by her sixth-generation grandparents. We're planning to build a house and move out here after the baby is born."

"You drawing the plans for the house?"

"I am. My wife wants a red brick two-story similar to the homes built during the old Nauvoo period. Living in Nauvoo will require some traveling in connection with my job, but I can do most of my work from here."

"That works out well," said Brantley.

Bridger nodded. "The move to Nauvoo should be good for us."

Carly beamed at me. "I'll bet you're excited," she said, nudging my shoulder.

"I am." I grinned.

"So how long are you planning on staying in Nauvoo this trip?" Brantley asked us.

Bridger gave my hand a squeeze. "A couple of days. We're here to do temple work for some of Savannah's ancestors. She's spent this whole last year and a half researching her family line. She has about seventy names ready to go."

"If you need any help with the men's names you've gathered, I'd be glad to lend a hand."

"Thanks, Brantley," I said, touched by his offer.

"You came all the way from Salt Lake City to do the work in the Nauvoo Temple, didn't you?" Carly said with pride.

"Yes. Some of my ancestors lived in Old Nauvoo. I thought it would be appropriate to do their work here. And the rebuilding of this temple has special meaning for me."

"Carly tells me you're a convert to the Church," Brantley said.

"That's right. It took me totally by surprise to find out some of my ancestors joined the Church in the 1840s."

"Yet none of your family are members?" he pursued.

"No. I've had to do a lot of digging to find out what happened to the family. My grandmother, six generations removed, died in Nauvoo before the exodus, and before she was able to receive her endowments in the temple. I found out later that her husband left Nauvoo with the Saints in 1846, but he died at Winter Quarters. Their five young children were apparently taken in by relatives who were not members of the Church, and so the children grew up outside the gospel. To my knowledge, no one in my family is a member except for me."

With the telling, my mind went back to what I'd read in Jeremiah Bolton's journal. His and Abigail's testimony of the gospel had burned brightly. But for their children, the gospel light was extinguished before it had a chance to flame. How glorious was the gospel plan that made provision for all of God's children, and how blessed I was to come into the gospel net. In the scheme of God's eternal plan, perhaps consistent with promises made before I came to earth, I had the extraordinary privilege to take part in sacred temple ordinances in behalf of my deceased relatives. I prayed that our family would continue in one eternal round, a circle that would one day enfold my own parents and brother.

I'd been doing all I could to mend the relationship with my family, but breaking down the barriers that had been in place for many long years was difficult. I constantly had to fight the impulse to be impatient and unforgiving. My brother and I still were not as close as I wanted us to be, but I'd recently enjoyed some frank, open communication with my parents, which seemed to be opening the door to a more loving relationship. I hadn't yet tried to explain in any detail the principles of the gospel to them. For the present, I hoped that the way Bridger and I conducted our lives would be a quiet example. I would never stop striving, however, to bring my family into the gospel. My heart's desire was to see them accept the gospel plan and come into the Church.

"I've never seen anything that's evoked such excitement and anticipation among Church members as this rebuilding project," Brantley was saying.

"Exactly. It's spurred a tremendous spiritual connection to the past," replied Bridger.

I thanked Carly for coming to help me with the baptisms for my ancestors. "Having you share in this means a lot to me," I said.

"I'm thrilled to be a part of it," she returned. "I only wish I could participate in the rest of the temple ordinances. Next time I will, after Brantley and I are married."

The four of us began walking the temple's perimeter, delighting in the building's beauty and the lush grounds surrounding it. Carly asked when McKell and her husband would arrive in Nauvoo. I had told Carly all about McKell, and both were looking forward to meeting at last.

"She and her husband, Travis, will be here tomorrow to help with the temple work," I said. "You're going to love her."

"You and Brantley will like her husband, as well," Bridger added.

Carly brushed against my shoulder. "Who would ever have predicted that an innocent road trip would lead to all of this?"

My eyes scaled the temple. "It's a miracle, isn't it? A total miracle," I said, recounting in my mind the circumstances which brought me into the gospel.

"Did you ever think our lives would take such an unexpected twist?" asked Carly, gazing from me to her fiancé with a glowing smile.

"Never even imagined it could," I returned. The many blessings Heavenly Father had given me cascaded across my mind. Feelings of gratitude filled my heart to overflowing.

"After everything that happened after your bike accident, I wouldn't have guessed you and Bridger would be standing here together." Carly grinned at me.

I reached for Bridger's hand. "Someone once told me that if you exercise a little faith, things eventually turn out for a person's best good," I said softly.

Bridger bent to kiss me.

"And now the two of you are starting a family. Have you decided on a name for the baby?" asked Carly.

"Yes," I said, squeezing my husband's hand. "We're going to call her Abigail."

About the Author

Laurel was born in Salt Lake City, Utah. She graduated from Brigham Young University with a degree in history and a minor in English literature. She has taught creative writing for adult education programs, and has also conducted classes in genealogy and family history. Because of her interest and education in the field of history, she has served as a tour guide at Wheeler Historic Farm, and visited many historical sites. Laurel is currently an instructor at a private school where she teaches reading and writing skills to young adults. She is the published author of several LDS novels and short stories. In addition to writing, Laurel enjoys skiing, horseback riding, and traveling with her family. She and her husband, Robert, have four children.